D0047696

"If you love cats—or think you might want to—pick up a copy of this book. Because of America's increasing urbanization, cats have become the pet of choice for the majority of Americans. *Great Cat Tales* is a charming collection of stories."—*Bookshelf*

GREAT CAT TALES

Edited by Lesley O'Mara

Foreword by
BERYL REID

Illustrations by
William Geldart

Carroll & Graf Publishers, Inc.
New York

For Suki and Yaki

Collection copyright © 1989 by Michael O'Mara Books Limited
All rights reserved

First Carroll & Graf hardcover edition 1989
First Carroll & Graf paperback edition 1990
Second paperback printing 1992

Carroll & Graf Publishers, Inc
260 Fifth Avenue
New York, NY 10001

ISBN: 0-88184-645-7

Manufactured in the United States of America

Contents

FOREWORD by Beryl Reid OBE   9

THE CAT'S PARADISE by Emile Zola   11

LILLIAN by Damon Runyon   16

SAHA by Colette   29

CHILDHOOD OF MISS CHURT by F.R. Buckley   42

THE FAT CAT by Q. Patrick   56

THE UNDOING OF MORNING GLORY ADOLPHUS
by N. Margaret Campbell   61

HOW A CAT PLAYED ROBINSON CRUSOE
by Charles G.D. Roberts   66

MING'S BIGGEST PREY by Patricia Highsmith   76

MRS BOND'S CATS by James Herriot   87

DICK BAKER'S CAT by Mark Twain   96

A CAT AFFAIR by Derek Tangye   100

KYM by Joyce Stranger   109

A FINE PLACE FOR THE CAT by Margaret Bonham   140

THE BLUE FLAG by Kay Hill   150

THE STORY OF WEBSTER by P.G. Wodehouse   161

TROUBLE EVERYWHERE by Doreen Tovey   182

HEATHCLIFF by Lloyd Alexander   194

THE CAT THAT WALKED BY HIMSELF
by Rudyard Kipling   207

A SHIP OF SOLACE by Eleanor Mordaunt   217

PARTICULARLY CATS by Doris Lessing   222

THE WHITE AND BLACK DYNASTIES
by Théophile Gautier   230

MIDSHIPMAN, THE CAT
by John Coleman Adams   239

THE BEST BED
by Syvlia Townsend Warner   248

ACKNOWLEDGEMENTS   253

Foreword

THERE is no greater treat for a cat lover like me than sifting through a new collection of cat stories. I am a bit like Mrs Bond in James Herriot's story. She had a houseful of cats though, whereas I only have ten! Each of my cats is entirely different from the others in shape, size, and personality but I never have a favourite—I just don't allow myself. I only wish I could think and talk like a cat the way Emile Zola does in his story, 'The Cat's Paradise'.

Cats have had a chequered history. In Ancient Egypt there was a cat goddess called Bast. Thousands of cat mummies have been discovered in Egypt, very often accompanied by mouse mummies which served as cat food in the afterlife. Then we had Elizabeth Ist and James Ist who put any cats they could find into leather bags or 'ferkins' and hung them in the trees for archers to practice on! This is where, I feel, the expression 'letting the cat out of the bag' originated because of course there were people who were fond of them and who had hearts.

Talking of hearts, the most amazing thing is that if you live with cats—or a cat—you are less likely to have heart trouble or high blood pressure. Therefore, we who love them and own them are really very lucky indeed.

I am sure that reading stories about cats is good for you also; especially if you read them with a cat purring on your lap! I can heartily recommend *Great Cat Tales*. It will give great enjoyment to people like me who think cats are sheer 'purr-fection'.
HAPPY READING.

BERYL REID OBE

The Cat's Paradise

EMILE ZOLA

I WAS then two years old, and was at the same time the fattest and most naive cat in existence. At that tender age I still had all the presumptuousness of an animal who is disdainful of the sweetness of home.

How fortunate I was, indeed, that providence had placed me with your aunt! That good woman adored me. I had at the bottom of a wardrobe a veritable sleeping salon, with feather cushions and triple covers. My food was equally excellent; never just bread, or soup, but always meat, carefully chosen meat.

Well, in the midst of all this opulence, I had only one desire, one dream, and that was to slip out of the upper window and escape on to the roofs. Caresses annoyed me, the softness of my bed nauseated me, and I was so fat that it was disgusting even to myself. In short, I was bored the whole day long just with being happy.

I must tell you that by stretching my neck a bit, I had seen the roof directly in front of my window. That day four cats were playing with each other up there; their fur bristling, their tails high, they were romping around with every indication of joy on the blue roof slates baked by the sun. I had never before watched such an extraordinary spectacle. And from then on I had a definitely fixed belief: out there on that roof was true happiness, out there beyond the window which was always closed so carefully. In proof of that contention I remembered that the doors of the chest in which the meat was kept were also closed, just as carefully!

I resolved to flee. After all there had to be other things in life besides a comfortable bed. Out there was the unknown, the

11

ideal. And then one day they forgot to close the kitchen window. I jumped out on to the small roof above it.

How beautiful the roofs were! The wide eaves bordering them exuded delicious smells. Carefully I followed those eaves, where my feet sank into fine mud that smelled tepid and infinitely sweet. It felt as if I were walking on velvet. And the sun shone with a good warmth that caressed my plumpness.

I will not hide from you the fact that I was trembling all over. There was something overwhelming in my joy. I remember particularly the tremendous emotional upheaval which actually made me lose my footing on the slates, when three cats rolled down from the ridge of the roof and approached with excited miaows. But when I showed signs of fear, they told me I was a silly fat goose and insisted that their miaowing was only laughter.

I decided to join them in their caterwauling. It was fun, even though the three stalwarts weren't as fat as I was and made fun of me when I rolled like a ball over the roof heated by the sun.

An old tomcat belonging to the gang honoured me particularly with his friendship. He offered to take care of my education, an offer which I accepted with gratitude.

Oh, how far away seemed all the soft things of your aunt! I drank from the gutters, and never did sugared milk taste half as fine! Everything was good and beautiful.

A female cat passed by, a ravishing she, and the very sight of her filled me with strange emotions. Only in my dreams had I up to then seen such an exquisite creature with such a magnificently arched back. We dashed forward to meet the newcomer, my three companions and myself. I was actually ahead of the others in paying the enchanting female my compliments; but then one of my comrades gave me a nasty bite in the neck, and I let out a shriek of pain.

'Pshaw!' said the old tomcat, dragging me away. 'You will meet plenty of others.'

After a walk that lasted an hour I had a ravenous appetite.

'What does one eat on these roofs?' I asked my friend the tom.

'Whatever one finds,' he replied laconically.

This answer embarrassed me somewhat for, hunt as I might,

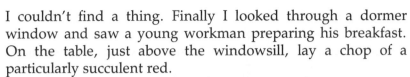

I couldn't find a thing. Finally I looked through a dormer window and saw a young workman preparing his breakfast. On the table, just above the windowsill, lay a chop of a particularly succulent red.

'There is my chance,' I thought, rather naively.

So I jumped on to the table and snatched the chop. But the workingman saw me and gave me a terrific wallop across my back with a broom. I dropped the meat, cursed rather vulgarly and escaped.

'What part of the world do you come from?' asked the tomcat. 'Don't you know that meat on tables is meant only to be admired from afar? What we've got to do is look in the gutters.'

I have never been able to understand why kitchen meat shouldn't belong to cats. My stomach began to complain quite bitterly. The tom tried to console me by saying it would only be necessary to wait for the night. Then, he said, we would climb down from the roofs into the streets and forage in the garbage heaps.

Wait for the night! Confirmed philosopher that he was, he said it calmly while the very thought of such a protracted fast made me positively faint.

Night came ever so slowly, a misty night that made me shiver. To make things worse, rain began to fall, a thin, penetrating rain whipped up by brisk howling gusts of wind.

How desolate the streets looked to me! There was nothing left of the good warmth, of the big sun, of those roofs where one could play so pleasantly. My paws slipped on the slimy pavement, and I began to think with some longing of my triple covers and my feather pillow.

We had hardly reached the street when my friend, the tom, began to tremble. He made himself small, quite small, and glided surreptitiously along the walls of the houses, warning me under his breath to be quick about it. When we reached the shelter of a house door, he hid behind it and purred with satisfaction. And when I asked him the reason for his strange conduct, he said:

'Did you see that man with the hook and the basket?'

'Yes.'

'Well, if he had seen us, we would have been caught, fried

13

on the spit and eaten!'

'Fried on the spit and eaten!' I exclaimed. 'Why, then the street is really not for the likes of us. One does not eat, but is eaten instead!'

In the meantime, however, they had begun to put the garbage out on the sidewalks. I inspected it with growing despair. All I found there were two or three dry bones that had obviously been thrown in among the ashes. And then and there I realized how succulent a dish of fresh meat really is!

My friend, the tom, went over the heaps of garbage with consummate artistry. He made me rummage around until morning, inspecting every cobblestone, without the least trace of hurry. But after ten hours of almost incessant rain my whole body was trembling. Damn the street, I thought, damn liberty! And how I longed for my prison!

When day came, the tomcat noticed that I was weakening.

'You've had enough, eh?' he asked in a strange voice.

'Oh, yes,' I replied.

'Do you want to go home?'

'I certainly do. But how can I find my house?'

'Come along. Yesterday morning when I saw you come out I knew immediately that a cat as fat as you isn't made for the joys of liberty. I know where you live. I'll take you back to your door.'

He said this all simply enough, the good, dignified tom. And when we finally got there, he added, without the slightest show of emotion:

'Goodbye, then.'

'No, no!' I protested. 'I shall not leave you like this. You come with me! We shall share bed and board. My mistress is a good woman . . .'

He didn't even let me finish.

'Shut up!' he said brusquely. 'You are a fool. I'd die in that stuffy softness. Your abundant life is for weaklings. Free cats will never buy your comforts and your featherbeds at the price of being imprisoned. Goodbye!'

With these words he climbed back on to the roof. I saw his proud thin shadow shudder deliciously as it began to feel the warmth of the morning sun.

When I came home your aunt acted the martinet and

administered a corrective which I received with profound joy. I revelled in being punished and voluptuously warm. And while she cuffed me, I thought with delight of the meat she would give me directly afterwards.

You see—an afterthought, while stretched out before the embers—true happiness, paradise, my master, is where one is locked up and beaten, wherever there is meat.

I speak for cats.

Lillian

DAMON RUNYON

WHAT I always say is that Wilbur Willard is nothing but a very lucky guy, because what is it but luck that has him teetering along Forty-ninth Street one cold snowy morning when Lillian is mer-owing around the sidewalk looking for her mamma?

And what is it but luck that has Wilbur Willard all mulled up to a million, what with him having been sitting out a few glasses of Scotch with a friend by the name of Haggerty in an apartment over in Fifty-ninth Street? Because if Wilbur Willard is not mulled up he will see Lillian is nothing but a little black cat, and give her plenty of room, for everybody knows that black cats are terribly bad luck, even when they are only kittens.

But being mulled up like I tell you, things look very different to Wilbur Willard, and he does not see Lillian as a little black kitten scrabbling around in the snow. He sees a beautiful leopard; because a copper by the name of O'Hara, who is walking past about then, and who knows Wilbur Willard, hears him say:

'Oh, you beautiful leopard!'

The copper takes a quick peek himself, because he does not wish any leopards running around his beat, it being against the law, but all he sees, as he tells me afterwards, is this rumpot ham, Wilbur Willard, picking up a scrawny little black kitten and shoving it in his overcoat pocket, and he also hears Wilbur say:

'Your name is Lillian.'

Then Wilbur teeters on up to his room on the top floor of an

16

old fleabag in Eighth Avenue that is called the Hotel de Brussels, where he lives quite a while, because the management does not mind actors, the management of the Hotel de Brussels being very broadminded, indeed.

There is some complaint this same morning from one of Wilbur's neighbours, an old burlesque doll by the name of Minnie Madigan, who is not working since Abraham Lincoln is assassinated, because she hears Wilbur going on in his room about a beautiful leopard, and calls up the clerk to say that a hotel which allows wild animals is not respectable. But the clerk looks in on Wilbur and finds him playing with nothing but a harmless-looking little black kitten, and nothing comes of the old doll's grouse, especially as nobody ever claims the Hotel de Brussels is respectable anyway, or at least not much.

Of course when Wilbur comes out from under the ether next afternoon he can see Lillian is not a leopard, and in fact Wilbur is quite astonished to find himself in bed with a little black kitten, because it seems Lillian is sleeping on Wilbur's chest to keep warm. At first Wilbur does not believe what he sees, and puts it down to Haggerty's Scotch, but finally he is convinced, and so he puts Lillian in his pocket, and takes her over to the Hot Box night club and gives her some milk, of which it seems Lillian is very fond.

Now where Lillian comes from in the first place of course nobody knows. The chances are somebody chucks her out of a window into the snow, because people are always chucking kittens, and one thing and another, out of windows in New York. In fact, if there is one thing this town has plenty of, it is kittens, which finally grow up to be cats, and go snooping around ash cans, and mer-owing on roofs, and keeping people from sleeping well.

Personally, I have no use for cats, including kittens, because I never seen one that has any too much sense, although I know a guy by the name of Pussy McGuire who makes a first-rate living doing nothing but stealing cats, and sometimes dogs, and selling them to old dolls who like such things for company. But Pussy only steals Persian and Angora cats, which are very fine cats, and of course Lillian is no such cat as this. Lillian is nothing but a black cat, and nobody will give you a dime a dozen for black cats in this town, as they are

generally regarded as very bad jinxes.

Furthermore, it comes out in a few weeks that Wilbur Willard can just as well name her Herman, or Sidney, as not, but Wilbur sticks to Lillian, because this is the name of his partner when he is in vaudeville years ago. He often tells me about Lillian Withington when he is mulled up, which is more often than somewhat, for Wilbur is a great hand for drinking Scotch, or rye, or bourbon, or gin, or whatever else there is around for drinking, except water. In fact, Wilbur Willard is a high-class drinking man, and it does no good telling him it is against the law to drink in this country, because it only makes him mad, and he says to the dickens with the law, only Wilbur Willard uses a much rougher word than dickens.

'She is like a beautiful leopard,' Wilbur says to me about Lillian Withington. 'Black-haired, and black-eyed, and all ripply, like a leopard I see in an animal act on the same bill at the Palace with us once. We are headliners then,' he says, 'Willard and Withington, the best singing and dancing act in the country.

'I pick her up in San Antonio, which is a spot in Texas,' Wilbur says. 'She is not long out of a convent, and I just lose my old partner, Mary McGee, who ups and dies on me of pneumonia down there. Lillian wishes to go on the stage, and joins out with me. A natural-born actress with a great voice. But like a leopard,' Wilbur says. 'Like a leopard. There is cat in her, no doubt of this, and cats and women are both ungrateful. I love Lillian Withington. I wish to marry her. But she is cold to me. She says she is not going to follow the stage all her life. She says she wishes money, and luxury, and a fine home, and of course a guy like me cannot give a doll such things.

'I wait on her hand and foot,' Wilbur says. 'I am her slave. There is nothing I will not do for her. Then one day she walks in on me in Boston very cool and says she is quitting me. She says she is marrying a rich guy there. Well, naturally it busts up the act and I never have the heart to look for another partner, and then I get to belting that old black bottle around, and now what am I but a cabaret performer?'

Then sometimes he will bust out crying, and sometimes I will cry with him, although the way I look at it, Wilbur gets a pretty fair break, at that, in getting rid of a doll who wishes things

LILLIAN

he cannot give her. Many a guy in this town is tangled up with a doll who wishes things he cannot give her, but who keeps him tangled up just the same and busting himself trying to keep her quiet.

Wilbur makes pretty fair money as an entertainer in the Hot Box, though he spends most of it for Scotch, and he is not a bad entertainer, either. I often go to the Hot Box when I am feeling blue to hear him sing Melancholy Baby, and Moonshine Valley, and other sad songs which break my heart. Personally, I do not see why any doll cannot love Wilbur, especially if they listen to him sing such songs as Melancholy Baby when he is mulled up well, because he is a tall, nice-looking guy with long eyelashes, and sleepy brown eyes, and his voice has a low moaning sound that usually goes very big with the dolls. In fact, many a doll does do some pitching to Wilbur when he is singing in the Hot Box, but somehow Wilbur never gives them a tumble, which I suppose is because he is thinking only of Lillian Withington.

Well, after he gets Lillian, the black kitten, Wilbur seems to find a new interest in life, and Lillian turns out to be right cute, and not bad-looking after Wilbur gets her fed up well. She is blacker than a yard up a chimney, with not a white spot on her, and she grows so fast that by and by Wilbur cannot carry her in his pocket any more, so he puts a collar on her and leads her around. So Lillian becomes very well known on Broadway, what with Wilbur taking her to many places, and finally she does not even have to be led around by Willard, but follows him like a pooch. And in all the Roaring Forties there is no pooch that cares to have any truck with Lillian, for she will leap aboard them quicker than you can say scat, and scratch and bite them until they are very glad indeed to get away from her.

But of course the pooches in the Forties are mainly nothing but Chows, and Pekes, and Poms, or little woolly white poodles, which are led around by blonde dolls, and are not fit to take their own part against a smart cat. In fact, Wilbur Willard is finally not on speaking terms with any doll that owns a pooch between Times Square and Columbus Circle, and they are all hoping that both Wilbur and Lillian will go lay down and die somewhere. Furthermore, Wilbur has a couple of battles with guys who also belong to the dolls, but Wilbur is no boob in a battle if he is not mulled up too much and leg-weary.

19

After he is through entertaining people in the Hot Box, Wilbur generally goes around to any speakeasies which may still be open, and does a little off-hand drinking on top of what he already drinks down in the Hot Box, which is plenty, and although it is considered very risky in this town to mix Hot Box liquor with any other, it never seems to bother Wilbur. Along toward daylight he takes a couple of bottles of Scotch over to his room in the Hotel de Brussels and uses them for a nightcap, so by the time Wilbur Willard is ready to slide off to sleep he has plenty of liquor of one kind and another inside him, and he sleeps pretty good.

Of course nobody on Broadway blames Wilbur so very much for being such a rumpot, because they know about him loving Lillian Withington, and losing her, and it is considered a reasonable excuse in this town for a guy to do some drinking when he loses a doll, which is why there is so much drinking here, but it is a mystery to one and all how Wilbur stands all this liquor without croaking. The cemeteries are full of guys who do a lot less drinking than Wilbur, but he never even seems to feel extra tough, or if he does he keeps it to himself and does not go around saying it is the kind of liquor you get nowadays.

He costs some of the boys around Mindy's plenty of dough one winter, because he starts in doing most of his drinking after hours in Good Time Charley's speakeasy, and the boys lay a price of four to one against him lasting until spring, never figuring a guy can drink very much of Good Time Charley's liquor and keep on living. But Wilbur Willard does it just the same, so everybody says the guy is just naturally superhuman, and lets it go at that.

Sometimes Wilbur drops into Mindy's with Lillian following him on the look-out for pooches, or riding on his shoulder if the weather is bad, and the two of them will sit with us for hours chewing the rag about one thing and another. At such times Wilbur generally has a bottle on his hip and takes a shot now and then, but of course this does not come under the head of serious drinking with him. When Lillian is with Wilbur she always lies as close to him as she can get and anybody can see that she seems to be very fond of Wilbur, and that he is very fond of her, although he sometimes forgets himself and

speaks of her as a beautiful leopard. But of course this is only a slip of the tongue, and anyway if Wilbur gets any pleasure out of thinking Lillian is a leopard, it is nobody's business but his own.

'I suppose she will run away from me some day,' Wilbur says, running his hand over Lillian's back until her fur crackles. 'Yes, although I give her plenty of liver and catnip, and one thing and another, and all my affection, she will probably give me the go-by. Cats are like women, and women are like cats. They are both very ungrateful.'

'They are both generally bad luck', Big Nip, the crap shooter, says. 'Especially cats, and most especially black cats.'

Many other guys tell Wilbur about black cats being bad luck, and advise him to slip Lillian into the North River some night with a sinker on her, but Wilbur claims he already has all the bad luck in the world when he loses Lillian Withington, and that Lillian, the cat, cannot make it any worse, so he goes on taking extra good care of her, and Lillian goes on getting bigger and bigger until I commence thinking maybe there is some St Bernard in her.

Finally I commence to notice something funny about Lillian. Sometimes she will be acting very loving towards Wilbur, and then again she will be very unfriendly to him, and will spit at him, and snatch at him with her claws, very hostile. It seems to me that she is all right when Wilbur is mulled up, but is as sad and fretful as he is himself when he is only a little bit mulled. And when Lillian is sad and fretful she makes it very tough indeed on the pooches in the neighbourhood of the Brussels.

In fact, Lillian takes to pooch-hunting, sneaking off when Wilbur is getting his rest, and running pooches bow-legged, especially when she finds one that is not on a leash. A loose pooch is just naturally cherry pie for Lillian.

Well, of course this causes great indignation among the dolls who own the pooches, particularly when Lillian comes home one day carrying a Peke as big as she is herself by the scruff of the neck, and with a very excited blonde doll following her and yelling bloody murder outside Wilbur Willard's door when Lillian pops into Wilbur's room through a hole he cuts in the door for her, still lugging the Peke. But it seems that instead of

being mad at Lillian and giving her a pasting for such goings on, Wilbur is somewhat pleased, because he happens to be still in a fog when Lillian arrives with the Peke, and is thinking of Lillian as a beautiful leopard.

'Why,' Wilbur says, 'this is devotion, indeed. My beautiful leopard goes off into the jungle and fetches me an antelope for dinner.'

Now of course there is no sense whatever to this, because a Peke is certainly not anything like an antelope, but the blonde doll outside Wilbur's door hears Wilbur mumble, and gets the idea that he is going to eat her Peke for dinner and the squawk she puts up is very terrible. There is plenty of trouble around the Brussels in cooling the blonde doll's rage over Lillian snagging her Peke, and what is more the blonde doll's ever-loving guy, who turns out to be a tough Ginney bootlegger by the name of Gregorio, shows up at the Hot Box the next night and wishes to put the slug on Wilbur Willard.

But Wilbur rounds him up with a few drinks and by singing Melancholy Baby to him, and before he leaves the Ginney gets very sentimental towards Wilbur, and Lillian, too, and wishes to give Wilbur five bucks to let Lillian grab the Peke again, if Lillian will promise not to bring it back. It seems Gregorio does not really care for the Peke, and is only acting quarrel-some to please the blonde doll and make her think he loves her dearly.

But I can see Lillian is having different moods, and finally I ask Wilbur if he notices it.

'Yes,' he says, very sad, 'I do not seem to be holding her love. She is getting very fickle. A guy moves on to my floor at the Brussels the other day with a little boy, and Lillian becomes very fond of this kid at once. In fact, they are great friends. Ah, well,' Wilbur says, 'cats are like women. Their affection does not last.'

I happen to go over to the Brussels a few days later to explain to a guy by the name of Crutchy, who lives on the same floor as Wilbur Willard, that some of our citizens do not like his face and that it may be a good idea for him to leave town, especially if he insists on bringing ale into their territory, and I see Lillian out in the hall with a youngster which I judge is the kid Wilbur is talking about. This kid is maybe three years old, and very

cute, what with black hair and black eyes, and he is mauling Lillian around the hall in a way that is most surprising, for Lillian is not such a cat as will stand for much mauling around, not even from Wilbur Willard.

I am wondering how anybody comes to take such a kid to a place like the Brussels, but I figure it is some actor's kid, and that maybe there is no mamma for it. Later I am talking to Wilbur about this, and he says:

'Well, if the kid's old man is an actor, he is not working at it. He sticks close to his room all the time, and he does not allow the kid to go anywhere but in the hall, and I feel sorry for the little guy, which is why I allow Lillian to play with him.'

Now it comes on a very cold spell, and a bunch of us are sitting in Mindy's along towards five o'clock in the morning when we hear fire engines going past. By and by in comes a guy by the name of Kansas, who is named Kansas because he comes from Kansas, and who is a gambler by trade.

'The old Brussels is on fire,' this guy Kansas says.

'She is always on fire,' Big Nig says, meaning there is always plenty of hot stuff going on around the Brussels.

About this time who walks in but Wilbur Willard, and anybody can see he is just naturally floating. The chances are he comes from Good Time Charley's, and is certainly carrying plenty of pressure. I never see Wilbur Willard mulled up more. He does not have Lillian with him, but then he never takes Lillian to Good Time Charley's because Charley hates cats.

'Hey, Wilbur,' Big Nig says, 'your joint, the Brussels, is on fire.'

'Well,' Wilbur says, 'I am a little firefly, and I need a light. Let us go where there is a fire.'

The Brussels is only a few blocks from Mindy's and there is nothing else to do just then, so some of us walk over to Eighth Avenue with Wilbur teetering along ahead of us. The old shack is certainly roaring away when we get in sight of it, and the firemen are tossing water into it, and the coppers have the fire lines out to keep the crowd back, although there is not much of a crowd at such an hour in the morning.

'Is it not beautiful?' Wilbur Willard says, looking up at the flames. 'Is it not like a fairy palace all lighted up this way?'

You see, Wilbur does not realise the place is on fire, although

23

guys and dolls are running out of it every which way, most of them half dressed, or not dressed at all, and the firemen are getting out the life nets in case anybody wishes to hop out of the windows.

'It is certainly beautiful,' Wilbur says, 'I must get Lillian so she can see this.'

And before anybody has time to think, there is Wilbur Willard walking into the front door of the Brussels as if nothing happens. The firemen and the coppers are so astonished all they can do is holler at Wilbur, but he pays no attention whatever. Well, naturally everybody figures Wilbur is a gone gosling, but in about ten minutes he comes walking out of this same door through the fire and smoke as cool as you please, and he has Lillian in his arms.

'You know,' Wilbur says, coming over to where we are standing with our eyes popping out, 'I have to walk all the way up to my floor because the elevators seem to be out of commission. The service is getting terrible in this hotel. I will certainly make a strong complaint to the management about it as soon as I pay something on my account.'

Then what happens but Lillian lets out a big mer-row, and hops out of Wilbur's arms and skips past the coppers and the firemen with her back all humped up, and the next thing anybody knows she is tearing through the front door of the old hotel and making plenty of speed.

'Well, well,' Wilbur says, looking much surprised, 'there goes Lillian.'

And what does this daffy Wilbur Willard do but turn and go marching back into the Brussels again, and by this time the smoke is pouring out of the front doors so thick he is out of sight in a second. Naturally he takes the coppers and firemen by surprise, because they are not used to guys walking in and out of fires on them.

This time anybody standing around will lay you plenty of odds—two and a half and maybe three to one that Wilbur never shows up again, because the old Brussels is now just popping with fire and smoke from the lower windows, although there does not seem to be quite so much fire in the upper storey. Everybody seems to be out of the building, and even the firemen are fighting the blaze from the outside

because the Brussels is so old and ramshackly there is no sense in them risking the floors.

I mean everybody is out of the place except Wilbur Willard and Lillian, and we figure they are getting a good frying somewere inside, although Feet Samuels is around offering to take thirteen to five for a few small bets that Lillian comes out okay, because Feet claims that a cat has nine lives and that is a fair bet at the price.

Well, up comes a swell-looking doll all heated up about something and pushing and clawing her way through the crowd up to the ropes and screaming until you can hardly hear yourself think, and about this same minute everybody hears a voice going ai-lee-hi-hee-hoo, like a Swiss yodeller, which comes from the roof of the Brussels, and looking up what do we see but Wilbur Willard standing up there on the edge of the roof, high above the fire and smoke, and yodelling very loud.

Under one arm he has a big bundle of some kind, and under the other he has the little kid I see playing in the hall with Lillian. As he stands up there going ai-lee-hi-hee-hoo, the swell-dressed doll near us begins screaming louder than Wilbur is yodelling, and the firemen rush over under him with a life net.

Wilbur lets go another ai-lee-hi-hee-hoo, and down he comes all spraddled out, with the bundle and the kid, but he hits the net sitting down and bounces up and back again for a couple of minutes before he finally settles. In fact, Wilbur is enjoying the bouncing, and the chances are he will be bouncing yet if the firemen do not drop their hold on the net and let him fall to the ground.

Then Wilbur steps out of the net, and I can see the bundle is a rolled-up blanket with Lillian's eyes peeking out of one end. He still has the kid under the other arm with his head stuck out in front, and his legs stuck out behind, and it does not seem to be that Wilbur is handling the kid as careful as he is handling Lillian. He stands there looking at the firemen with a very sneering look, and finally he says:

'Do not think you can catch me in your net unless I wish to be caught. I am a butterfly, and very hard to overtake.'

Then all of a sudden the swell-dressed doll who is doing so much hollering, piles on top of Wilbur and grabs the kid from

25

him and begins hugging and kissing it.

'Wilbur,' she says, 'God bless you, Wilbur, for saving my baby! Oh, thank you, Wilbur, thank you! My wretched husband kidnaps and runs away with him, and it is only a few hours ago that my detectives find out where he is.'

Wilbur gives the doll a funny look for about half a minute and starts to walk away, but Lillian comes wiggling out of the blanket, looking and smelling pretty much singed up, and the kid sees Lillian and begins hollering for her, so Wilbur finally hands Lillian over to the kid. And not wishing to leave Lillian, Wilbur stands around somewhat confused, and the doll gets talking to him, and finally they go away together, and as they go Wilbur is carrying the kid, and the kid is carrying Lillian, and Lillian is not feeling so good from her burns.

Furthermore, Wilbur is probably more sober than he ever is before in years at this hour in the morning, but before they go I get a chance to talk some to Wilbur when he is still rambling somewhat, and I make out from what he says that the first time he goes to get Lillian he finds her in his room and does not see hide or hair of the little kid and does not even think of him, because he does not know what room the kid is in, anyway, having never noticed such a thing.

But the second time he goes up, Lillian is sniffing at the crack under the door of a room down the hall from Wilbur's and Wilbur says he seems to remember seeing a trickle of something like water coming out of the crack.

'And,' Wilbur says, 'as I am looking for a blanket for Lillian, and it will be a bother to go back to my room, I figure I will get one out of this room. I try the knob but the door is locked, so I kick it in, and walk in to find the room is full of smoke, and fire is shooting through the windows very lovely, and when I grab a blanket off the bed for Lillian, what is under the blanket but the kid?

'Well,' Wilbur says, 'the kid is squawking, and Lillian is merowing, and there is so much confusion generally that it makes me nervous, so I figure we better go up on the roof and let the stink blow off us, and look at the fire from there. It seems there is a guy stretched out on the floor of the room alongside an upset table between the door and the bed. He has a bottle in one hand, and he is dead. Well, naturally there is nothing to be

26

gained by lugging a dead guy along, so I take Lillian and the kid and go up on the roof, and we just naturally fly off like humming birds. Now I must get a drink,' Wilbur says. 'I wonder if anybody has anything on their hip?'

Well, the papers are certainly full of Wilbur and Lillian the next day, especially Lillian, and they are both great heroes.

But Wilbur cannot stand publicity very long, because he never has no time to himself for his drinking, what with the scribes and the photographers hopping on him every few minutes wishing to hear his story, and to take more pictures of him and Lillian, so one night he disappears, and Lillian disappears with him.

About a year later it comes out that he marries his old doll, Lillian Withington-Harmon, and falls into a lot of dough, and what is more he cuts out the liquor and becomes quite a useful citizen one way and another. So everybody has to admit that black cats are not always bad luck, although I say Wilbur's case is a little exceptional because he does not start out knowing Lillian is a black cat, but thinking she is a leopard.

I happen to run into Wilbur one day all dressed up in good clothes and jewellery and cutting quite a swell.

'Wilbur,' I say to him, 'I often think how remarkable it is the way Lillian suddenly gets such an attachment for the little kid and remembers about him being in the hotel and leads you back there a second time to the right room. If I do not see this come off with my own eyes, I will never believe a cat has brains enough to do such a thing, because I consider cats are extra dumb.'

'Brains nothing,' Wilbur says. 'Lillian does not have brains enough to grease a gimlet. And what is more she has no more attachment for the kid than a jack rabbit. The time has come,' Wilbur says, 'to expose Lillian. She gets a lot of credit which is never coming to her. I will now tell you about Lillian, and nobody knows this but me.

'You see,' Wilbur says, 'when Lillian is a little kitten I always put a little Scotch in her milk, partly to help make her good and strong, and partly because I am never no hand to drink alone, unless there is nobody with me. Well, at first Lillian does not care so much for this Scotch in her milk, but finally she takes a liking to it, and I keep making her toddy stronger until in the

27

end she will lap up a good big snort without any milk for a chaser, and yell for more. In fact, I suddenly realize that Lillian becomes a rumpot, just like I am in those days, and simply must have her grog, and it is when she is good and rummed up that Lillian goes off snatching Pekes, and acting tough generally.

'Now,' Wilbur says, 'the time of the fire is about the time I get home every morning and give Lillian her schnapps. But when I go into the hotel and get her the first time I forget to Scotch her up, and the reason she runs back into the hotel is because she is looking for her shot. And the reason she is sniffing at the kid's door is not because the kid is in there but because the trickle that is coming through the crack under the door is nothing but Scotch running out of the bottle in the dead guy's hand. I never mention this before because I figure it may be a knock to a dead guy's memory,' Wilbur says. 'Drinking is certainly a disgusting thing, especially secret drinking.'

'But how is Lillian getting along these days?' I ask Wilbur Willard.

'I am greatly disappointed in Lillian,' he says. 'She refuses to reform when I do and the last I hear of her she takes up with Gregorio, the Ginney bootlegger, who keeps her well Scotched up all the time so she will lead his blonde doll's Peke a dog's life.'

28

Saha

COLETTE

ONE July evening, as they were both waiting for Alain to
come home, Camille and the cat sat quietly at the same
railing, the cat sitting on her elbows, the girl leaning
over, her arms crossed. Camille did not like this balcony,
reserved for the cat, and shut in by two cement walls which
protected it from the wind and from all communication with
the front terrace.

Each gave the other a quick, searching glance and Camille
said nothing to Saha. On her elbows, she leaned out as though
to count the flights of yellow, slackened awnings, from the top
to the bottom of the dizzying façade of the apartment house;
stroked the cat, who got up, drew away, and lay down again a
little farther along on the railing.

The moment Camille was alone she always looked very
much like the little girl who would not say 'how-do-you-do'.
Her face took on its childlike expression of merciless innocence, that hard perfection which gives children's faces the
look of angels. With an expression impartially severe, which
could have no reproach in it, she was gazing on Paris, from
whose sky the light was dying earlier each day. She yawned
nervously, got up, took several aimless steps, leaned over the
railing again, obliging the cat to jump down to the floor. Saha
drew off, preferring to go back into the bedroom. But the door
of the three-cornered room had been closed and so Saha sat
down in front of it, patiently. A moment later she had to yield
the entrance to Camille, who began to walk back and forth
from one wall to the other with long, quick strides; and the cat
jumped back on the railing. As though teasing her, Camille

29

dislodged her again as she leaned on her elbows and gazed across Paris. Once again Saha drew back and took up her station before the closed door.

Her eye on the horizon, her back to the cat, Camille stood motionless as a statue. But as Saha stared at that back, her breath came faster and faster. She got up, turned around two or three times, sniffed inquiringly at the closed door. . . . Camille had not stirred. The cat distended her nostrils; she had that distressed look which accompanies nausea. A long-drawn-out, desolate 'Meow', the plaintive reaction to a menacing and unexpressed design, escaped her; and Camille wheeled squarely around.

She was a little pale; that is, her rouge outlined two oval moons on her cheeks. She feigned the preoccupied air she would have had under the glance of a human being. At the same time she began to hum, her mouth tightly closed. Then she resumed her walk from one wall to the opposite one, back and forth, moving to the rhythm of the tune after her voice could no longer carry it. She drove the cat first to regain with one leap her narrow place of observation on the railing, and next to sit tightly pressed against the bedroom door.

Saha did not lose her composure; she would have died rather than utter a second cry. Closing in on the cat but pretending not to see her, Camille walked back and forth in complete silence. Saha did not jump on to the railing until she saw Camille's feet coming close; and when she jumped down on the balcony floor, it was only to avoid the arm which, if extended, would have thrown her down from a height of five stories.

She was not confused. She fled with design, jumped carefully, kept her eyes fixed on the enemy; and she stooped neither to anger nor to pleading. Extreme emotion, the fear of death, moistened her paws with sweat; they stamped flower-like imprints on the cement balcony floor.

Camille seemed to be the first to weaken, to dissipate her murderous power. She made the mistake of noticing that the sun was setting; glanced at her wristwatch; listened to the tinkling of glasses inside the apartment. A few seconds more, and her resolution, slipping from her as sleep does from a sleepwalker, would have left her guiltless and exhausted. . . .

Sensing her enemy's wavering strength of purpose, Saha hesitated a second on the railing; and Camille, spreading her arms wide apart, pushed the cat off into space.

She had time to hear the scratching of the claws on the cement, to see Saha's blue body, curved into an 'S', clutch at the air with the upward leap of a trout. Then the girl drew back and leaned against the wall.

She showed no desire to look below into the little garden outlined in fresh pebbles. Back in the bedroom, she put her hands over her ears, withdrew them again, shook her head as though troubled by the buzzing of mosquitoes, sat down and nearly fell asleep. But the oncoming night roused her, and she chased away the twilight by lighting squares of glass, shining grooves, blinding, mushroom-shaped crystals, and also the chromium bar which threw an opaline light across the bed.

She moved lithely from place to place, and as she passed them, touched each object lightly, dexterously, dreamily.

'I feel as though I had grown thin,' she said aloud.

She changed her clothes, dressed herself all in white.

'My fly in the ointment,' she said, imitating the voice in which Alain had said it to her. Colour returned to her cheeks again at a sensual memory which brought her back to reality, and she looked forward to Alain's homecoming.

She bent her head toward the buzzing of the elevator and trembled at every sound—the irritating squeaks, the metallic scrapings of a ship at anchor, strangled music—all the discordant sounds which a new house emits. But an expression of fright came into her face only when the sepulchral tinkling of the bell in the entrance hall followed the fumbling of a key in the door. She ran, and opened it herself.

'Shut the door,' Alain ordered. 'If only I were sure that she's not hurt! Come, turn on some light.'

He was carrying the still breathing Saha in his arms. He went straight to the bedroom, pushed aside the trinkets on the disguised dressing table, and carefully put the cat down on its glass top. She managed to stand on her feet and kept her balance, but her deep-set eyes glanced around the room as if she were in some unfamiliar house.

'Saha!' Alain called to her in a low tone. 'If she's not hurt it's a miracle . . . Saha!'

31

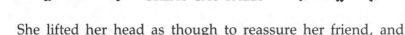

She lifted her head as though to reassure her friend, and leaned her cheek against his hand.

'Take a step or two for me, Saha. . . . She's walking! Ah, good. . . . A fall of five stories! . . . It was the awnings on the second floor that broke her fall. . . . From there she bounced off onto the caretaker's little grass patch. He saw her dropping. He said to me, "I thought it was an umbrella falling!" . . . What's that in her ear? . . . No, it's just something white from the wall. Wait a moment till I listen to her heart.'

He laid the cat down on her side and examined the heaving ribs; the irregular, faint movement of the mechanism. His fair hair pushed back, his eyes shut, he seemed to be sleeping on Saha's fur. Then he opened his eyes and noticed Camille standing by, silent, looking down on the impervious pair.

'Can you believe it? She hasn't any . . . at least, I can't find anything but a heart terribly excited; still a cat's heart is normally excited. But how could this have happened to her? I'm asking you as though you could know, my poor little Camille. She fell from this side here,' he said, looking at the wide-open French window. 'Jump down, Saha, if you can.'

She hesitated, then jumped, but lay down again on the rug. She was breathing quickly and still had that lost expression in her eyes as she looked around the room.

'I've a mind to telephone Chéron. . . . And still, look . . . she's cleaning herself. She wouldn't be stirring as much as that if she had hurt herself inside, somewhere. . . . Ah, thank heaven . . .'

He withdrew, threw his waistcoat on the bed, and went over to Camille.

'What a scare! . . . There you are, very pretty, all in white. . . . Give me a kiss, my little fly in the ointment.'

She gave herself up to the arms that had at last become aware of her; but she could not hold back the sobs that shook her.

'Why . . . you're crying?'

He himself became upset and buried his face in her thick black hair.

'I did not realize you were so tender-hearted . . . Imagine . . .'

She had the courage not to release herself at that word.

Alain, moreover, turned quickly back to Saha, to take her out into the cool air of the balcony. But the cat resisted; she preferred to lie down near the window sill and look into the sky, as blue as herself. From time to time she shivered slightly and turned to question the depths of the triangular bedroom.

'It's the shock,' Alain explained. 'I would like to make her comfortable outside.'

'Let her alone,' answered Camille feebly, 'if she doesn't want to.'

'Her whims are my commands. Especially today. Can there possibly be anything left fit to eat at this hour? Half past nine!'

Buque rolled the table out on to the terrace and they dined looking out on East Paris, the Paris most thickly dotted with lights. Alain talked a good deal, drank reddened water, accused Saha of awkwardness, of imprudence, of what he called 'cat mistakes'.

'Cat mistakes are the kind of "accidental" errors, biological "setbacks" chargeable to civilization and to domestication. They have nothing in common with clumsy, blunt actions that are almost intentional . . .'

But Camille did not ask, 'How do you know that?'

Dinner over, he carried Saha and led Camille into the studio where the cat consented to drink the milk she had refused before. As she drank she shivered all through her body as cats do when they are drenched with cold water.

'The shock,' Alain said again. 'Even so, I'll ask Chéron to look at her tomorrow morning. Oh, I forgot,' he said gaily. 'Please telephone the superintendent. I forgot to bring up the roll that Massart, our accursed decorator, left for me there.'

Camille obeyed, while Alain fell exhausted into one of the armchairs, relaxed, and closed his eyes.

'Hello,' Camille said into the telephone. 'Yes, that must be it . . . a large roll . . . thank you.'

His eyes closed, he grinned. She had come back near him and saw him smiling.

'That tiny voice of yours! What's this new little voice? "A large roll . . . thank you," ' he mimicked. 'Do you keep such a thin small voice just for the superintendent? Come on, the two of us are not too many to tackle Massart's latest creations.'

He spread a large sheet of water-colour paper on the ebony table. Immediately Saha, enamoured of everything made of paper, leapt on to the design.

'Isn't she good?' Alain exclaimed. 'She wants to show me that she isn't really hurt anywhere. . . . Isn't that a swelling on her head, though? Camille, feel her head. . . . No, it isn't. Still, just feel her head anyway, Camille.'

A miserable little murderess, obedient, she tried to pull herself out of the exile into which she had been sinking. She put out her hand with a meek sort of hatred, and gently touched the cat's forehead.

The most savage scream, a snarl, an epileptic spasm responded to her touch. Camille said 'Oh!' as if she had been burned. Standing on the spread-out paper, the cat glowered at the young woman with flaming accusation, stiffened the fur on her back, showed her teeth and the dry red of her jaw.

Alain had risen, ready to protect the one from the other— Saha and Camille.

'Careful. She is . . . perhaps she's mad. Saha!'

She stared at him fiercely, yet the lucid look in her eyes proved that she had her reason.

'What's the matter with her? Where did you touch her?'

'I didn't touch her.'

They spoke in low tones, the words coming from the edges of their lips.

'Now that I don't understand,' Alain said. 'Put out your hand again.'

'No, I don't want to,' Camille protested. 'Perhaps she is mad,' she added.

Alain took the risk of caressing Saha, who stopped bristling, shaped herself to her friend's palm, but still glared at Camille.

'So, that's it,' Alain said slowly. 'Wait a moment. She has a scratch on her nose; I hadn't seen that. And that's dried blood. Quiet, Saha, quiet,' he said, noticing the fury gathering in her yellow eyes. The puffing out of her cheeks, the huntress-like stiffness of the whiskers brought forward, made the infuriated cat look as though she were laughing. The conflicts within her, coming one after the other in such quick succession, drew down the mauve corners of her jaw, stiffened her trembling chin; and all her feline face was straining itself toward a

universal language, toward a word forgotten of men. . . .

'What's that?' asked Alain sharply.

'What's what?'

The cat's glare brought back Camille's bravado and her instinct of defence. Bending over the drawing, Alain deciphered some moist pink spots in groups of four around a central irregular spot.

'Her paws . . . moist?' he said, very low.

He turned towards his wife.

'She must have stepped in some water,' Camille said. 'You exaggerate every little thing so.'

Alain lifted up his head toward the dry, blue night.

'In water? In what water?'

His round, staring eyes made him look singularly ugly as he turned toward his wife.

'Don't you know what those marks are?' he said bitterly. 'No, you don't know anything about it. That's fear, you understand, the sweat that comes from fright—a cat's sweat, the only moisture a cat has. That means she's been through some terrible fright. . . .'

Delicately he took one of Saha's front paws, and with his fingers wiped off the fleshy sole of the foot. Then he pushed back the living white tissue covering her retractive claws.

'All her claws are broken. . . .' he said, talking to himself. 'She caught herself . . . tried to stop herself . . . tried to cling to the stone. She—'

He stopped suddenly, took the cat under his arm, and carried her into the kitchen.

Alone, perfectly still, Camille listened. She clasped her hands tightly together and, though free, looked as if bound by shackles.

'Buque,' said Alain, 'have you any milk?'

'Yes, sir, in the icebox.'

'Then it's cold?'

'But I can heat it on the stove. . . . I can heat it in a jiffy. It's for the cat? Nothing the matter with her, I hope?'

'No, she's. . . .'

Alain stopped himself, and changed to: 'Some food must have disagreed with her in this hot weather. Thank you, Buque. Yes, you may leave now.'

Camille heard her husband turning on a faucet, and knew

that he was giving the cat food and fresh water. A diffused shadow above a metal lamp shade showed the slow movement of her big eyeballs.

Alain came back, automatically tightened his leather belt and sat down at the black table. But he was oblivious of Camille's presence, and it was she who had to speak first.

'You told Buque she could go?'

'Yes. Shouldn't I have?'

He lighted a cigarette and blinked above the flames of the lighter.

'I was going to ask her if she would bring . . . Oh, it's not important; don't excuse yourself.'

'But I wasn't excusing myself. Perhaps I should.'

Lured by the blue depth of the night, he went to the open French window. He noted in himself an agitation which did not have its birth in this recent emotion, a trembling comparable to the quavering of an orchestra, deafening, prophetic. A skyrocket shot up from the Folie-Sainte-James, burst into shimmering petals which faded out, one by one, as they fell, and peace came back into the powdery depth of the blue night. In the park of the Folie, a rocky grotto, a colonnade, and a cascade were illuminated with incandescent white. Camille drew near.

'Is this a gala night? Let's watch the fireworks. Do you hear the guitars?'

Absorbed in his own nervous trembling, he did not answer her. His wrists, his tingling hands, his tired backbone prickled with a thousand torments. It all brought back to him a hated feeling of fatigue, the fatigue of the athletic competitions in his high-school days—foot races, boat races—from which he emerged vindictive, despising both his victory and his defeat, breathless and stumbling with exhaustion. He was not at peace, except about one thing: he no longer felt any anxiety for Saha. A long moment ago—or a very short moment ago—since the discovery of the broken claws, since Saha's burning fright, he had not exactly been aware of time.

'It's not fireworks,' he said. 'More likely dancing.'

By the movement Camille made near him in the shadow, he gathered that she wasn't expecting him to answer. But she grew bolder and came nearer still; he felt no dread at her

36

coming. Out of the corner of his eye he saw the white dress; one bare arm; one half of her face tinged with yellow from the lamps indoors, the other half blue, absorbed from the clear night; two half-faces divided by the same straight nose, each one endowed with one big eye which blinked very little.

'Yes, dancing, of course,' she agreed. 'Those are mandolins, not guitars. Listen. *"Les donneurs . . . de . . sé-é-réna . . des. Et les bel-les é-écouteu . . ." '*

Her voice stumbled on the highest note and fell, and she coughed to cover her defeat.

'What a thin voice!' Alain marvelled. 'What has she done with her voice, as big as her eyes? She sings like a little girl, and she's hoarse.'

The mandolins stopped playing, the breeze brought a faint murmur of human pleasure and applause. In a moment a rocket went up, and broke like an umbrella of violet rays from which dropped tears of living fire.

'Oh!' Camille exclaimed.

Both of them had emerged from the darkness like two statues: Camille like lilac marble; Alain white, his hair greenish, his pupils faded. When the rocket burst, Camille sighed.

'They never last long enough,' she said plaintively.

The distant music started up again. But the capricious wind transformed the sound of the instruments to a sharp resonance, and the lingering glare of one of the accompanying brasses, on two notes, rose discordantly up to the balcony where the two were watching.

'That's too bad,' Camille said. 'Probably they play the best jazz. . . . That's "Love in the Night" they're playing. . . .'

She tried to hum the tune, but her voice—it seemed to come in the wake of tears—was too high and trembling. . . . This new voice redoubled Alain's uneasiness; it engendered in him a necessity for revelation, a desire to break through the thing which—a long moment ago or a very short moment—was being built up between Camille and himself; a thing which as yet had no name, but was growing quickly; the thing which kept him from taking Camille by the neck as though she were a small boy; the thing which held him immovable, vigilant, leaning against the wall, warm still with the day's heat. He

became impatient, and said:

'Sing some more. . . .'

A long, three-cornered shower dropping in sprays like boughs of weeping willow lit up the sky above the park, and revealed to Alain a Camille surprised, already defiant.

'Sing what?'

' "Love in the Night" or . . . anything.'

She hesitated a moment; then refused.

'Let me listen to the jazz . . . even from where we are you can hear how mellow it is.'

He did not urge her, but restrained his impatience and tried to control the tingling that went through his entire body.

When night closed down, he hesitated no longer, and slipped his bare arm under Camille's. In touching it he seemed to see it quite white, hardly tinted by the summer sun, covered with fine soft hairs, reddish brown on the forearm, paler near the shoulder. . . .

'You're cold,' he murmured. 'You're not ill?'

She wept softly, but so immediately that Alain suspected her of having had her tears in readiness.

'No . . . it's you. It's you . . . you don't love me.'

He backed up to the wall and pressed Camille against his hip. He could feel her shaking and cold from her shoulder to her knees, bare above the rolled stockings. She did not hold back; she yielded her whole body to him, faithfully.

'Ah, ah! I don't love you. So that's it! Another jealous scene on account of Saha?'

He could feel that whole body, pressed against his, stiffen— Camille recapturing her self-defence, her resistance; and he went on, encouraged by the moment and the opportunity.

'Instead of loving that charming animal the way I do. . . . Are we the only young married couple to bring up a cat or a dog? Would you like a parrot, a marmoset, a pair of lovebirds to make me jealous?'

She shook her shoulders and protested by making a peevish sound in her closed mouth. His head high, Alain controlled his own voice and spurred himself on.

'Come now, come on. One or two more childish bickerings, and we'll get somewhere.' She's like a jar I have to turn upside down in order to empty it completely. But come on. . . .

'Would you like a little lion, a baby crocodile, say, fifty years old or so? You'd do better to adopt Saha. If you'll just take the trouble, you'll see. . . .'

Camille wrenched herself from his arms so furiously that he tottered.

'No,' she cried. 'That? Never. You hear what I say? Never!'

She drew a long sigh of rage and repeated in a lower tone:

'No. . . . never!'

'That's that,' he said to himself delightedly.

He pushed her into the bedroom, lowered the blinds, turned on the square ceiling lights, closed the window. With a quick movement Camille went to the window, which Alain reopened.

'On the condition that you don't scream,' he said.

He rolled up the single armchair for Camille; he himself straddled the one small chair at the foot of the wide, turned-down, freshly sheeted bed. The glazed chintz curtains, drawn for the night, cast a shade of green over Camille's pallor and her crumpled white dress.

'So?' Alain began. 'Impossible to settle? Horrible situation? Either she or you?'

An abrupt shake of the head was her answer and Alain was made to realize that he had better drop his bantering manner.

'What do you want me to tell you?' he began, after a silence. 'The only thing I can't say? You know very well I won't give up that cat. I'd be ashamed to. Ashamed for my own sake, ashamed for her. . . .'

'I know,' Camille said.

'And ashamed in your eyes,' he finished.

'Oh, as for me . . .' Camille said, raising her hand.

'You count too,' he went on severely. 'When all is said and done, I'm the one you're really angry with. The only grudge you've got against Saha is that she loves me.'

Her sole answer was a troubled and hesitant expression, and it annoyed him to have to go on putting questions to her. He had thought that one short, decisive scene would force the entire issue, he was relying on that easy disposal of the matter. Not at all. After the first cry had been uttered, Camille recoiled; she did nothing to feed the flames. He resorted to patience.

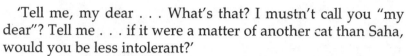

'Tell me, my dear . . . What's that? I mustn't call you "my dear"? Tell me . . . if it were a matter of another cat than Saha, would you be less intolerant?'

'Naturally; of course I would,' she replied very quickly. 'You wouldn't love it as you do this one.'

'That's true,' he agreed, with studied loyalty.

'Even a woman,' Camille went on, indignantly, 'even a woman, you would probably not love so much.'

'That's true.'

'You're not like people who love animals . . . you . . . Take Pat, now, he loves animals. He grabs big dogs by the neck, tumbles them over; imitates cats to see the faces they'll make; whistles to birds . . .'

'Yes, but he's not hard to please,' Alain answered.

'But with you, it's not the same thing. You love Saha . . .'

'I've never hidden it from you, but neither did I lie when I told you that Saha is not your rival.'

He stopped and lowered his lids upon his secret, that secret concerning purity.

'There are rivals and rivals,' Camille said sarcastically.

She reddened suddenly, inflamed with sharp rage.

'I've seen you,' she cried. 'In the morning after you had spent the night on your little cot. Before daybreak, I've seen you both . . .'

She stretched her trembling arm out toward the balcony.

'Sitting there, both of you. You didn't even hear me. . . . You were like this, your cheeks against each other . . .'

She went to the window, took a breath of air and came back to Alain.

'It's for you to say, honestly, if I'm wrong in disliking that cat . . . wrong in suffering . . .'

He kept silent so long that she was angry again.

'Go on, say something. What are you waiting for?'

'The sequel,' Alain said. 'The end of the story.'

He got up deliberately, bent over his wife and lowered his voice as he indicated the French window.

'It was you, wasn't it? You pushed her off?'

She made a swift movement and put the bed between them, but she denied nothing.

With a kind of indulgent smile, he watched her flee.

'You threw her,' he said dreamily. 'I felt that you had changed everything between us. You pushed her. She broke her claws trying to catch hold of the wall . . .'

He lowered his head, seeming to picture the crime. 'But how did you throw her? By clutching her by the skin of her neck? By taking advantage of her sleeping on the balcony? Have you been planning the attack for a long time? Did you two quarrel beforehand?'

He raised his head, looked at Camille's hands and arms.

'No, you haven't any marks. It was she who accused you when I asked you to touch her. She was magnificent.'

He turned from Camille to look at the night, the burnt-out stars, the tops of the three poplars with the bedroom lights shining upon them.

'Well,' he said simply, 'I'm leaving.'

'Oh, listen . . . listen . . .' Camille begged in a low voice.

But she did not hinder him from leaving the bedroom. He opened closet doors, talked to the cat in the bathroom, and from the sound of his footsteps Camille knew that he had just put on his street shoes. Mechanically she looked at the clock. He came back into the room, carrying Saha in a wide basket which Buque used when she went to market. Hastily dressed, his hair hardly combed, a handkerchief around his neck, he had the look of a lover after a quarrel. Wide eyed, Camille stared at him. But she heard Saha move in the basket and her lips tightened.

'There you are; I'm leaving,' Alain said again.

He lowered his eyes, raised the basket slightly and, with designed cruelty, corrected himself:

'We're leaving.'

41

Childhood of Miss Churt

F. R. BUCKLEY

MISS Churt—British, like everyone else aboard the *Malvern*—sat on the storm sill of the galley and with glazed eyes surveyed the North Atlantic.

Miss Churt was meditating sombrely on the rump steak the cook had given her. 'Eat it up, Kitty; good!' the cook had said, and Miss Churt had followed the suggestion.

Now—although the steak had been delicious—Miss Churt was experiencing certain qualms; a sensation, as of cannon balls in the midriff, had assailed her. . . .

Miss Churt decided that she would get a little fresh air and drop in on her friend Mr Wharton.

She dropped from her perch and, with tail at its meridian height, walked unsteadily toward the cuddy stairway.

The *Malvern* was moving unsteadily also, and likewise because of a heavy feeling in the midriff; caused not by cannon balls but by much more modern munitions of war. Never on very cordial terms with her rudder, she had now been be-shelled and be-packing-cased and be-airplane-parted until she would just as soon go anywhere as anywhere else, and was constantly trying to do so.

In a room on the boat deck, the first officer and the chief engineer were discussing this phenomenon and others related to the comfort and well-being of the ship's company. Mr McIvor, who was naturally the engineer, had joined in New York and was absorbing pessimism from Mr Wharton.

'He's a kind of mixed product of the flu and the board room,' said the first mate, alluding to his captain. 'He's—well, you saw him.'

42

'I saw *something*,' said Mr McIvor, cautiously.

'That'd be him. Chairman's nephew; on the beach for years; war come along—old Stokes gets flu—hand o' Providence—an' here I am sayin' "Aye, aye, sir!" to *that*. If he'd got eyelashes I wouldn't mind it so much, but—'

Mr McIvor nodded, and his unclean pipe said, 'Cluck, cluck.'

'Have any trouble comin' over?'

'Subs, you mean? Naw. Hello, sweetheart! Hello! Come to see Poppa?'

Mr McIvor, thunderstruck, made an instinctive motion to smooth his hair, but it was only Miss Churt. Mr Wharton went over, picked her up out of the aperture of the hooked door and before sitting down again on his berth spread a month-old newspaper carefully on the carpet. The page uppermost bore a picture of Lady Somebody's wedding to Captain Gossakes-Whosis of the guards; Mr Wharton, bending with Miss Churt sprawled over his palm, surveyed orange blossoms, smiles, teeth, tonsils and the arch of swords with a nitric eye.

'There, sweetheart,' he said, putting Miss Churt down on them.

'You a married mon?' asked Mr McIvor.

'Nah. But I *will* be. That's her.'

The engineer rolled an eye at the picture on the bureau.

'Nice gurrul.'

'You said it. Canon Hobson an' all. Speakin' of cannon, have you seen our 4.7 on the poop deck?'

'To my grief. But what's this', said Mr McIvor, whose intake of personal news was disproportionate to his output, 'aboot a canon? The young leddy's no got a smash on um?'

'On old Hobson? Not *that* kind,' said Mr Wharton; and his look made Mr McIvor wonder whether he should have asked. 'Fact is—that's a good little sweetheart! Come to Poppa! 'At's a girlie!'

'Ye seem fond o' yon kitten.'

'I'm mad about her. And she's just wild about Harry, aren't you, pet?'

Miss Churt licked a gnarled and knotted hand. It tasted something like the rump steak, flavoured with tar, salt, tobacco and Mallinson's Wonder Ointment for superficial cuts and bruises. . . .

'Then whaur *does* this canon come in?'

'All the girls round our way in Liverpool are mad about him. See—he had us all in Sunday school; children's choral guild, he called it; us boys got away after we'd been confirmed, of course, but you can believe it or not, I've never been the swearer I ought to have.'

'I noticed that when we was warpin' into the stream,' said Mr McIvor. 'I thocht maybe ye was a nance.'

A sudden squeezing of Miss Churt's ribs evoked a mew.

'Did I hurt ums bellah?' asked Mr Wharton. 'Dere Snuzzle down, a good girlie; such a full ickle tummy . . . Ho, you did, hah?'

'Until we met,' said Mr McIvor in haste. 'But—he canna be a young mon, this parson?'

'Canon,' said Mr Wharton. 'Naw, an' he's no beauty neither. But he's the bee's knees so far's Annie's concerned, an' she's goin' to be married by him or nobody, so so far it's been nobody—an' now they go an' put this pink-whiskered nincompoop in over my head—'

'What's it matter who morries ye? It takes no longer than havin' a tooth out.'

'Ho, doesn't it? That's where *you* drop your tow. Old Hobson's strong for the ritual and all that; and that means veils an' orange flowers for Annie an' a top hat an' tails for me.'

'But not in wartime!'

'How do *you* know?'

'I'd go,' said Mr McIvor after reflection, 'an' see the old mon an' say "Fush!" to um.'

'You would *not*,' said Mr Wharton darkly, 'not if you saw him. He's only five foot six, but I've seen him sober, an' askin' for coffee. He's got one o' those kissers you carve out o' granite with a road drill. Looks something like you.'

The chief engineer considered this judicially, and put his glass down.

'Awheel,' he said, rising. 'It's the wull o' Allah, I suppawse, that some of us should be morried an' hae bairns, while ithers lovish their possions on tobby cots. Guid nicht, Mr Wharton.'

In the doorway he turned to see the burst of this Glaswegian bomb. Miss Churt, who had been awakened by something that

felt like an earth tremor, blinked at him and went to sleep again.

'We've naval ratings aboard to work yon gun?' McIvor asked, to cover his more morbid curiosity.

'We have,' said Mr Wharton, 'an' if anybody asks you who's in command o' that gun crew, it's me. Naval reserve.'

'You bein' in turn commanded by Captain Timbs. Weel—guid nicht.'

'You heard about that timber ship gettin' torpedoed?' Wharton asked.

'No. What was that?'

'Oh, just that they thought she mightn't have sunk properly, an' be derelict hereabouts. Timbs has been radioin' everybody bar Churchill an' President Roosevelt, but nobody's seen her. Dark night, too. Well—pleasant dreams.'

A certain pensiveness marked Mr McIvor's departure but the first mate seemed to feel better.

He extracted Miss Churt gently fron the land of nod, held her up with forelegs dangling, treated her to a gigantic smile and kissed her unhygienically on the nose.

'Azza booful girlie!' said Mr Wharton. 'You like Poppa go home to his other girl an' get married, please, an' zen you have lovely house an' garden to scratch in?'

Miss Churt was exceedingly drowsy; moreover that rump steak seemed still to be clogging her articulation. She opened her pink mouth, but no sound issued.

'I'll bet you,' said Mr Wharton. 'And that reminds me—'

He had just risen to pick up the newspaper with the wedding on it when from for'ard, out in the starry dark, there came a thunderous crash.

The *Malvern* stopped in her tracks like a dowager smitten in the breadbasket.

Simultaneously, the lights went out.

It was, of course, that derelict, floating bottom up at what the French so prettily call the flower of the water, or, in Anglo-Saxon sea talk, awash.

Having accomplished the destiny given her by those heavenly lights overhead—Neptune afflicted by Mars, perhaps; who knows?—and buckled the *Malvern*'s blunt bows backward like the bellows of a concertina, the timber ship rolled, spewed a few hundred thousand board feet from a new gash and sank; while down behind the forepeak of the *Malvern*, Mr Wharton and a number of nearly naked shipmates strove to save their tub from doing likewise.

It was a question of strengthening a bulkhead, and strengthening bulkheads is uneasy work in the pitch dark.

It was an hour before Mr McIvor and his horde got the uprooted dynamo going again; and then what was revealed by hand lights led into the hold was the reverse of encouraging.

Not only was the bulkhead spouting water through the holes of deracinated rivets; it was bulging bodily and visibly inward, so that it was obvious that no time remained for carpenter work and fancy shoring.

Mr Wharton's eyes, under a mop of embattled hair, shuttled desperately about the hold. The port and starboard sides were solid-packed with minor munitions, forming admirable buttresses for the wings of the forward wall. But in the midst stood two cases that had taxed the stevedores; they were large and heavy enough to have contained whippet tanks, and the *Malvern*'s notorious instability had caused them to be stowed well aft of the bulkhead.

The space between was filled with this and that, in packets weighing mere hundreds of pounds.

'Get that junk out o' the way!' roared Mr Wharton. 'C'mon, boys!'

He himself was about to seize a crate when the third mate grabbed his shoulder.

'I say—Wharton—'

'The hell you do. Muck in an' shift something. I'm going' to shove these locomotives up, or whatever they are'.

'Listen! The Old Man's in a sweat of funk—sendin' out SOS till the ether's got clots in it—'

'To hell with him!'

'An' now he's getting ready to abandon ship.'

Mr Wharton disposed of his current crate and dashed forward to cut the key case out of a jam. Somehow or other his shirt had disintegrated, and his trousers consisted of but a breechclout and one leg, but still he was not swearing.

Canon Hobson, at that moment asleep in far-off Liverpool,

47

his craglike nose in a soft pillow made for him by a parishioner, would have been gratified could he have known.

'What are you going' to do?' demanded the third officer. 'He's got all the ship's papers ready, an' he says his duty's to his men, an' unless we get help by dawn he's gonna take to the boats.'

'If you don't get outa my dog-rammed way we won't be afloat till dawn,' said Mr Wharton. 'Hey—'

'But you got to stop him!'

'An' risk my ticket—mutiny? No, sir; I obey—get that stuff movin',' you bunch o' lobsters! Come along aft here, you knobeyed slackers—want me to shove this myself? You Fawdry—you Wilson—'

A cleared space now lay between the bulkhead and the first tank, which, of course, was not really a tank, it just felt like one. Anyway, the problem was to get it up to that bulkhead—and the other one up behind it, if possible. And the bulkhead was remarking, in the language of tortured steel, that it would be damned if it was going to wait for such support much longer.

'You can't shift 'em,' said the third mate weakly, 'an' if you do, you'll shove her bow down an' we'll slide.'

'Like the *Tornado* at Coney Island,' gasped Mr Wharton, grinning. ' "Down went McGinty"—ready, boys? Line up, get your shoulders against it. It's shove or grow gills! Now—one—two—'

The case didn't move.

'The Old Man says—' gasped the third mate.

'Give us a shanty,' grunted one of the men; and Mr Wharton obliged. It might almost be said that out of the fullness of the heart the mouth spoke. It could hardly be called singing, and the verbiage was bald and incomplete; yet in topicality, direction and—yes—the passion of love denied, Mr Wharton's shanty might have claimed kinship with the romances of the troubadours.

'Ca-a-a-ptain Ti-i-i-mbs,' he emitted in a wavering roar, 'is a son of a—*heave!*'

The men had had their leave stopped in Staten Island.

'Ca-a-a-ptain Ti-i-i-mbs,' they agreed fulsomely, 'is a son of a—*heave!*'

The case budged.

'Ca-a-a-ptain Timbs—*heave!*'

It moved six inches.

'—son of a—*heave!*'

Six inches more.

Up on the bridge, the subject of the shanty was talking to three naval ratings who seemed not to like him. They were the men responsible for the 4.7 aft, and they seemed to be suffering from the spirit of Nelson, or Collingwood or somebody.

All they did about it, though, was to say they didn't think—

'You don't have to think!' said Captain Timbs.

'You're not our officer, sir,' said the senior rating.

'You're under my orders! If I say to abandon ship, we'll abandon ship!'

This made it the turn of the junior rating.

'Aye, aye, sir,' said he. 'If you say so.'

Captain Timbs swallowed a large and visible lump in the throat. 'That's the order,' he said. 'Soon's it's dawn. We're ripped wide open.'

'Roughish sea, sir,' said the senior rating impassively.

'I've got a Swedish freighter on the radio—she'll be here by then, standing by. Who the hell are you, questioning my orders?'

'Nobody, sir,' said the second rating.

'Get to hell out!'

'Aye, aye, sir,' said the third; and out they went.

What they said as they went below is nobody's business; such low speculations about the sums payable by government to bereaved ship owners; so much plain, vulgar swearing. One may, however, make extracts to the extent that the senior remarked that dawn was breaking already; the second said that the old gal felt like taking the high dive, at that; while the junior, peering aft, remarked sentimentally that anyhow she'd go down with her flag up and her gun shotted.

'Might go an' fire her off for once,' said he.

'Might go down an' give Wharton a hand,' said his senior severely; and so they did.

Some time later, Miss Churt, whose rump steak had filled

slumber with dreams of gigantic rats chasing her down unending alleyways, awoke with a start and a bad taste in her mouth.

She yawned and decided that a little fresh air, again, would do her good. Jumping down from the settee, she found that the floor was not exactly where she had left it—it sloped downward now, and before she could correct her stance her for'ard legs had given way and she had rolled into a corner.

Picking herself thence, and reaching the door-sill, she rolled forth in search of company. It was light, so she gave the yawn and stretch by which cats thank God for each night spent in shelter—but something appeared to be wrong.

Where was everybody, to start with?

And why wasn't the deck vibrating as it always had, except just before and after mother left? And then the cargo winches had been working, with a roar that set one's ears back; now there was stillness—and behold! as one crossed behind the charthouse the bulwark of boats was gone and the wind smote one unimpeded.

Just some ropes trailing . . .

Miss Churt walked forward a few more paces and sat down, like the treble clef in a musical stave. Far in the misty distance she could see a ship standing still; and as for the *Malvern's* boats, they were on the water—swimming, actually, and swimming away from her.

And in one of them, along with the three naval ratings and some other able-bodied gentlemen who disapproved of Captain Timbs and were saying so, Mr Wharton was at this identical moment remembering that he had left Miss Churt aboard.

'Noah's nails!' he ejaculated; and Canon Hobson, still sleeping, smiled in his distant dreams. 'Why—'

The oars lifted.

'Forgot something, sir?' asked the senior rating.

'Forgotten something?' said Mr Wharton. 'I've left my cat behind!'

From the bow of the boat came an imperfectly stifled chuckle.

'You laugh at me and I'll put a head on you,' said the first officer; and silence redescended on the ocean.

'Want to go back, sir?'

'I—think I will,' said Mr Wharton. 'If we're to save our dirty hides when there's no need to, I don't see why a poor dumb animal should suffer. Unless these gentlemen object? Pull stabbud, back port! Come on, you bunch of tailors!'

'Captain's boat's stopped rowin', sir,' said the bow oar.

'Ne'er mind,' said Mr Wharton, 'we can rat just as well in ten minutes' time. An' that Swede can wait. Some expensive nephew for—c'mon, put some beef into it!'

A distant hail came over the water—which, by the way, was now astonishingly calm.

'I'll just swarm up the falls an' be back in a jiffy,' said Mr Wharton—not knowing that a mile the other side of the *Malvern* the sea, hidden from him by the wallowing bulk of that ship, was just being broken by the conning tower of a submarine.

Her commander, a pleasant enough fellow named Koenig, usually resident in Munich, Glocknergasse No. 8, had heard the frantic distress signals wirelessed by Captain Timbs and had wondered if perchance they might portend something in his line of business. There was, he knew, a temporary scarcity of destroyers in this area, but the event was turning out better than his hopes. Through the periscope he had watched the crew abandoning ship, and, when the *Malvern* failed to slide precipitately out of sight, had commented soul-ticklingly to his men on the unsea-to-dare-worthiness of British sailors.

That this was no Q-ship he was well assured, both by the presence of the Swedish ship and the perilous trim of the *Malvern* herself. So it was his intent to combine business with pleasure by letting the fleeing crew watch him use their vessel for target practice. He thought he would use percussion fuse and blow the funnel out of her first.

As the submarine came awash her gun crew tumbled up, ran for'ard and proceeded to clear their gun.

And simultaneously, the longing gaze of Miss Churt was gratified by the spectacle of Mr Wharton, shaggier than ever. Miss Churt liked shagginess, it gave one more corners to nestle in.

Her master, landing on the boat deck from the falls, didn't seem as cheery as usual; something seemed to be bothering him; he didn't smile.

But Miss Churt knew how to remedy that. When anybody looked sad, she ran away, and Mr Wharton ran after her and picked her up and called her a little devil and corrected himself and said 'weevil' and kissed her on the end of the nose.

Miss Churt therefore ran away now, skidding slightly because of the slant of the deck; her ears cocked for the sound of beloved footsteps pursuing.

And here they came.

But here came something else.

Something terrible. A long, increasing noise, coming out of the middle of a distant thump, boring into her ears—so terrifying—and then—a vast flash of light, taking up the whole world and tearing it to pieces, shaking her stomach so that the steak didn't matter any more. . . .

Mr Wharton, rushing from behind the wireless house, paused a moment.

He saw a very large scorched hole in the boat deck planking, around which he had to pick his way.

While thus engaged, he saw Captain Koenig's submarine, lying perhaps three quarters of a mile off.

But what he was looking for was a small ball of soiled fur; and this he found, very limp, just for'ard of the bridge deck ladder. The curious thing is that Captain Koenig also adored cats, and had three at home in the Glocknergasse.

But that's war.

Mr Wharton took up in his very large hand what war had left of Miss Churt, and he laid the other hand over her like the lid of a little coffin and cursed Captain Koenig and his superiors and inferiors; and then he lifted both his arms and, still holding the limp form in his right hand, raised in a voice that almost carried the distance.

Indeed—in St Mary's Rectory, Canon Hobson awoke with a start; looked at his bedside clock and found it was 5.25; rolled over—but somehow was disinclined to go to sleep again.

'You bloody, sneaking *bloody* butcher!' Mr Wharton was now shouting; and there came a sudden crack in his voice. 'My little—'

A voice spoke from just behind him. It had not seemed quite proper to the naval ratings that their officer should go aboard without escort, so they had swarmed up the falls also and here

52

they were. The voice was the voice of the senior rating, as was proper.

'How about giving 'em a packet, sir?' he inquired.

Mr Wharton had forgotten the 4.7 gun aft. Now he remembered and gave a perfect snarl of assent.

The body of Miss Churt he crammed into the side pocket of his coat; and then down the ladder he went, and after him came the ratings.

They had to descend another ladder and cross the aft well-deck and then climb the poop; and it was now that Captain Koenig saw them.

With a welter of ow sounds and a swamp of terminations in ch, he directed his men to shift target and give Wharton *et al.* a packet; so that the question resolved itself roughly into one of who should give whom a packet first.

The U-boat, being in the groove, got her shot off the earlier; but the hastily altered aim was high and the shell went to miss the Swedish ship by no more than half a mile. (Memorandum of 27 March 1940, paragraph 2.)

Meantime, the senior rating had done various manipulations of various things; and now, with a nod of the head, he expressed himself satisfied. Quite unnecessarily, he looked at Mr Wharton, opened his mouth and was just about to ask if he should open fire when the officer (not a regular navy man, of course) shoved him aside, seized the firing lever and got the shot off himself.

It was just luck, blind luck, for all concerned; but the fact remains that the unconventional, almost illegitimate, shell flew as through a tube to the barrel of the U-boat's gun, bent it, zoomed thereoff without touching Captain Koenig or his men, and smote the lip of the conning tower, where it exploded with the abandon peculiar to high explosive.

Nobody was hurt, save Seaman Albrecht Otto of Bremen (deafness and scratches)—but the conning tower was impossible to close. That meant no submersion—

And on the southern sky line there had appeared, and was approaching, a smudge of smoke, which betokened destroyers. The ratings pointed this out to one another.

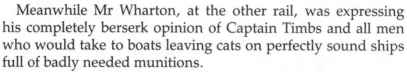

Meanwhile Mr Wharton, at the other rail, was expressing his completely berserk opinion of Captain Timbs and all men who would take to boats leaving cats on perfectly sound ships full of badly needed munitions.

This expression, in addition to blistering (if the third officer may be believed) the paint on the thwarts of Lifeboat No. 1, left Mr Wharton rather exhausted. And softened in mood.

He put his hand into his pocket and pulled out the mortal envelope of Miss Churt. The bluish eyes were closed, the furry head rolled on the neck, and all her whiskers had been singed away.

'You want us to come back, sir?' came a hail from the boats.

'You can go to hell!' roared Mr Wharton; so they started toward him.

But a voice pitched to carry a quarter of a mile is tremendous at close range.

Miss Churt vibrated in every cell.

Her stomach began to trouble her again. There was a familiar smell in her nostrils, seeping past the stench of burned whiskers—tobacco, tar and Mallinson's—

She opened her eyes and said: 'Mew!'

For all it was wartime, the parish church of St Mary's was properly decorated for this wedding; though in view of the circumstances, Canon Hobson had consented to relax the clothing rules so far as the bridegroom was concerned.

Miss Woollard, however, was in the prescribed raiment even down to the seventy-ninth orange blossom; albeit inclined, apparently, to take nervous bites out of her veil. She was more nervous than brides usually are; more nervous even than seemed warranted by the fact that her bridegroom had three best men—the senior, junior and middle naval ratings, all with medals but one degree inferior to that which had been bestowed on Mr Wharton.

The cause for this uneasiness came to light when Canon Hobson, opening his prayer book, first glanced, then looked, then stared at the bridegroom's right-hand coat pocket.

It should perhaps be mentioned here that in addition to a granite face and an extraordinarily soft heart, the reverend gentleman was equipped with eyes that seemed to have been chipped out of adamant and ground to fine points.

He furled the prayer book and spoke in a low, dazed voice.

'Henry,' said he, while the congregation craned, 'that cannot be a cat you have in your coat pocket? Not a *cat?*'

This was rather an exaggeration of the status of Miss Churt, who was six weeks old that day and had just put her shell-shaven face out for a little air. But the general proposition was undeniable.

'Yes,' said Mr Wharton. 'It is.'

'He *would* bring it—he *would*—I said—' quavered the bride; but Canon Hobson paid no attention to her, though she began to sob.

Meeting the bluish eyes of Miss Churt, however, his adamantine orbs underwent a peculiar process. First they flickered from their condemning stare; then, as it were, they liquefied, so that their penetrative qualities became nil.

He spoke:

'Am I to presume that—this—is some kind of mascot? Connected perhaps with the recent—? What has happened to her whiskers?'

'I'll tell you about it in the vestry,' said Mr Wharton; and, meeting the canon's gaze, mourned for the misjudgments of his youth.

Canon Hobson nodded; opened the book which he had closed on a probationary thumb, and cleared his throat.

'Dearly beloved,' he proclaimed, 'we are gathered to-gether—'

Miss Churt could not quite identify all the smells (largely lilies) or sounds (mostly Canon Hobson) that were going on.

They were interesting, and she had a vague idea that something of the same general purport might be her personal concern one day.

But not now.

Not for a long time yet.

And meantime she had had enough air.

She withdrew her head from the atmosphere of St Mary's into the warm tweediness of Mr Wharton's pocket and composed herself to sleep.

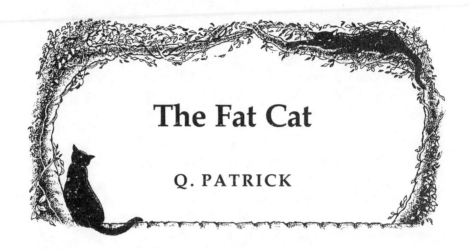

The Fat Cat

Q. PATRICK

T HE marines found her when they finally captured the old mission house at Fufa. After two days of relentless pounding, they hadn't expected to find anything alive there—least of all a fat cat.

And she was a very fat cat, sandy as a Scotsman, with enormous agate eyes and a fat amiable face. She sat there on the mat—or rather what was left of the mat—in front of what had been the mission porch, licking her paws as placidly as if the shell-blasted jungle were a summer lawn in New Jersey.

One of the men, remembering his childhood primer, quoted: 'The fat cat sat on the mat.'

The other men laughed; not that the remark was really funny, but laughter broke the tension and expressed their relief at having at last reached their objective, after two days of bitter fighting.

The fat cat, still sitting on the mat, smiled at them, as if to show she didn't mind the joke being on her. Then she saw Corporal Randy Jones, and for some reason known only to herself ran toward him as though he was her long-lost master. With a refrigerator purr, she weaved in and out of his muddy legs.

Everyone laughed again as Randy picked her up and pushed his ugly face against the sleek fur. It was funny to see any living thing show a preference for the dour, solitary Randy.

A sergeant flicked his fingers. 'Kitty. Come here. We'll make you B Company mascot.'

But the cat, perched on Randy's shoulder like a queen on her throne, merely smiled down majestically as much as to say:

56

 THE FAT CAT

'You can be my subjects if you like. But this is my man—my royal consort.'

And never for a second did she swerve from her devotion. She lived with Randy, slept with him, ate only food provided by him. Almost every man in Co. B tried to seduce her with caresses and morsels of canned ration, but all advances were met with a yawn of contempt.

For Randy this new love was ecstasy. He guarded her with the possessive tenderness of a mother. He combed her fur sleek; he almost starved himself to maintain her fatness. And all the time there was a strange wonder in him. The homeliest and ungainliest of ten in a West Virginia mining family, he had never before aroused affection in man or woman. No one had counted for him until the fat cat.

Randy's felicity, however, was short-lived. In a few days B Company was selected to carry out a flanking movement to surprise and possibly capture the enemy's headquarters, known to be twenty miles away through dense, sniper-infested jungle. The going would be rugged. Each man would carry his own supply of food and water, and sleep in foxholes with no support from the base.

The C.O. was definite about the fat cat: the stricken Randy was informed that the presence of a cat would seriously endanger the safety of the whole company. If it were seen following him, it would be shot on sight. Just before their scheduled departure, Randy carried the fat cat over to the mess of Co. H, where she was enthusiastically received by an equally fat cook. Randy could not bring himself to look back at the reproachful stare which he knew would be in the cat's agate eyes.

But all through that first day of perilous jungle travel, the thought of the cat's stare haunted him, and he was prey to all the heartache of parting; in leaving the cat, he had left behind wife, mother, and child.

Darkness, like an immense black parachute, had descended hours ago on the jungle, when Randy was awakened from exhausted sleep. Something soft and warm was brushing his cheek; and his foxhole resounded to a symphony of purring. He stretched out an incredulous hand, but this was no dream.

Real and solid, the cat was curled in a contented ball at his shoulder.

His first rush of pleasure was chilled as he remembered his C.O.'s words. The cat, spurning the blandishments of H. Co.'s cuisine, had followed him through miles of treacherous jungle, only to face death the moment daylight revealed her presence. Randy was in an agony of uncertainty. To carry her back to the base would be desertion. To beat and drive her away was beyond the power of his simple nature.

The cat nuzzled his face again and breathed a mournful meow. She was hungry, of course, after her desperate trek. Suddenly Randy saw what he must do. If he could bring himself not to feed her, hunger would surely drive her back to the sanctuary of the cook.

She meowed again. He shushed her and gave her a half-hearted slap. 'Aain't got nothing for you, honey. Scram. Go home. Scat.'

To his mingled pleasure and disappointment, she leaped silently out of the foxhole. When morning came there was no sign of her.

As B Company inched its furtive advance through the dense undergrowth, Randy felt the visit from the cat must have been a dream. But on the third night it came again. It brushed against his cheek and daintily took his ear in its teeth. When it meowed, the sound was still soft and cautious, but held a pitiful quaver of beseechment which cut through Randy like a Jap bayonet.

On its first visit, Randy had not seen the cat, but tonight some impulse made him reach for his flashlight. Holding it carefully downward, he turned it on. What he saw was the ultimate ordeal. The fat cat was fat no longer. Her body sagged; her sleek fur was matted and mud-stained, her paws torn and bloody. But it was the eyes, blinking up at him, that were the worst. There was no hint of reproach in them, only an expression of infinite trust and pleading.

Forgetting everything but those eyes, Randy tugged out one of his few remaining cans of ration. At the sight of it, the cat weakly licked its lips. Randy moved to open the can. Then the realization that he would be signing the cat's death warrant surged over him. And, because the pent-up emotion

in him had to have some outlet, it turned into unreasoning anger against this animal whose suffering had become more than he could bear. 'Skat,' he hissed. But the cat did not move.

He lashed out at her with the heavy flashlight. For a second she lay motionless under the blow. Then with a little moan she fled.

The next night she did not come back and Randy did not sleep.

On the fifth day they reached really dangerous territory. Randy and another marine, Joe, were sent forward to scout for the Jap command headquarters. Suddenly, weaving through the jungle, they came upon it.

A profound silence hung over the glade, with its two hastily erected shacks. Peering through the dense foliage, they saw traces of recent evacuation—waste paper scattered on the grass, a pile of fresh garbage, a Jap army shirt flapping on a tree. Outside one of the shacks, under an awning, stretched a rough table strewn with the remains of a meal. 'They must have got wind of us and scrammed,' breathed Joe.

Randy edged forward—then froze as something stirred in the long grasses near the door of the first shack. As he watched, the once fat cat hobbled out into the sunlight.

A sense of heightened danger warred with Randy's pride that she had not abandoned him. Stiff with suspense, he watched it disappear into the shack. Soon it padded out.

'No Japs,' said Joe. 'That cat'd have raised 'em sure as shooting.'

He started boldly into the glade. 'Hey, Randy, there's a whole chicken on that table. Chicken's going to taste good after K ration.'

He broke off, for the cat had seen the chicken too, and with pitiful clumsiness had leaped on to the table. With an angry yell Joe stooped for a rock and threw it.

Indignation blazed in Randy. He'd starved and spurned the cat, and yet she'd followed him with blind devotion. The chicken, surely, should be her reward. In his slow, simple mind it seemed the most important thing in the world for his beloved to have her fair share of the booty.

The cat, seeing the rock coming, lumbered off the table just

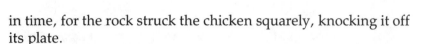

in time, for the rock struck the chicken squarely, knocking it off its plate.

Randy leaped into the clearing. As he did so, a deafening explosion made him drop to the ground. A few seconds later, when he raised himself, there was no table, no shack, nothing but a blazing wreckage of wood.

Dazedly he heard Joe's voice: 'Booby trap under that chicken. Gee, if that cat hadn't jumped for it, I wouldn't have hurled the rock; we'd have grabbed it ourselves—and we'd be in heaven now.' His voice dropped to an awed whisper. 'That cat. I guess it's blown to hell . . . But it saved our lives.' Randy couldn't speak. There was a constriction in his throat. He lay there, feeling more desolate than he'd ever felt in his life before.

Then from behind came a contented purr.

He spun round. Freakishly, the explosion had hurled a crude rush mat out of the shack. It had come to rest on the grass behind him.

And, seated serenely on the mat, the cat was smiling at him.

The Undoing of Morning Glory Adolphus

N. MARGARET CAMPBELL

ORNING Glory Adolphus is our oldest and most sedate cat. He has his own hunting preserves in a wooded ravine at the back of our house, and woe to the cat or dog who invades it. In his early youth he won an enviable reputation as a hunter of big game, and he had his own method of securing due recognition for his exploits. Whenever he captures a rabbit, a squirrel, a water-rat, or a snake, he hunts until he finds his mistress and lays the tribute proudly at her feet. This determination to be cited for bravery and prowess becomes a trifle embarrassing at times, especially when he drags a five-foot snake into the music-room and lets it wriggle on the rug to the horror and confusion of guests. But whatever the hazards, Adolphus is not to be thwarted of due publicity for his skill. If he were a man, he would be accompanied on all of his hunting-trips by a press-agent, and would have luncheon with the editors of all the sporting journals upon his return. As it is, without even a correspondence course in advertising, Adolphus manages quite well.

For the study of majestic dignity, tinged on occasions with lofty disdain, interpreters of muscular expression would do well to seek out Adolphus. He walks the highway without haste or concern for his personal survival in the midst of tooting automobiles and charging dogs. When a strange dog appears and mistakes Adolphus for an ordinary cat who may be chased for the sport of the thing, it is the custom of Adolphus to slow his pace somewhat and stretch out in the path of the oncoming enemy, assuming the pose and the expression of the sphinx. He is the graven image of repose and

perfect muscular control. Only his slumbrous amber eyes burn unblinkingly, never leaving the enraged countenance of his enemy, who bears down upon him with exposed fangs and hackles erect. When the assault is too ferocious to be in good taste even among dogs, accompanied by hysterical yapping and snapping, Adolphus has been known to yawn in the face of his assailant, quite deliberately and very politely, as a gentleman of good breeding might when bored by an excessive display of emotion. Usually the dog mysteriously halts within a foot or so of those calm yellow eyes and describes a semi-circle within the range of those twin fires, filling the air with defiant taunts that gradually die away to foolish whimpering as he begins an undignified withdrawal, while Adolphus winks solemnly and stares past his cowering foe into a mysterious space undesecrated by blustering dogs.

A few dogs there have been who have failed to halt at the hypnotic command of those yellow eyes. Then there came a lightning-like flash of fur through the air, and Adolphus landed neatly on his victim's neck, his great claws beginning to rip with businesslike precision through the soft ears and forehead of the terrified dog. Perhaps the rumour of these encounters spread among the canine population of our neighbourhood, for it is never counted against the reputation of any dog as a fighter if he makes a wide detour of the regions frequented by Adolphus.

For years the rule of Adolphus among the cats of his own household had been undisputed. Then came Silver Paws, a handsome young rogue whose satiny coat was beautiful with broken silver and blue lights. There was no question about it, Silver Paws had a way with the ladies. While Adolphus still looked upon him as a frolicsome kitten whose sense of humour was unbalanced by a proper sense of dignity, he artfully won all hearts and easily became the centre of attraction wherever he appeared. It was plainly disgusting to Adolphus to see the way the conceited young thing arched his back expectantly whenever a human hand came near enough to caress him.

If Adolphus had had the small mind of a punster, he might have observed, after the cynical manner of others who have lost their place in the public affections to an unworthy rival, that the glory was passing out of his name. But he was never

62

one to surrender without a struggle. He went to his nightly hunt with cold murder in his heart and a high resolve to force the spotlight back upon himself. Daily he laid at the feet of his mistress older and wilder rabbits, fiercer-eyed rats, and longer snakes. All to no purpose. He even played the heroic role of the deliverer when his hated rival was treed by the grocer's dog. He simply walked calmly up to the tree where the dog was dancing wildly under the limb where the trembling Silver Paws clung, and the dog suddenly remembered that he really ought to catch up to the grocer's wagon and it wasn't much fun to bark at a silly kitten, anyway! When the frightened Silver Paws slid down the tree, Adolphus walked up to him with the self-righteous air of a benevolent gentleman who has rescued a lost soul not because the soul deserved it, but because he himself was made that way. This magnanimous act gave Adolphus a momentary advantage over his rival, but the fickle attentions of the household were soon centred upon the handsome young charmer again. Then Adolphus took to sitting about the house,

gazing solemnly past the spot where Silver Paws was receiving the choicest bits of meat with many endearing words, and smoothing his whiskers with a reflective paw.

It was about this time that Silver Paws, to the consternation of the household, disappeared. A search was instituted in the neighbourhood, but he was gone without a trace, just as though he had been whisked away on a magic broom. Mournfully we gathered up the playthings he had left scattered over the house—a bit of fur on a string, a bright-coloured ball, some dried beans that rattled in the pod when batted about by a velvet paw—and of these remembrances we made a heap in his favourite rocking-chair. 'He'll want them if he ever comes back,' we said.

A remarkable change had come over Morning Glory Adolphus. We had long honoured him as a crafty hunter and first-rate fighting-man, but we had judged him to be somewhat lacking in sentiment, a trifle indifferent and unresponsive, as was natural enough in one who had achieved no small amount of fame. What was our astonishment to find that he had become, overnight, warmly demonstrative in his affections and sympathetically desirous of turning our thoughts from useless brooding over the lost one. It was really touching to see the way he followed us about the house, sitting at our feet to sing with rapturous abandon wherever we happened to pause. Forgotten were the joys of the chase, the pleasant pastime of disciplining unmannerly dogs. For three whole days he gave himself up wholly to the business of love-making. If we attempted to ignore him, he threw himself at our feet and lay on his back at our mercy, as one who would say that he bared his faithful heart that we might kill him if we could not love him. He walked about the house with the proudly possessive air of a haughty ruler who has returned to his domains after an enforced absence, and he curled up blissfully on the cushions where his late rival had been accustomed to take his ease. Once we found him stretched contemptuously over the playthings that lay in a little heap in the rocking-chair. It must have been a bumpy sort of bed, but Adolphus looked happy and comfortable.

Suspicion instantly seized upon his mistress. 'Adolphus,' she said sternly, 'I believe you know what has become of our beautiful Silver Paws!' The accused rose stiffly to his full height, regarded her with the gravely innocent expression of an outraged deacon, and then, turning his back deliberately upon her, gave himself up again to the slumbers of the just.

But the suspicions of the household were not laid. 'Adolphus is trying too hard to be good,' they argued. 'It is not natural. There must be something on his conscience!' For this was Adolphus's way of raising a smoke-screen, as it were, to hide his evil deeds. They had observed this in the past. It was all very humiliating to a proud soul like Adolphus, and he showed his resentment by stalking out of the house and letting the screen-door slam behind him after the manner of any offended male.

The household followed him from afar. He walked straight to the ravine, where he was accustomed to hunt, and stood peering intently down into it over the edge of a cliff, his ears pricked forward, every line of him expressing gloating satisfaction, from his agitated whiskers to the tip of his quivering tail. It was hard to believe that he was the same kindly creature who had been making affectionate advances to us a few hours before. As we drew near we could hear a faint crying, pleading and pitiful, and down among the bushes we discovered our lost Silver Paws, too weak from loss of food to stand, and rather battered from the rough treatment he had received from his jailor.

The moment that Adolphus saw us looking into the ravine he withdrew in disgust, for he knew that his game was up. With lofty scorn he watched us gather up his banished rival, revive him with warm milk, caress and comfort him. With what dire threats had Adolphus kept his captive down in the ravine, within sound of our voices, all the long hours while he wooed us at his leisure, and what spell had he cast over him that the hungry kitten had not dared to come at our call?

While we rejoiced and scolded, the grocer's dog was observed coming around the corner of the house. He had grown bold during those days of weakness when Adolphus had been courting the ladies. But one look into the amber eyes of Adolphus, and he was off with a shriek, for he could see that the fighter was once more the master of his emotions.

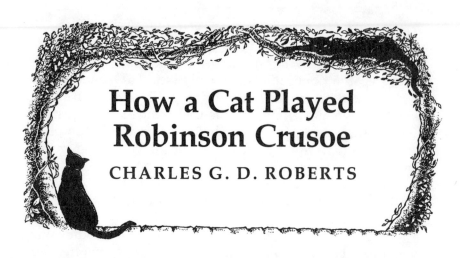

How a Cat Played Robinson Crusoe

CHARLES G. D. ROBERTS

THE island was a mere sandbank off the low, flat coast. Not a tree broke its bleak levels—not even a shrub. But the long, gritty stalks of the marsh grass clothed it everywhere above tide-mark; and a tiny rivulet of sweet water, flowing from a spring at its centre, drew a ribbon of inland herbage and tenderer green across the harsh and sombre yellow grey of the grass. Few would have chosen the island as a place to live, yet at its seaward end, where the changing tides were never still, stood a spacious, one-storied, wide-verandaed cottage, with a low shed behind it. The virtue of this lone plot of sand was coolness. When the neighbour mainland would be sweltering day and night alike under a breathless heat, out here on the island there was always a cool wind blowing. Therefore a wise city dweller had appropriated the sea waif and built his summer home thereon, where the tonic airs might bring back the rose to the pale cheeks of his children.

The family came to the island toward the end of June. In the first week of September they went away, leaving every door and window of house and shed securely shuttered, bolted or barred against the winter's storms. A roomy boat, rowed by two fishermen, carried them across the half mile of racing tides that separated them from the mainland. The elders of the household were not sorry to get back to the world of men, after two months of mere wind, and sun, and waves, and waving grass tops. But the children went with tear-stained faces. They were leaving behind them their favourite pet, the accustomed comrade of their migrations, a handsome, moon-faced cat, striped like a tiger. The animal had mysteriously disappeared

66

two days before, vanishing from the face of the island without leaving a trace behind. The only reasonable explanation seemed to be that she had been snapped up by a passing eagle. The cat, meanwhile, was a fast prisoner at the other end of the island, hidden beneath a broken barrel and some hundred-weight of drifted sand.

The old barrel, with the staves battered out of one side, had stood, half buried, on the crest of a sand ridge raised by a long prevailing wind. Under its lee the cat had found a sheltered hollow, full of sun, where she had been wont to lie curled up for hours at a time, basking and sleeping. Meanwhile the sand had been steadily piling itself higher and higher behind the unstable barrier. At last it had piled too high; and suddenly, before a stronger gust, the barrel had come toppling over beneath a mass of sand, burying the sleeping cat out of sight and light. But at the same time the sound half of the barrel had formed a safe roof to her prison, and she was neither crushed nor smothered. When the children in their anxious search all over the island chanced upon the mound of fine, white sand they gave it but one careless look. They could not hear the faint cries that came, at intervals, from the close darkness within. So they went away sorrowfully, little dreaming that their friend was imprisoned almost beneath their feet.

For three days the prisoner kept up her appeals for help. On the third day the wind changed and presently blew up a gale. In a few hours it had uncovered the barrel. At one corner a tiny spot of light appeared.

Eagerly the cat stuck her paw through the hole. When she withdrew it again the hole was much enlarged. She took the hint and fell to scratching. At first her efforts were rather aimless; but presently, whether by good luck or quick sagacity, she learned to make her scratching more effective. The opening rapidly enlarged, and at last she was able to squeeze her way out.

The wind was tearing madly across the island, filled with flying sand. The seas hurled themselves trampling up the beach, with the uproar of a bombardment. The grasses lay bowed flat in long quivering ranks. Over the turmoil the sun stared down from a deep, unclouded blue. The cat, when first she met the full force of the gale, was fairly blown off her feet.

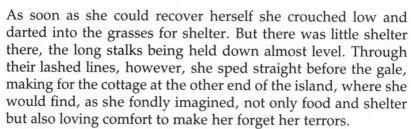

As soon as she could recover herself she crouched low and darted into the grasses for shelter. But there was little shelter there, the long stalks being held down almost level. Through their lashed lines, however, she sped straight before the gale, making for the cottage at the other end of the island, where she would find, as she fondly imagined, not only food and shelter but also loving comfort to make her forget her terrors.

Still and desolate in the bright sunshine and the tearing wind, the house frightened her. She could not understand the tight-closed shutters, the blind, unresponding doors that would no longer open to her anxious appeal. The wind swept her savagely across the naked veranda. Climbing with difficulty to the dining-room windowsill, where so often she had been let in, she clung there a few moments and yowled heartbrokenly. Then, in a sudden panic, she jumped down and ran to the shed. That, too, was closed. Never before had she seen the shed doors closed, and she could not understand it. Cautiously she crept around the foundations—but those had been built honestly: there was no such thing as getting in that way. On every side it was nothing but a blank, forbidding face that the old familiar house confronted her with.

The cat had always been so coddled and pampered by the children that she had had no need to forage for herself; but, fortunately for her, she had learned to hunt the marsh mice and grass sparrows for amusement. So now, being ravenous from her long fast under the sand, she slunk mournfully away from the deserted house and crept along under the lee of a sand ridge to a little grassy hollow which she knew. Here the gale caught only the tops of the grasses; and here, in the warmth and comparative calm, the furry little marsh folk, mice and shrews, were going about their business undisturbed.

The cat, quick and stealthy, soon caught one and eased her hunger. She caught several. And then, making her way back to the house, she spent hours in heartsick prowling around it and around, sniffing and peering, yowling piteously on the threshold and windowsill; and every now and then being blown ignominiously across the smooth, naked expanse of the veranda floor. At last, hopelessly discouraged, she curled herself up beneath the children's window and went to sleep.

In spite of her loneliness and grief the life of the island

prisoner during the next two or three weeks was by no means one of hardship. Besides her abundant food of birds and mice she quickly learned to catch tiny fish in the mouth of the rivulet, where salt water and fresh water met. It was an exciting game, and she became expert at dashing the grey tom-cod and blue-and-silver sand-lance far up the slope with a sweep of her armed paw. But when the equinoctial storms roared down upon the island, with furious rain, and low, black clouds torn to shreds, then life became more difficult for her. Game all took to cover, where it was hard to find. It was difficult to get around in the drenched and lashing grass; and, moreover, she loathed wet. Most of the time she went hungry, sitting sullen and desolate under the lee of the house, glaring out defiantly at the rush and battling tumult of the waves.

The storm lasted nearly ten days before it blew itself clean out. On the eighth day the abandoned wreck of a small Nova Scotia schooner drove ashore, battered out of all likeness to a ship. But hulk as it was it had passengers of a sort. A horde of rats got through the surf and scurried into the hiding of the grass roots. They promptly made themselves at home, burrowing under the grass and beneath old, half-buried timbers, and carrying panic into the ranks of the mice and shrews.

When the storm was over the cat had a decided surprise in her first long hunting expedition. Something had rustled the grass heavily and she trailed it, expecting a particularly large, fat marsh mouse. When she pounced and alighted upon an immense old ship's rat, many-voyaged and many-battled, she got badly bitten. Such an experience had never before fallen to her lot. At first she felt so injured that she was on the point of backing out and running away. Then her latent pugnacity awoke, and the fire of far-off ancestors. She flung herself into the fight with a rage that took no accounting of the wounds she got; and the struggle was soon over. Her wounds, faithfully licked, quickly healed themselves in that clean and tonic air; and after that, having learned how to handle such big game, she no more got bitten.

During the first full moon after her abandonment—the first week in October—the island was visited by still weather with sharp night frosts. The cat discovered then that it was most exciting to hunt by night and do her sleeping in the daytime.

She found that now, under the strange whiteness of the moon, all her game was astir—except the birds, which had fled to the mainland during the storm, gathering for the southward flight. The blanched grasses, she found, were now everywhere a-rustle; and everywhere dim little shapes went darting with thin squeaks across ghostly-white sands. Also she made the acquaintaince of a new bird, which she regarded at first uneasily and then with vengeful wrath. This was the brown marsh owl, which came over from the mainland to do some autumn mouse hunting. There were two pairs of these big, downy-winged, round-eyed hunters, and they did not know there was a cat on the island.

The cat, spying one of them as it swooped soundlessly hither and thither over the silvered grass tops, crouched with flattened ears. With its wide spread of wing it looked bigger than herself; and the great round face, with hooked beak and wild, staring eyes, appeared extremely formidable. However, she was no coward; and presently, though not without reasonable caution, she went about her hunting. Suddenly the owl caught a partial glimpse of her in the grass—probably of her ears or head. He swooped; and at the same instant she sprang upward to meet the assault, spitting and growling harshly and striking with unsheathed claws. With a frantic flapping of his great wings the owl checked himself and drew back into the air, just escaping the clutch of those indignant claws. After that the marsh owls were careful to give her a wide berth. They realized that the black-striped animal with the quick spring and the clutching claws was not to be interfered with. They perceived that she was some relation to that ferocious prowler, the lynx.

In spite of all this hunting, however, the furry life of the marsh grass was so teeming, so inexhaustible, that the depredations of cat, rats and owls were powerless to make more than a passing impression upon it. So the hunting and the merry-making went on side by side under the indifferent moon.

As the winter deepened—with bursts of sharp cold and changing winds that forced the cat to be continually changing her refuge—she grew more and more unhappy. She felt her homelessness keenly. Nowhere on the whole island could she find a nook where she might feel secure from both wind and rain. As for the old barrel, the first cause of her misfortunes, there was no help in that. The winds had long ago turned it completely over, open to the sky, then drifted it full of sand and reburied it. And in any case the cat would have been afraid to go near it again. So it came about that she alone of all the island dwellers had no shelter to turn to when the real winter arrived, with snows that smothered the grass tops out of sight, and frosts that lined the shore with grinding ice cakes. The rats had their holes under the buried fragments of wreckage; the mice and shrews had their deep, warm tunnels; the owls had nests in hollow trees far away in the forests of the mainland. But the cat, shivering and frightened, could do nothing but crouch against the blind walls of the unrelenting house and let the snow whirl itself and pile itself about her.

And now, in her misery, she found her food cut off. The mice ran secure in their hidden runways, where the grass roots on each side of them gave them easy and abundant provender. The rats, too, were out of sight—digging burrows themselves in the soft snow in the hope of intercepting some of the tunnels of the mice, and now and then snapping up an unwary passer-by. The ice fringe, crumbling and heaving under the ruthless tide, put an end to her fishing. She would have tried to capture one of the formidable owls in her hunger, but the owls no longer came to the island. They would return, no doubt, later in the season when the snow had hardened and the mice had begun to come out and play on the surface. But for the present they were following an easier chase in the deeps of the upland forest.

When the snow stopped falling and the sun came out again there fell such keen cold as the cat had never felt before. The day, as it chanced, was Christmas; and if the cat had had any idea as to the calendar she would certainly have marked the day in her memory as it was an eventful one for her. Starving as she was she could not sleep, but kept ceaselessly on the prowl. This was fortunate, for had she gone to sleep without any more shelter than the wall of the house she would never have wakened again. In her restlessness she wandered to the farther side of the island where, in a somewhat sheltered and sunny recess of the shore facing the mainland, she found a patch of bare sand, free of ice cakes and just uncovered by the tide. Opening upon this recess were the tiny entrances to several of the mouse tunnels.

72

Close beside one of these holes in the snow the cat crouched, quiveringly intent. For ten minutes or more she waited, never so much as twitching a whisker. At last a mouse thrust out its little pointed head. Not daring to give it time to change its mind or take alarm, she pounced. The mouse, glimpsing the doom ere it fell, doubled back upon itself in the narrow runway. Hardly realizing what she did in her desperation the cat plunged head and shoulders into the snow, reaching blindly after the vanished prize. By great good luck she caught it.

It was her first meal in four bitter days. The children had always tried to share with her their Christmas cheer and enthusiasm, and had usually succeeded in interesting her by an agreeable lavishness in the matter of cream; but never before had she found a Christmas feast so good.

Now she had learned a lesson. Being naturally clever and her wits sharpened by her fierce necessities, she had grasped the idea that it was possible to follow her prey a little way into the snow. She had not realized that the snow was so penetrable. She had quite wiped out the door of this particular runway; so she went and crouched beside a similar one, but here she had to wait a long time before an adventurous mouse came to peer out. But this time she showed that she had grasped her lesson. It was straight at the side of the entrance that she pounced, where instinct told her that the body of the mouse would be. One outstretched paw thus cut off the quarry's retreat. Her tactics were completely successful; and as her head went plunging into the fluffy whiteness she felt the prize between her paws.

Her hunger now fairly appeased, she found herself immensely excited over this new fashion of hunting. Often before had she waited at mouse holes, but never had she found it possible to break down the walls and invade the holes themselves. It was a thrilling idea. As she crept toward another hole a mouse scurried swiftly up the sand and darted into it. The cat, too late to catch him before he disappeared, tried to follow him. Scratching clumsily but hopefully she succeeded in forcing the full length of her body into the snow. She found no sign of the fugitive, which was by this time racing in safety down some dim transverse tunnel. Her eyes, mouth, whiskers and fur full of the powdery white particles, she backed out, much disappointed. But in that moment she had realized that it was much warmer in there beneath the snow than out in the stinging air. It was a second and vitally important lesson; and though she was probably unconscious of having learned it she instinctively put the new lore into practice a little while later.

Having succeeded in catching yet another mouse for which her appetite made no immediate demand, she carried it back to the house and laid it down in tribute on the veranda steps while she meowed and stared hopefully at the desolate, snow-draped door. Getting no response she carried the mouse down with her to the hollow behind the drift which had been caused by the bulging front of the bay-window on the end of the house. Here she curled herself up forlornly, thinking to have a wink of sleep.

But the still cold was too searching. She looked at the sloping wall of snow beside her and cautiously thrust her paw into it. It was very soft and light. It seemed to offer practically no resistance. She pawed away in an awkward fashion till she had scooped out a sort of tiny cave. Gently she pushed herself into it, pressing back the snow on every side till she had room to turn around.

Then turn around she did several times, as dogs do in getting their beds arranged to their liking. In this process she not only packed down the snow beneath her, but she also rounded out for herself a snug chamber with a comparatively narrow doorway. From this snowy retreat she gazed forth with a solemn air of possession; then she went to sleep with a sense of comfort, of 'homeyness', such as she had never before felt since the disappearance of her friends.

Having thus conquered misfortune and won herself the freedom of the winter wild, her life though strenuous was no longer one of any terrible hardship. With patience at the mouse holes she could catch enough to eat; and in her snowy den she slept warm and secure. In a little while, when a crust had formed over the surface, the mice took to coming out at night and holding revels on the snow. Then the owls, too, came back; and the cat, having tried to catch one, got sharply bitten and clawed before she realized the propriety of letting it go. After this experience she decided that owls, on the whole, were meant to be let alone. But for all that she found it fine hunting, out there on the bleak, unfenced, white reaches of the snow.

Thus, mistress of the situation, she found the winter slipping by without further serious trials. Only once, toward the end of January, did Fate send her another bad quarter of an hour. On the heels of a peculiarly bitter cold snap a huge white owl from the Arctic Barrens came one night to the island. The cat, taking observations from the corner of the veranda, caught sight of him. One look was enough to assure her that this was a very different kind of visitor from the brown marsh owls. She slipped inconspicuously down into her burrow; and until the great white owl went away, some twenty-four hours later, she kept herself discreetly out of sight.

When spring came back to the island, with the nightly shrill chorus of fluting frogs in the shallow, sedgy pools and the young grass alive with nesting birds, the prisoner's life became almost luxurious in its easy abundance. But now she was once more homeless, since her snug den had vanished with the snow. This did not much matter to her, however, for the weather grew warmer and more tranquil day by day; and moreover, she herself, in being forced back upon her instincts, had learned to be as contented as a tramp. Nevertheless, with all her capacity for learning and adapting herself she had not forgotten anything. So when, one day in June, a crowded boat came over from the mainland, and children's voices, clamouring across the grass tops, broke the desolate silence of the island, the cat heard and sprang up out of her sleep on the veranda steps.

For one second she stood, listening intently. Then, almost as a dog would have done, and as few of her supercilious tribe ever condescend to do, she went racing across to the landing place—to be snatched up into the arms of four happy children at once, and to have her fine fur ruffled to a state which it would cost her an hour's assiduous toilet to put in order.

Ming's Biggest Prey

PATRICIA HIGHSMITH

MING was resting comfortably on the foot of his mistress's bunk, when the man picked him up by the back of the neck, stuck him out on the deck and closed the cabin door. Ming's blue eyes widened in shock and brief anger, then nearly closed again because of the brilliant sunlight. It was not the first time Ming had been thrust out of the cabin rudely, and Ming realized that the man did it when his mistress, Elaine, was not looking.

The sailboat now offered no shelter from the sun, but Ming was not yet too warm. He leapt easily to the cabin roof and stepped on to the coil of rope just behind the mast. Ming liked the rope coil as a couch, because he could see everything from the height, the cup shape of the rope protected him from strong breezes, and also minimized the swaying and sudden changes of angle of the *White Lark*, since it was more or less the centre point. But just now the sail had been taken down, because Elaine and the man had eaten lunch, and often they had a siesta afterward, during which time, Ming knew, that man didn't like him in the cabin. Lunchtime was all right. In fact, Ming had just lunched on delicious grilled fish and a bit of lobster. Now, lying in a relaxed curve on the coil of rope, Ming opened his mouth in a great yawn, then with his slant eyes almost closed against the strong sunlight, gazed at the beige hills and the white and pink houses and hotels that circled the bay of Acapulco. Between the *White Lark* and the shore where people plashed inaudibly, the sun twinkled on the water's surface like thousands of tiny electric lights going on and off. A water-skier went by, skimming up white spray behind him.

Such activity! Ming half dozed, feeling the heat of the sun sink into his fur. Ming was from New York, and he considered Acapulco a great improvement over his environment in the first weeks of his life. He remembered a sunless box with straw on the bottom, three or four other kittens in with him, and a window behind which giant forms paused for a few moments, tried to catch his attention by tapping, then passed on. He did not remember his mother at all. One day a young woman who smelled of something pleasant came into the place and took him away—away from the ugly, frightening smell of dogs, of medicine and parrot dung. Then they went on what Ming now knew was an aeroplane. He was quite used to aeroplanes now and rather liked them. On aeroplanes he sat on Elaine's lap, or slept on her lap, and there were always titbits to eat if he was hungry.

Elaine spent much of the day in a shop in Acapulco, where dresses and slacks and bathing suits hung on all the walls. This place smelled clean and fresh, there were flowers in pots and in boxes out front, and the floor was of cool blue and white tiles. Ming had perfect freedom to wander out into the patio behind the shop, or to sleep in his basket in a corner. There was more sunlight in front of the shop, but mischievous boys often tried to grab him if he sat in front, and Ming could never relax there.

Ming liked best lying in the sun with his mistress on one of the long canvas chairs on their terrace at home. What Ming did not like were the people she sometimes invited to their house, people who spent the night, people by the score who stayed up very late eating and drinking, playing the gramophone or the piano—people who separated him from Elaine. People who stepped on his toes, people who sometimes picked him up from behind before he could do anything about it, so that he had to squirm and fight to get free, people who stroked him roughly, people who closed a door somewhere, locking him in. *People!* Ming detested people. In all the world, he liked only Elaine. Elaine loved him and understood him.

Especially this man called Teddie Ming detested now. Teddie was around all the time lately. Ming did not like the way Teddie looked at him, when Elaine was not watching. And sometimes Teddie, when Elaine was not near, muttered something which Ming knew was a threat. Or a command to leave the room. Ming took it calmly. Dignity was to be preserved. Besides, wasn't his mistress on his side? The man was the intruder. When Elaine was watching, the man sometimes pretended a fondness for him, but Ming always moved gracefully but unmistakably in another direction.

Ming's nap was interrupted by the sound of the cabin door opening. He heard Elaine and the man laughing and talking. The big red-orange sun was near the horizon.

'Ming!' Elaine came over to him. 'Aren't you getting *cooked*, darling? I thought you were *in!*'

'So did I!' said Teddie.

Ming purred as he always did when he awakened. She picked him up gently, cradled him in her arms, and took him below into the suddenly cool shade of the cabin. She was talking to the man, and not in a gentle tone. She set Ming down in front of his dish of water, and though he was not thirsty, he drank a little to please her. Ming did feel addled by the heat, and he staggered a little.

Elaine took a wet towel and wiped Ming's face, his ears and his four paws. Then she laid him gently on the bunk that smelled of Elaine's perfume but also of the man whom Ming detested.

Now his mistress and the man were quarrelling, Ming could tell from the tone. Elaine was staying with Ming, sitting on the edge of the bunk. Ming at last heard the splash that meant Teddie had dived into the water. Ming hoped he stayed there, hoped he drowned, hoped he never came back. Elaine wet a bathtowel in the aluminium sink, wrung it out, spread it on the bunk, and lifted Ming on to it. She brought water, and now Ming was thirsty, and drank. She left him to sleep again while she washed and put away the dishes. These were comfortable sounds that Ming liked to hear.

But soon there was another *plash* and *plop*, Teddie's wet feet on the deck, and Ming was awake again.

The tone of quarrelling recommenced. Elaine went up the few steps on to the deck. Ming, tense but with his chin still resting on the moist bathtowel, kept his eyes on the cabin door. It was Teddie's feet that he heard descending. Ming lifted his head slightly, aware that there was no exit behind him, that he was trapped in the cabin. The man paused with a towel in his hands, staring at Ming.

Ming relaxed completely, as he might do preparatory to a yawn, and this caused his eyes to cross. Ming then let his tongue slide a little way out of his mouth. The man started to say something, looked as if he wanted to hurl the wadded towel at Ming, but he wavered, whatever he had been going to say never got out of his mouth, and he threw the towel in the sink, then bent to wash his face. It was not the first time Ming had let his tongue slide out at Teddie. Lots of people laughed when Ming did this, if they were people at a party, for instance, and Ming rather enjoyed that. But Ming sensed that Teddie took it as a hostile gesture of some kind, which was why Ming did it deliberately to Teddie, whereas among other people, it was often an accident when Ming's tongue slid out.

The quarrelling continued. Elaine made coffee. Ming began to feel better, and went on deck again, because the sun had now set. Elaine had started the motor, and they were gliding slowly towards the shore. Ming caught the song of birds, the odd screams, like shrill phrases, of certain birds that cried only at sunset. Ming looked forward to the adobe house on the cliff that was his and his mistress's home. He knew that the reason she did not leave him at home (where he would have been more comfortable) when she went on the boat, was because she was afraid that people might trap him, even kill him. Ming understood. People had tried to grab him from almost under Elaine's eyes. Once he had been suddenly hauled away in a cloth bag and, though fighting as hard as he could, he was not sure he would have been able to get out if Elaine had not hit the boy herself and grabbed the bag from him.

Ming had intended to jump up on the cabin roof again but, after glancing at it, he decided to save his strength, so he crouched on the warm, gently sloping deck with his feet tucked in, and gazed at the approaching shore. Now he could hear guitar music from the beach. The voices of his mistress and the man had come to a halt. For a few moments, the loudest sound was the *chug-chug-chug* of the boat's motor. Then Ming heard the man's bare feet climbing the cabin steps. Ming did not turn his head to look at him, but his ears twitched back a little, involuntarily. Ming looked at the water just the distance of a short leap in front of him and below him. Strangely, there was no sound from the man behind him. The hair on Ming's neck prickled, and Ming glanced over his right shoulder.

At that instant, the man bent forward and rushed at Ming with his arms outspread.

Ming was on his feet at once, darting straight towards the man, which was the only direction of safety on the rail-less deck, and the man swung his left arm and cuffed Ming in the chest. Ming went flying backward, claws scraping the deck, but his hind legs went over the edge. Ming clung with his front feet to the sleek wood which gave him little hold, while his hind legs worked to heave him up, worked at the side of the boat which sloped to Ming's disadvantage.

The man advanced to shove a foot against Ming's paws, but Elaine came up the cabin steps just then.

'What's happening? *Ming!*'

Ming's strong hind legs were getting him on to the deck little by little. The man had knelt as if to lend a hand. Elaine had fallen on to her knees also, and had Ming by the back of the neck now.

Ming relaxed, hunched on the deck. His tail was wet.

'He fell overboard!' Teddie said. 'It's true, he's groggy. Just lurched over and fell when the boat gave a dip.'

'It's the sun. Poor *Ming!*' Elaine held the cat against her breast, and carried him into the cabin. 'Teddie—could you steer?'

The man came down into the cabin. Elaine had Ming on the bunk and was talking softly to him. Ming's heart was still beating fast. He was alert against the man at the wheel, even though Elaine was with him. Ming was aware that they had entered the little cove where they always went before getting off the boat.

Here were the friends and allies of Teddie, whom Ming detested by association, although these were merely Mexican boys. Two or three boys in shorts called 'Señor Teddie!' and offered a hand to Elaine to climb on to the dock, took the rope attached to the front of the boat, offered to carry *'Ming!—Ming!'* Ming leapt on to the dock himself and crouched, waiting for Elaine, ready to dart away from any other hand that might reach for him. And there were several brown hands making a rush for him, so that Ming had to keep jumping aside. There were laughs, yelps, stomps of bare feet on wooden boards. But there was also the reassuring voice of Elaine warning them off. Ming knew she was busy carrying off the plastic satchels, locking the cabin door. Teddie with the aid of one of the Mexican boys was stretching the canvas over the cabin now. And Elaine's sandalled feet were beside Ming. Ming followed her as she walked away. A boy took the things Elaine was carrying, then she picked Ming up.

They got into the big car without a roof that belonged to Teddie, and drove up the winding road towards Elaine's and Ming's house. One of the boys was driving. Now the tone in which Elaine and Teddie were speaking was calmer, softer. The man laughed. Ming sat tensely on his mistress's lap. He could feel her concern for him in the way she stroked him and touched the back of his neck. The man reached out to put his fingers on Ming's back, and Ming gave a low growl that rose and fell and rumbled deep in his throat.

'Well, well,' said the man, pretending to be amused, and took his hand away.

Elaine's voice had stopped in the middle of something she

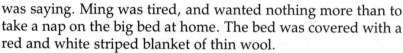

was saying. Ming was tired, and wanted nothing more than to take a nap on the big bed at home. The bed was covered with a red and white striped blanket of thin wool.

Hardly had Ming thought of this, when he found himself in the cool, fragrant atmosphere of his own home, being lowered gently on to the bed with the soft woollen cover. His mistress kissed his cheek, and said something with the word hungry in it. Ming understood, at any rate. He was to tell her when he was hungry.

Ming dozed, and awakened at the sound of voices on the terrace a couple of yards away, past the open glass doors. Now it was dark. Ming could see one end of the table, and could tell from the quality of the light that there were candles on the table. Concha, the servant who slept in the house, was clearing the table. Ming heard her voice, then the voices of Elaine and the man. Ming smelled cigar smoke. Ming jumped to the floor and sat for a moment looking out of the door towards the terrace. He yawned, then arched his back and stretched, and limbered up his muscles by digging his claws into the thick straw carpet. Then he slipped out to the right of the terrace and glided silently down the long stairway of broad stones to the garden below. The garden was like a jungle or a forest. Avocado trees and mango trees grew as high as the terrace itself, there were bougainvillaea against the wall, orchids in the trees, and magnolias and several camellias which Elaine had planted. Ming could hear birds twittering and stirring in their nests. Sometimes he climbed trees to get at their nests, but tonight he was not in the mood, though he was no longer tired. The voices of his mistress and the man disturbed him. His mistress was not a friend of the man's tonight, that was plain.

Concha was probably still in the kitchen, and Ming decided to go in and ask her for something to eat. Concha liked him. One maid who had not liked him had been dismissed by Elaine. Ming thought he fancied barbecued pork. That was what his mistress and the man had eaten tonight. The breeze blew fresh from the ocean, ruffling Ming's fur slightly. Ming felt completely recovered from the awful experience of nearly falling into the sea.

Now the terrace was empty of people. Ming went left, back into the bedroom, and was at once aware of the man's

presence, though there was no light on and Ming could not see him. The man was standing by the dressing table, opening a box. Again involuntarily Ming gave a low growl which rose and fell, and Ming remained frozen in the position he had been in when he first became aware of the man, his right front paw extended for the next step. Now his ears were back, he was prepared to spring in any direction, although the man had not seen him.

'Ssss-st! Damn you!' the man said in a whisper. He stamped his foot, not very hard, to make the cat go away.

Ming did not move at all. Ming heard the soft rattle of the white necklace which belonged to his mistress. The man put it into his pocket, then moved to Ming's right, out of the door that went into the big living-room. Ming now heard the clink of a bottle against glass, heard liquid being poured. Ming went through the same door and turned left towards the kitchen.

Here he miaowed, and was greeted by Elaine and Concha. Concha had her radio turned on to music.

'Fish?—Pork. He likes pork,' Elaine said, speaking the odd form of words which she used with Concha.

Ming, without much difficulty, conveyed his preference for pork, and got it. He fell to with a good appetite. Concha was exclaiming 'Ah-eee-ee!' as his mistress spoke with her, spoke at length. Then Concha bent to stroke him, and Ming put up with it, still looking down at his plate, until she left off and he could finish his meal. Then Elaine left the kitchen. Concha gave him some of the tinned milk, which he loved, in his now empty saucer, and Ming lapped this up. Then he rubbed himself against her bare leg by way of thanks and went out of the kitchen, made his way cautiously into the living-room en route to the bedroom. But now Elaine and the man were out on the terrace. Ming had just entered the bedroom, when he heard Elaine call:

'Ming? Where are you?'

Ming went to the terrace door and stopped, and sat on the threshold.

Elaine was sitting sideways at the end of the table, and the candlelight was bright on her long fair hair, on the white of her trousers. She slapped her thigh, and Ming jumped on to her lap.

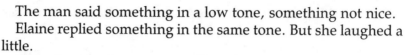

The man said something in a low tone, something not nice.

Elaine replied something in the same tone. But she laughed a little.

Then the telephone rang.

Elaine put Ming down, and went into the living-room towards the telephone.

The man finished what was in his glass, muttered something at Ming, then set the glass on the table. He got up and tried to circle Ming, or to get him towards the edge of the terrace, Ming realized, and Ming also realized that the man was drunk— therefore moving slowly and a little clumsily. The terrace had a parapet about as high as the man's hips, but it was broken by grilles in three places, grilles with bars wide enough for Ming to pass through, though Ming never did, merely looked through the grilles sometimes. It was plain to Ming that the man wanted to drive him through one of the grilles, or grab him and toss him over the terrace parapet. There was nothing easier for Ming than to elude him. Then the man picked up a chair and swung it suddenly, catching Ming on the hip. That had been quick, and it hurt. Ming took the nearest exit, which was down the outside steps that led to the garden.

The man started down the steps after him. Without reflecting, Ming dashed back up the few steps he had come, keeping close to the wall which was in shadow. The man hadn't seen him, Ming knew. Ming leapt to the terrace parapet, sat down and licked a paw once to recover and collect himself. His heart beat fast as if he were in the middle of a fight. And hatred ran in his veins. Hatred burned his eyes as he crouched and listened to the man uncertainly climbing the steps below him. The man came into view.

Ming tensed himself for a jump, then jumped as hard as he could, landing with all four feet on the man's right arm near the shoulder. Ming clung to the cloth of the man's white jacket, but they were both falling. The man groaned. Ming hung on. Branches crackled. Ming could not tell up from down. Ming jumped off the man, became aware of direction and of the earth too late, and landed on his side. Almost at the same time, he heard the thud of the man hitting the ground, then of his body rolling a little way, then there was silence. Ming had to breathe fast with his mouth open until his chest stopped hurting. From

the direction of the man, he could smell drink, cigar, and the sharp odour that meant fear. But the man was not moving.

Ming could now see quite well. There was even a bit of moonlight. Ming headed for the steps again, had to go a long way through the bush, over stones and sand, to where the steps began. Then he glided up and arrived once more upon the terrace.

Elaine was just coming on to the terrace.

'Teddie?' she called. Then she went back into the bedroom where she turned on a lamp. She went into the kitchen. Ming followed her. Concha had left the light on, but Concha was now in her own room, where the radio played.

Elaine opened the front door.

The man's car was still in the driveway, Ming saw. Now Ming's hip had begun to hurt, or now he had begun to notice it. It caused him to limp a little. Elaine noticed this, touched his back, and asked him what was the matter. Ming only purred.

'Teddie?—Where are you?' Elaine called.

She took a torch and shone it down into the garden, down among the great trunks of the avocado trees, among the orchids and the lavender and pink blossoms of the bougain-villaeas. Ming, safe beside her on the terrace parapet, followed the beam of the torch with his eyes and purred with content. The man was not below here, but below and to the right. Elaine went to the terrace steps and carefully, because there was no rail here, only broad steps, pointed the beam of the light downward. Ming did not bother looking. He sat on the terrace where the steps began.

'Teddie!' she said. '*Teddie!*' Then she ran down the steps.

Ming still did not follow her. He heard her draw in her breath. Then she cried:

'*Concha!*'

Elaine ran back up the steps.

Concha had come out of her room. Elaine spoke to Concha. Then Concha became excited. Elaine went to the telephone, and spoke for a short while, then she and Concha went down the steps together. Ming settled himself with his paws tucked under him on the terrace, which was still faintly warm from the day's sun. A car arrived. Elaine came up the steps, and went and opened the front door. Ming kept out of the way on the terrace, in a shadowy corner, as three or four strange men came out on the terrace and tramped down the steps. There was a great deal of talk below, noises of feet, breaking of bushes, and then the smell of all of them mounted the steps, the smell of tobacco, sweat, and the familiar smell of blood. The man's blood. Ming was pleased, as he was pleased when he killed a bird and created this smell of blood under his own teeth. This was big prey. Ming, unnoticed by any of the others, stood up to his full height as the group passed with the corpse, and inhaled the aroma of his victory with a lifted nose.

Then suddenly the house was empty. Everyone had gone, even Concha. Ming drank a little water from his bowl in the kitchen, then went to his mistress's bed, curled against the slope of the pillows, and fell fast asleep. He was awakened by the *rr-rr-r* of an unfamiliar car. Then the front door opened, and he recognized the step of Elaine and then Concha. Ming stayed where he was. Elaine and Concha talked softly for a few minutes. Then Elaine came into the bedroom. The lamp was still on. Ming watched her slowly open the box on her dressing table, and into it she let fall the white necklace that made a little clatter. Then she closed the box. She began to unbutton her shirt, but before she had finished, she flung herself on the bed and stroked Ming's head, lifted his left paw and pressed it gently so that the claws came forth.

'Oh, Ming—Ming,' she said.

Ming recognized the tones of love.

Mrs Bond's Cats

JAMES HERRIOT

'I WORK for cats.'

That was how Mrs Bond introduced herself on my first visit, gripping my hand firmly and thrusting out her jaw defiantly as though challenging me to make something of it. She was a big woman with a strong, high-cheekboned face and a commanding presence and I wouldn't have argued with her anyway, so I nodded gravely as though I fully understood and agreed, and allowed her to lead me into the house.

I saw at once what she meant. The big kitchen-living room had been completely given over to cats. There were cats on the sofas and chairs and spilling in cascades on to the floor, cats sitting in rows along the window sills and, right in the middle of it all, little Mr Bond, pallid, wispy-moustached, in his shirt sleeves reading a newspaper.

It was a scene which was going to become very familiar. A lot of the cats were obviously uncastrated Toms because the atmosphere was vibrant with their distinctive smell—a fierce pungency which overwhelmed even the sickly wisps from the big saucepans of nameless cat food bubbling on the stove. And Mr Bond was always there, always in his shirt sleeves and reading his paper, a lonely little island in a sea of cats.

I had heard of the Bonds, of course. They were Londoners who for some obscure reason had picked on North Yorkshire for their retirement. People said they had a 'bit o' brass' and they had bought an old house on the outskirts of Darrowby where they kept themselves to themselves—and the cats. I had heard that Mrs Bond was in the habit of taking in strays and feeding them and giving them a home if they wanted it and this

had predisposed me in her favour, because in my experience the unfortunate feline species seemed to be fair game for every kind of cruelty and neglect. They shot cats, threw things at them, starved them and set their dogs on them for fun. It was good to see somebody taking their side.

My patient on this first visit was no more than a big kitten, a terrified little blob of black and white crouching in a corner.

'He's one of the outside cats,' Mrs Bond boomed.

'Outside cats?'

'Yes. All these you see here are the inside cats. The others are the really wild ones who simply refuse to enter the house. I feed them of course but the only time they come indoors is when they are ill.'

'I see.'

'I've had frightful trouble catching this one. I'm worried about his eyes—there seemed to be a skin growing over them, and I do hope you can do something for him. His name, by the way, is Alfred.'

'Alfred? Ah yes, quite.' I advanced cautiously on the little half-grown animal and was greeted by a waving set of claws and a series of open-mouthed spittings. He was trapped in his corner or he would have been off with the speed of light.

Examining him was going to be a problem. I turned to Mrs Bond. 'Could you let me have a sheet of some kind? An old ironing sheet would do. I'm going to have to wrap him up.'

'Wrap him up?' Mrs Bond looked very doubtful but she disappeared into another room and returned with a tattered sheet of cotton which looked just right.

I cleared the table of an amazing variety of cat feeding dishes, cat books, cat medicines and spread out the sheet, then I approached my patient again. You can't be in a hurry in a situation like this and it took me perhaps five minutes of wheedling and 'Puss-pussing' while I brought my hand nearer and nearer. When I got as far as being able to stroke his cheek I made a quick grab at the scruff of his neck and finally bore Alfred, protesting bitterly and lashing out in all directions, over to the table. There, still holding tightly to his scruff, I laid him on the sheet and started the wrapping operation.

This is something which has to be done quite often with obstreperous felines and, although I say it, I am rather good at

it. The idea is to make a neat, tight roll, leaving the relevant piece of cat exposed; it may be an injured paw, perhaps the tail, and in this case of course the head. I think it was the beginning of Mrs Bond's unquestioning faith in me when she saw me quickly enveloping that cat till all you could see of him was a small black and white head protruding from an immovable cocoon of cloth. He and I were now facing each other, more or less eyeball to eyeball, and Alfred couldn't do a thing about it.

As I say, I rather pride myself on this little expertise and even today my veterinary colleagues have been known to remark: 'Old Herriot may be limited in many respects but by God he can wrap a cat.'

As it turned out, there wasn't a skin growing over Alfred's eyes. There never is.

'He's got a paralysis of the third eyelid, Mrs Bond. Animals have this membrane which flicks across the eye to protect it. In this case it hasn't gone back, probably because the cat is in low condition—maybe had a touch of cat flu or something else which has weakened him. I'll give him an injection of vitamins and leave you some powder to put in his food if you could keep him in for a few days. I think he'll be all right in a week or two.'

The injection presented no problems with Alfred furious but helpless inside his sheet and I had come to the end of my first visit to Mrs Bond's.

It was the first of many. The lady and I established an immediate rapport which was strengthened by the fact that I was always prepared to spend time over her assorted charges; crawling on my stomach under piles of logs in the outhouses to reach the outside cats, coaxing them down from trees, stalking them endlessly through the shrubbery. But from my point of view it was rewarding in many ways.

For instance there was the diversity of names she had for her cats. True to her London upbringing she had named many of the Toms after the great Arsenal team of those days. There was Eddie Hapgood, Cliff Bastin, Ted Drake, Wilf Copping, but she did slip up in one case because Alex James had kittens three times a year with unfailing regularity.

Then there was her way of calling them home. The first time I saw her at this was on a still summer evening. The two cats she wanted me to see were out in the garden somewhere and I

walked with her to the back door where she halted, clasped her hands across her bosom, closed her eyes and gave tongue in a mellifluous contralto.

'Bates, Bates, Bates, Ba-hates.' She actually sang out the words in a reverent monotone except for a delightful little lilt on the 'Ba-hates'. Then once more she inflated her ample rib cage like an operatic prima donna and out it came again, delivered with the utmost feeling.

'Bates, Bates, Bates, Ba-hates.'

Anyway it worked, because Bates the cat came trotting from behind a clump of laurel. There remained the other patient and I watched Mrs Bond with interest.

She took up the same stance, breathed in, closed her eyes, composed her features into a sweet half-smile and started again.

'Seven-times-three, Seven-times-three, Seven-times-three-hee.' It was set to the same melody as Bates with the same dulcet rise and fall at the end. She didn't get the quick response this time, though, and had to go through the performance again and again, and as the notes lingered on the still evening air the effect was startlingly like a muezzin calling the faithful to prayer.

At length she was successful and a fat tortoiseshell slunk apologetically along the wall-side into the house.

'By the way, Mrs Bond,' I asked, making my voice casual. 'I didn't quite catch the name of that last cat.'

'Oh, Seven-times-three?' She smiled reminiscently. 'Yes, she is a dear. She's had three kittens seven times running, you see, so I thought it rather a good name for her, don't you?'

'Yes, yes, I do indeed. Splendid name, splendid.'

Another thing which warmed me towards Mrs Bond was her concern for my safety. I appreciated this because it is a rare trait among animal owners. I can think of the trainer after one of his racehorses had kicked me clean out of a loose box examining the animal anxiously to see if it had damaged its foot; the little old lady dwarfed by the bristling, teeth-bared Alsatian saying: 'You'll be gentle with him won't you and I hope you won't hurt him—he's very nervous'; the farmer, after an exhausting calving which I feel certain has knocked about two years off my life expectancy, grunting morosely: 'I doubt you've tired that cow out, young man.'

Mrs Bond was different. She used to meet me at the door with an enormous pair of gauntlets to protect my hands against scratches and it was an inexpressible relief to find that somebody cared. It became part of the pattern of my life; walking up the garden path among the innumerable slinking, wild-eyed little creatures which were the outside cats, the ceremonial acceptance of the gloves at the door, then the entry into the charged atmosphere of the kitchen with little Mr Bond and his newspaper just visible among the milling furry bodies of the inside cats. I was never able to ascertain Mr Bond's attitute to cats—come to think of it he hardly ever said anything—but I had the impression he could take them or leave them.

The gauntlets were a big help and at times they were a veritable godsend. As in the case of Boris. Boris was an enormous blue-black member of the outside cats and my bête noire in more senses than one. I always cherished a private conviction that he had escaped from a zoo; I had never seen a domestic cat with such sleek, writhing muscles, such dedicated ferocity. I'm sure there was a bit of puma in Boris somewhere.

It had been a sad day for the cat colony when he turned up. I have always found it difficult to dislike any animal; most of the ones which try to do us a mischief are activated by fear, but Boris was different; he was a malevolent bully and after his arrival the frequency of my visits increased because of his habit of regularly beating up his colleagues. I was forever stitching up tattered ears, dressing gnawed limbs.

We had one trial of strength fairly early. Mrs Bond wanted me to give him a worm dose and I had the little tablet all ready held in forceps. How I ever got hold of him I don't quite know, but I hustled him on to the table and did my wrapping act at lightning speed, swathing him in roll upon roll of stout material. Just for a few seconds I thought I had him as he stared up at me, his great brilliant eyes full of hate. But as I pushed my loaded forceps into his mouth he clamped his teeth viciously down on them and I could feel claws of amazing power tearing inside the sheet. It was all over in moments. A long leg shot out and ripped its way down my wrist, I let go my tight hold of the neck and in a flash Boris sank his teeth through the gauntlet into the ball of my thumb and was away. I was left standing

there stupidly, holding the fragmented worm tablet in a bleeding hand and looking at the bunch of ribbons which had once been my wrapping sheet. From then on Boris loathed the very sight of me and the feeling was mutual.

But this was one of the few clouds in a serene sky. I continued to enjoy my visits there and life proceeded on a tranquil course except, perhaps, for some legpulling from my colleagues. They could never understand my willingness to spend so much time over a lot of cats. And of course this fitted in with the general attitude because Siegfried didn't believe in people keeping pets of any kind. He just couldn't understand their mentality and propounded his views to anybody who cared to listen. He himself, of course, kept five dogs and two cats. The dogs, all of them, travelled everywhere with him in the car and he fed dogs and cats every day with his own hands—wouldn't allow anybody else to do the job. In the evening all seven animals would pile themselves round his feet as he sat in his chair by the fire. To this day he is still as vehemently anti-pet as ever, though another generation of waving dogs' tails almost obscures him as he drives around and he also has several cats, a few tanks of tropical fish and a couple of snakes.

Tristan saw me in action at Mrs Bond's on only one occasion. I was collecting some long forceps from the instrument cupboard when he came into the room.

'Anything interesting, Jim?' he asked.

'No, not really. I'm just off to see one of the Bond cats. It's got a bone stuck between its teeth.'

The young man eyed me ruminatively for a moment. 'Think I'll come with you. I haven't seen much small animal stuff lately.'

As we went down the garden at the cat establishment I felt a twinge of embarrassment. One of the things which had built up my happy relationship with Mrs Bond was my tender concern for her charges. Even with the wildest and the fiercest I exhibited only gentleness, patience and solicitude; it wasn't really an act, it came quite naturally to me. However, I couldn't help wondering what Tristan would think of my cat bedside manner.

Mrs Bond in the doorway had summed up the situation in a

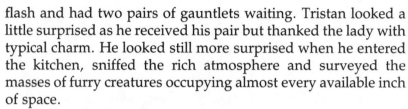

flash and had two pairs of gauntlets waiting. Tristan looked a little surprised as he received his pair but thanked the lady with typical charm. He looked still more surprised when he entered the kitchen, sniffed the rich atmosphere and surveyed the masses of furry creatures occupying almost every available inch of space.

'Mr Herriot, I'm afraid it's Boris who has the bone in his teeth,' Mrs Bond said.

'Boris!' My stomach lurched. 'How on earth are we going to catch him?'

'Oh I've been rather clever,' she replied. 'I've managed to entice him with some of his favourite food into a cat basket.'

Tristan put his hand on a big wicker cage on the table. 'In here, is he?' he asked casually. He slipped back the catch and opened the lid. For something like a third of a second the coiled creature within and Tristan regarded each other tensely, then a sleek black body exploded silently from the basket past the young man's left ear on to the top of a tall cupboard.

'Christ!' said Tristan. 'What the hell was that?'

'That,' I said, 'was Boris, and now we've got to get hold of him again.' I climbed on to a chair, reached slowly on to the cupboard top and started 'Puss-puss-puss'ing in my most beguiling tone.

After about a minute Tristan appeared to think he had a better idea; he made a sudden leap and grabbed Boris's tail. But only briefly, because the big cat freed himself in an instant and set off on a whirlwind circuit of the room; along the tops of cupboards and dressers, across the curtains, careering round and round like a wall-of-death rider.

Tristan stationed himself at a strategic point and as Boris shot past he swiped at him with one of the gauntlets.

'Missed the bloody thing!' he shouted in chagrin. 'But here he comes again . . . take that, you black sod! Damn it, I can't nail him!'

The docile little inside cats, startled by the scattering of plates and tins and pans and by Tristan's cries and arm wavings, began to run around in their turn, knocking over whatever Boris had missed. The noise and confusion even got through to Mr Bond because just for a moment he raised his head and looked around him in mild surprise at the hurtling bodies before returning to his newspaper.

Tristan, flushed with the excitement of the chase, had really begun to enjoy himself. I cringed inwardly as he shouted over to me happily.

'Send him on, Jim, I'll get the bugger next time round!'

We never did catch Boris. We just had to leave the piece of bone to work its own way out, so it wasn't a successful veterinary visit. But Tristan as we got back into the car smiled contentedly.

'That was great, Jim. I didn't realize you had such fun with your pussies.'

Mrs Bond on the other hand, when I next saw her, was rather tight-lipped over the whole thing.

'Mr Herriot,' she said, 'I hope you aren't going to bring that young man with you again.'

Dick Baker's Cat

MARK TWAIN

ONE of my comrades there—another of those victims of eighteen years of unrequited toil and blighted hopes—was one of the gentlest spirits that ever bore its patient cross in a weary exile; grave and simple Dick Baker, pocket-miner of Dead-Horse Gulch. He was forty-six, grey as a rat, earnest, thoughtful, slenderly educated, slouchily dressed and clay-soiled, but his heart was finer metal than any gold his shovel ever brought to light—than any, indeed, that ever was mined or minted.

Whenever he was out of luck and a little down-hearted, he would fall to mourning over the loss of a wonderful cat he used to own (for where women and children are not, men of kindly impulses take up with pets, for they must love something). And he always spoke of the strange sagacity of that cat with the air of a man who believed in his secret heart that there was something human about it—maybe even supernatural.

I heard him talking about this animal once. He said:

'Gentlemen, I used to have a cat here, by the name of Tom Quartz, which you'd 'a' took an interest in, I reckon—most anybody would. I had him here eight year—and he was the remarkablest cat I ever see. He was a large grey one of the Tom specie, an' he had more hard, natchral sense than any man in this camp—'n' a *power* of dignity—he wouldn't let the Gov'ner of Californy be familiar with him. He never ketched a rat in his life—'peared to be above it. He never cared for nothing but mining. He knowed more about mining, that cat did, than any man I ever, ever see. You couldn't tell *him* noth'n' 'bout placer-diggin's—'n' as for pocket-mining, why he was just born for it.

He would dig out after me an' Jim when we went over the hills prospect'n', and he would trot along behind us for as much as five mile, if we went so fur. An' he had the best judgment about mining-ground—why, you never see anything like it. When we went to work, he'd scatter a glance round, 'n' if he didn't think much of the indications, he would give a look as much as to say, "Well, I'll have to get you to excuse *me*"—'n' without another word he'd hyste his nose in the air 'n' shove for home. But if the ground suited him, he would lay low 'n' keep dark till the first pan was washed, 'n' then he would sidle up 'n' take a look, an' if there was about six or seven grains of gold *he* was satisfied—he didn't want no better prospect 'n' that—'n' then he would lay down on our coats and snore like a steamboat till we'd struck the pocket, an' then get up 'n' superintend. He was nearly lightnin' on superintending.

'Well, by an' by, up comes this yer quartz excitement. Everybody was into it—everybody was pick'n' 'n' blast'n' instead of shovellin' dirt on the hillside—everybody was putt'n' down a shaft instead of scrapin' the surface. Noth'n' would do Jim, but *we* must tackle the ledges, too, 'n' so we did. We commenced putt'n' down a shaft, 'n' Tom Quartz he begin to wonder what in the dickens it was all about. *He* hadn't ever seen any mining like that before, 'n' he was all upset, as you may say—he couldn't come to a right understanding of it no way—it was too many for *him*. He was down on it too, you bet you—he was down on it powerful—'n' always appeared to consider it the cussedest foolishness out. But that cat, you know, was *always* agin' new-fangled arrangements—somehow

he never could abide 'em. *You* know how it is with old habits. But by an' by Tom Quartz begin to git sort of reconciled a little though he never *could* altogether understand that eternal sinkin' of a shaft an' never pannin' out anything. At last he got to comin' down in the shaft, hisself, to try to cipher it out. An' when he'd git the blues, 'n' feel kind o' scruffy, 'n' aggravated 'n' disgusted—knowin' as he did, that the bills was runnin' up all the time an' we warn't makin' a cent—he would curl up on a gunny-sack in the corner an' go to sleep. Well, one day when the shaft was down about eight foot, the rock got so hard that we had to put in a blast—the first blast'n' we'd ever done since Tom Quartz was born. An' then we lit the fuse 'n' clumb out 'n' got off 'bout fifty yards—'n' forgot 'n' left Tom Quartz sound asleep on the gunny-sack. In 'bout a minute we seen a puff of smoke bust up out of the hole, 'n' then everything let go with an awful crash, 'n' about four million ton of rocks 'n' dirt 'n' smoke 'n' splinters shot up 'bout a mile an' a half into the air, an' by George, right in the dead centre of it was old Tom Quartz a-goin' end over end, an' a-snortin' an' a-sneez'n, an' a-clawin' an' a-reach'n' for things like all possessed. But it warn't no use, you know, it warn't no use. An' that was the last we see of *him* for about two minutes 'n' a half, an' then all of a sudden it begin to rain rocks and rubbage an' directly he come down ker-whoop about ten foot off f'm where we stood. Well, I reckon he was p'raps the orneriest-lookin' beast you ever see. One ear was sot back on his neck, 'n' his tail was stove up, 'n' his eye-winkers was singed off, 'n' he was all blacked up with powder an' smoke, an' all sloppy with mud 'n' slush f'm one end to the other. Well, sir, it warn't no use to try to apologize— we couldn't say a word. He took a sort of a disgusted look at hisself, 'n' then he looked at us—an' it was just exactly the same as if he had said—"Gents, maybe *you* think it's smart to take advantage of a cat that ain't had no experience of quartz-minin', but *I* think *different*"—an' then he turned on his heel 'n' marched off home without ever saying another word.

'That was jest his style. An' maybe you won't believe it, but after that you never see a cat so prejudiced agin' quartz-mining as what he was. An' by an' by when he *did* get to goin' down in the shaft agin', you'd 'a' been astonished at his sagacity. The minute we'd tetch off a blast 'n' the fuse'd begin to sizzle, he'd

give a look as much as to say, "Well, I'll have to git you to excuse *me*," an' it was surpris'n' the way he'd shin out of that hole 'n' go f'r a tree. Sagacity? It ain't no name for it. 'Twas inspiration!'

I said, 'Well, Mr. Baker, his prejudice against quartz-mining *was* remarkable, considering how he came by it. Couldn't you ever cure him of it?'

'*Cure him!* No! When Tom Quartz was sot once, he was *always* sot—and you might 'a' blowed him up as much as three million times 'n' you'd never 'a' broken him of his cussed prejudice agin' quartz-mining.'

A Cat Affair

DEREK TANGYE

JEANNIE'S sister Barbara came to stay with us in May from her home at Coton-in-the Clay near Derby. She had always referred to Lama as the Princess; and when she arrived on this occasion she exclaimed that she had never seen the Princess look so pretty. It was easy to agree. The Princess was plump, her coat glossy like a ripe blackberry, and her fat tail made a mockery of the object that belonged to Oliver. Her little face, except for the drooping white whiskers, looked as young as a kitten; and she was often as playful. I would suddenly spy her tapping a paw at a feather which had come from one of the gulls on the roof, or I would watch her indoors chasing a demon under a rug, pushing her head underneath in an effort to catch it. She was still young, it seemed, and there was no sign of the years she had been with us since that day she arrived at the door in a storm. Except that Barbara saw one, though it was a sign which, at the time, I preferred to ignore.

Often, when she settled on my lap after breakfast, lunch or dinner, pinning me down in a corner of the sofa until the time came when she decided to release me, I would make use of the situation by combing her. The comb was kept in the drawer of the small Regency table on the left of the sofa, and I would twist my body into contortions so that I could extract the comb from the drawer without disturbing the Princess on my lap.

I would then gently begin my task. First a comb along the ridge of the back, then another between the ears but with such care that she still proceeded to look sleepily at Jeannie in the chair opposite; and next a bolder comb in the thicker fur regions of her side, a move which, if successful, reaped a

harvest of silky, rich down; and this I would sometimes keep, putting it in a box decorated with sea shells, because I thought that one day I would want a tangible memory of her. I had done the same when I used to comb Monty, and his is still there in a small pot-pourri bowl of Swansea china which stands on top of the bookshelves. Thus I would sit in my corner delicately performing my task until Lama told me she had had enough by crossly attacking the comb. I would immediately stop.

The cross attacks, however, had recently become more frequent. She showed an increasing dislike of my combing the denser parts of her fur, and the reason was easy to understand for, although the surface of her coat appeared to be in perfect condition, underneath it was becoming matted. This was a sign of her age that Barbara pointed out to me.

Others pointed it out to me in another way. Visitors who made remarks like:

'Lama's getting on, isn't she?'

'Have you *still* got Lama?'

'She's a good age.'

Age, age, age. The British are besotted about age. If a woman walks down a street, slips on a banana peel, falls and breaks her leg, be sure the press will begin the report: 'Fifty-five year old Mrs So-and-So . . .' Age had to be tagged on to any news. It's a ritual. It had become a ritual to ask Lama's age . . . and I found myself going back over the years and remembering the same questions being asked about Monty. Nothing had changed. The same dismay at the questions, the same sadness, the same stifled awareness that I was blinding myself to the truth. Yes, I knew that Lama was coming to the end of her time and that she would become a black comma in my memory, but I did not want to be reminded of this by such questions. I could touch her now, pick her up, listen to her purr, and I did not want to be told that these subtle pleasures would one day be only a dream.

Such moments of depression, however, were only a shallow layer on the happiness of that summer. There was, for instance, the amusement, and confusion, caused by Oliver and Ambrose. We had already become accustomed to those who excitedly exclaimed: 'We saw Lama as we were coming up the

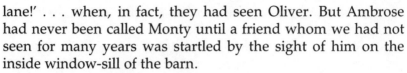

lane!' . . . when, in fact, they had seen Oliver. But Ambrose had never been called Monty until a friend whom we had not seen for many years was startled by the sight of him on the inside window-sill of the barn.

'I thought Monty was dead!'

'So he is . . . years ago.'

'I must have just seen his ghost!'

It has often seemed to me that many people, especially those who are leaders of a country, of a community, or of a cause, treat logic as a kind of lifebelt. They are desperately anxious to believe that they are masters of their own destinies, and that they can control the paths of these destinies by neat planning. Thus logic, backed up by elaborately documented facts and figures, provides the basis of any report on any subject you can name; and the imponderables are ignored because they are too mysterious to contemplate.

The imponderables, in this case, were represented by Oliver and Ambrose. How can anyone, however astute and logical in their thinking, explain the arrival at Minack of two wild, uninvited cats which were the doubles of the only two cats I have ever known?

Sensible people, no doubt, might explain it away by saying that it was a coincidence, and no more. Sensible people are inclined to ignore the existence of those unseen, untouchable, extra-sensory forces which push us this way and that during the course of our lives; and this is because the Western world believes itself so civilized that to consider magic as a reality is beneath its dignity. Yet many of us know of incidents that have no rational explanation.

A parson told me the other day of a little girl in his parish of whom he was particularly fond, who was found unconscious by her parents one morning. She had shown no previous symptoms, and when she reached hospital doctors were unable to diagnose the cause of her illness. Two days later hope for her life was given up; and the parents asked the parson to hurry to the hospital and give her a blessing. Just before he set off the parson rang up a healer who was a friend of his, and told him of his mission. An hour later he reached the hospital only to be greeted with the news that the child, who had never regained consciousness, was not expected to live more than a

few minutes. He hurried to the ward, and stood by the girl's bed, then quietly said: 'Who is here, Jill? Who is here?' There was stillness for a moment, then the girl stirred, and to the astonishment of everyone murmured: 'It's you Father.' From that instant the recovery began, and a month or so later she was riding her pony again in the fields near her home. Was it prayer, the healer, or magic which achieved this?

As for my own experience in these mysterious matters, one incident which sticks in my mind concerns the one and only time I have had my hand read by a palmist. I was on a steamer sailing from Sydney to Hong Kong when one of my fellow passengers, a burly engineer on his way to a job in Hong Kong

dockyard, offered to tell me my fortune saying that he had once studied with Cheiro, a renowned palmist. So there I was on deck one balmy evening, the steamer sailing through the Aragura Sea, with my hands held out in front of me . . . and the engineer telling me that I would marry a slender, dark-haired girl whose initials were J.E. Five years later I was walking up the aisle of Richmond Church with Jean Everald Nicol.

Anyhow, whatever the explanation for the arrival of Oliver and Ambrose, I the anti-cat man was now besieged by three cats; and I was endlessly on guard. Lama, although she was no longer frightened by Oliver, understandably disliked his presence; and so we continued to do our best to keep them apart. Thus I was perpetually saying: 'No sign of Oliver, Lama can go out.' Or: 'Keep Lama in. Oliver is around the corner.' As for Ambrose, he continued to be elusive, *maddeningly* elusive.

'Come here, Ambrose,' I would call, waggling a finger towards him.

Or:

'I have something for you, Ambrose,' Jeannie would say, holding a saucer of fish in one hand while hoping to stroke him with the other.

Not a chance.

'Ambrose,' I would remark sternly, 'pay your rent!'

His markings, month by month, became more beautiful, lines of autumn bracken colours with shapes which reminded me of currents on a quiet sea. True that at times his head, because of his youth, looked scraggy, even his body sometimes looked scraggy, but suddenly for some reason like the change of light, or of mood, he looked his potential. This was going to be a champion cat, just like Monty. Beautiful to look at, and highly intelligent though still viewing the human race, and ourselves despite all that we were wanting to offer, with suspicion.

The relationship between him and Lama developed into a quiet understanding so that I would catch sight of them side by side at Monty's Leap, sipping from the trickle of the summer stream; and when they had finished they would walk back together. Of course Ambrose would not dare to take any advantage of her. He recognized that she was the Queen.

Affection he could offer, but no question of taking liberties.

Oliver, meanwhile, was becoming benign. He was still the outsider, longing to be the insider, and sometimes he took physical steps to achieve his aim. We had this wire-framed contraption, first used to prevent Monty from jumping out of the bedroom window at night, which we still erected to stop Lama from doing the same. It was an insecurely fixed, clumsy contraption, but firm enough to achieve its purpose. But one night I was woken from a deep sleep by a terrible battering noise at the window, followed by a crash on the floor, then a thump. Oliver, from the outside, had knocked down the contraption, and jumped on the bed.

Jeannie was half awake.

'What's happened? What's happened?'

She spoke in that half-hysterical fashion that half-awake people are inclined to do.

'Keep calm,' I hissed, 'leave it to me. It's an emergency.'

An emergency indeed. Oliver had crawled up to me on my left side, roaring out purrs like the sound of a low-flying piston-engined aircraft, while on my right side lay Lama.

'Don't wake her,' I hissed again, 'hold her gently, and I'll deal with Oliver.'

'You're panicking.'

'Of course I'm panicking . . . the two of them within a foot of each other, and one roaring his head off an inch from my face.'

I now seized Oliver firmly in my hands, got out of bed, carried him to the sitting-room door, opened it, then opened the porch door into the little garden, and dumped him there. I went back to bed.

'A bit cruel, weren't you?'

'Heavens,' I answered, 'what else could I do?'

Not a movement from Lama. She was still curled on the bed, making the clickety-click noise which was peculiar to her when she was sleeping.

'I just think it was a bit hard on him,' said Jeannie sleepily, adding, 'he only wants to be loved.'

'Oh Jeannie, you do sometimes say such silly things.'

'Shut up, I'm just going off.'

I myself didn't go off for an hour or more. I lay awake wondering what Oliver was thinking, and how he was spending the night. Back sharing a straw-filled box with Ambrose, I guessed.

The donkeys viewed Oliver and Ambrose with tolerant amusement. Oliver, they realised, was like Lama, possessing a middle-aged seriousness which forbade any prospect of playing silly games. Nevertheless they would sometimes try. If Oliver was in sight as we led the two of them from the stable meadow up past the cottage, one of them would be sure to advance head down, like a dog following a scent, and try to pull towards him. Oliver, of course, would skedaddle away; and Penny or Fred, whichever it was, would take a bite at the escallonia instead.

Ambrose was a different matter. Ambrose provoked them, especially Fred. Ambrose was like a saucy small boy who taunted his friends to attack him, then ran away before they were able to do so. Ambrose courted danger. Ambrose would find Fred munching grass in the donkey field above the cottage, and proceed to stalk him. This was a dangerous form of Russian roulette because Fred was often in the middle of the field, so that the nearer Ambrose crept the further he had to run to escape. Perhaps this was Ambrose's deliberate purpose, to experience the sheer thrill of being chased a hundred yards by a donkey. It certainly gave Fred pleasure, it was bliss chasing Ambrose at speed across a field.

Thus there were three cat lives running parallel to each other at Minack that summer. Ambrose, of course, was the most innocent, the years of adventure ahead of him, and the fun, and idiotic predicaments. Oliver, understandably, was bewildered as to what more he had to do to become acceptable . . . choosing to come back in the first place, the cold nights in the Wren House and on branches of gorse when his house was flooded, the efforts to show his affection, the wonderous production by him that Sunday October morning of the double of Monty, his gentle insistence that all he wanted from us was to be loved . . . it wasn't difficult to understand why he was puzzled that we didn't allow him to become a natural part of our life. Yet he had time on his side. He could wait. He could pursue a policy of quietly infiltrating into our lives because he had the edge on Lama. He was younger. He might be made to feel, by our manner towards him, that he was a second-class

106

citizen, but he was prepared to put up with it. He had Ambrose, in any case, as a companion. He wasn't lonely.

Lama, meanwhile, spent more and more of her time in sleep. She would curl herself in her favourite places, on the carpet beside my desk close to the storage heater, or she would lie on the newly washed clothes airing on top of the storage heater in the spare bedroom, or she would settle herself in the dark of the cupboard among my shirts. Not that she showed any serious signs of her age. Her appetite was as good as ever, and she still loved her walks, the walk to the cliff especially.

I remember one hot, early September morning, and Jeannie and I decided to take time off, and to go down to the rocks to bathe; and we hadn't walked a dozen yards down the path towards Fred's field when to our surprise Lama rushed past us, then suddenly stopped, and looked back at us. This was the old game of chase and stop which we knew so well. A spontaneous gesture of pleasure and excitement.

'I didn't really want her to come,' I said.

'Why ever not?'

'I wanted to lie on the rocks and bathe,' I said, 'I wanted to be on my own without bothering about Lama.'

'You old misery.'

I accepted that. I was an old misery not to be happy that Lama had chosen to come with us. But I was right about having to bother about her. For the path wending its way down through the daffodil meadows became steeper when it neared the rocks, and at that point Lama would always stop. She would not walk on the rocks. Hence when we wanted to bathe, one of us had always to stay with her, or otherwise she would join the gulls' cries with her miaows.

That September morning I let Jeannie go ahead with her bathe, while I stayed behind with Lama, lying on the same spot as when she warned me that an adder was about to attack me. She sat on my tummy purring; and I lay there with that sound in my ears and the sound of the sea caressing the rocks, a gull or two soulfully calling, and the poignant trilling of oyster catchers over to my left below Carn Barges. A moment of great happiness, complete, breeding no greedy wish for something better. This was the kind of moment for which men and women, in old-fashioned wars, were ready to die for, believing

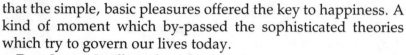

that the simple, basic pleasures offered the key to happiness. A kind of moment which by-passed the sophisticated theories which try to govern our lives today.

Dear Lama, I still can hear her purring.

Kym

JOYCE STRANGER

THERE have always been cats in my life as well as dogs. Many people are partisan, preferring one to the other. Numerous friends express surprise because I like both, fitting people into slots; cat people or dog people. They express even greater surprise when they visit my home now and find two cats and two dogs living amicably together. The cats often curl up against the dogs to keep warm. There is no need whatever to deprive oneself of one species because the house contains the other.

We have introduced a puppy into a house with an older cat; and a kitten into a home which already has a grown dog; we have had puppies and kittens at the same time. There is an initial settling-down period but, handled properly and introduced wisely, they do settle together, and often become great friends.

The first cat I remember really well was Nipper, who co-existed with our Airedale dog, Turk. Nipper must have had a fairly difficult life, as he came to us when my twin brother and sister were small and my younger sister was a baby. We all lugged him round constantly. I can't bear, now, to see a cat hoisted painfully by a little child, and insist that in our home the animals are treated with respect and not used as substitute toys. They usually endure without complaint, but should they rebel, unable to stand any more, the child may be badly hurt, and the animal will be blamed.

Once, when I was about eight, we dressed Nipper up in doll's clothes, and took him round the shops in my doll's pram. We were very careful to avoid our mother, as she would have been furious and stopped the game immediately, but we evaded her. She saw us go, thinking my big doll was in the pram.

In the very middle of Bexleyheath High Street, a dog pushed his nose under the hood. Nipper gave an eldritch yell and bolted, long clothes, bonnet, and all, into the street, where cars braked violently, tyres screaming. A tram was bearing down on both him and the dog.

There was pandemonium until a policeman fielded the cat, and brought him back to us. He was a very large and a very angry policeman, who shook me thoroughly, as I was the eldest of the three—the twins were only six. His anger taught me more than my mother's anger would have done; no one in those days questioned the authority of the police. Had my parents known of the incident they would both have said 'Serve you right,' and added another punishment, such as no visit to the Zoo, or stopping our pocket money.

We took Nipper home and undressed him hastily. I am not sure that my mother ever did hear of this incident. I took very good care that it never happened to any of our cats when my own children were young.

Nipper was extremely large, very heavy, and coal black with green eyes. He had a number of unendearing habits, possibly provoked by us, as we loved him far too much, handled him far too much and he was rarely left in peace to get on with his own life. Someone always wanted to cuddle him.

One of his most annoying games was to lurk in the black shadows under the stairs, waiting for white-socked schoolgirl legs to run by. As they did, he leaped out, sank claws and teeth into our calves, and thoroughly enjoyed the resulting noise; leaping to the safety of the top of the hall cupboard, where he looked down with the greatest interest at whoever was yelling or bellowing at him.

He had another extremely maddening habit. We moved house when he was about six years old. We went to live only a mile away from our original home, Lyndhurst, in Bexleyheath to a much bigger house called Broomwood. Nipper preferred our first home. Time after time during our first summer in the new house, I arrived back from school and was greeted by my mother.

'Nipper's gone back again. Will you go and get him, dear?'

Feeling must un-dear-like, I trudged across the dusty fields of cabbages along the footpath to Lyndhurst. I had to carry Nipper, protesting loudly and struggling vigorously, for over a mile.

Those cabbages never seemed to be harvested. Some years the price was too high for cutting them, and the profit too low, so they were left to rot and they stank. Other years they were soaked in continual rain and the crop was ruined and they rotted and they stank.

Black cats and the smell of rotting cabbages are irretrievably linked in my memory.

Nipper died at fifteen, and was succeeded by Sherry, a large and very beautiful tawny cat who spent most of his life lying in the sun.

Somewhere in the past there was also Snowball, so named because he was white. This was a misnomer, as he was born without the instinct to wash, and was the dirtiest cat I have ever seen.

I love cats. I love their grace and their elegance. I love their independence and their arrogance, and the way they lie and look at you, summing you up, surely to your detriment, with that unnerving, unwinking, appraising stare.

The war years were catless and dogless for me, except when I went home to my parents. I was away in hostel. I never passed a cat without stopping to make friends. With dogs I am more wary. One needs to know a dog before taking advantage; he may treat you as an intruder on his territory. However long one lives with dogs, it is never wise to go up to a strange one without reading his face and his tail, and parents who let children stroke my dogs without asking first if they may are fools. My dogs are safe approached the right way. Not all dogs are trustworthy by a long chalk. Many are unused to children, and alarmed by their noise and sudden uncontrolled movements. Many children are downright dangerous, unaware of animal needs.

After the war came marriage and babies. Twins, arriving when our elder son was only twenty months old, ensured there was no time for animals, however much I needed them. I knew I could not give a dog the exercise, training and companionship that he required. But I hankered for a cat.

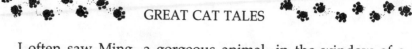

I often saw Ming, a gorgeous animal, in the window of a local sweet shop. I made friends with him and coveted him. He was the most beautiful creature.

So that when my husband asked me, just before a birthday, what I wanted most in all the world, I answered without even stopping to think.

'A Siamese kitten.'

I did not expect to be provided with my dream. But Kenneth occasionally surprises me by producing the unexpected, choosing something rather exotic that I did not know I wanted.

So, six weeks later, feeling as if I had been given the crown jewels, I found myself sitting in our old car, holding a minute and bewildered scrap that was only big enough to balance on the palm of my hand. He was very beautiful and, like all handsome creatures, he was aware of this throughout his long and crowded life.

His mask and ears were just beginning to colour. There was a hint of soot, as there was also on his paws and his kinked tail. The rest of him was a rich milky colour. His vivid blue eyes crossed when he was angry, and even at that age, reft from mother and litter mates, taken into the vast outside world at a mere nine weeks, he was not pining or pathetic.

He was furious.

He did not like us. He did not like the car. He intended that we should feel his resentment, and he yowled, long, loudly and determinedly, exclaiming at the arrangements we had made for him.

He hated us, he said. Very clearly and very plainly. He tried to scratch. I wrapped him tightly in an old jersey I had brought to keep him warm. It was a bitterly cold day. We were on the high bare moors, where he had been born in a very beautiful and luxurious home.

He hated the car. It made awful noises, and there were other noises as dinosaurian monsters hurtled towards us, far bigger than we were, obviously about to ram us and destroy us.

Even at that age he had a piercing voice and a habit of keeping up a running commentary in most expressive tones. He protested ever more loudly.

He was cold.

Rain lashed down the windscreen and obscured the bleak

road. The few stunted, wintry trees were bare and twisted. The road wound among barren hills, where last year's bracken was a dismal dank rust which gave the moors an aura of despair. Years later, they were the scene of the Moors murders. I hate them now. They are haunted by horror and children's dying screams.

The car was old and had no heater. Kym huddled into the jersey, but it lacked comfort. He tried to warm himself, but there was no fur against him. Wool felt different. There was no contact of familiar bodies; nor was there his mother's swift tongue to reassure him. He was minute, among giants, who meant nothing to him, and who had stolen him from his home.

He escaped from the jersey and explored my lap, looking for a hiding place, wanting to be in the dark, which did not reveal so many new and frightening things to him.

He discovered a much better resting place.

This was also a jersey, but the jersey had a gap at the bottom that could be lifted by an exploratory paw. He could crawl under it, and under it was something that breathed as his mother had breathed, rhythmically, hypnotically. It didn't smell as nice as his mother. And it wasn't furry. But it was close and dark and comforting, and the hand above it smoothed his fur gently, reassuring him a little.

The protests died.

They were succeeded by a faint rusty sound we decided was a purr.

Thereafter sanctuary for Kym while he was small was a hurried scurry up inside my jersey. There he could lie against me, trembling, secure in the knowledge that no one and nothing could possibly get him there.

We reached home.

We now owned a small kitten, a huge piece of paper on which was written his pedigree, and a diet sheet, and had instructions to provide him with a tray of sand. The sand and the tray were bought on the way home. He dashed to it. His mother had taught him well. We put him on the tray, showing him how to scratch with his paw, so that he knew what it was for. He never once made a mistake, even when very ill. Kittens are much more endearing in that respect than puppies.

He sat with his back to us. He was always very modest.

Until that day pets had not been part of our children's lives. We had had stick insects, but they are not exactly appealing. Ours were rather stupid and invariably strangled themselves with their old skin when they moulted. There was nothing we could do about that. They were too fragile to handle.

We also, briefly, acquired a female newt as part of a swapping deal at school. She was named, outrageously, Ivanhoe, after the TV serial at that time. Ivanhoe languished, in spite of a diet of daphne and ants' eggs, and one morning, convinced she would die on us, and hating having her captive in a goldfish bowl, I persuaded her owner to come with me and return her to the pond, where we hope she recovered. She simply sat on a stone, looking intensely miserable, all the time we had her.

Our boy and girl twins were seven years old when we bought Kym. They had come with us and helped to choose the kitten from a litter of five, a choice which had been easy, as Kym had been the one to approach us of his own free will and make friends, which he hadn't minded doing at all with his litter mates around him.

Our elder son was at a party. We decided we would surprise him, so he did not know we would have a new member of the family by the time he reached home. For that matter, I had not known until we arrived at our destination that afternoon.

The surprise was greater than we had intended as our son came in to find us all in the kitchen and the washing machine in pieces all over the floor. He was told that the reason for this was that somewhere inside, unhappily, in the dark, was a very small, very angry Siamese kitten that had made a bolt for the one safe hole when he saw his daunting new surroundings.

At that point the kitten spoke, confirming our story, which up to then had been thought to be rather an elaborate legpull.

We spent most of the evening in the kitchen, among the increasingly plentiful pieces of oily machinery. Kym had re-treated right into the middle of the inside of the wretched machine. He had no desire to come out into the open and face the shrill, noisy, strange-smelling giants who now surrounded him. We had to block the hole at the back of the washing machine, and the hole behind the refrigerator, and the oven ventilator, and all the chimneys.

Some time later, after the children had gone to bed, he was

extricated, a totally unrecognizable bedraggled scrap, shrieking in fury, hissing, scratching, and covered in oil. We did our best, but it was days before he was clean again.

He did not want food.

He did not want us.

He did not really want to be alone, but we could not provide him with his most urgent need, which was his old home, his mother and his litter brothers and sisters. I soothed him; I cuddled him; I petted him. I coaxed him to feed, just a few mouthfuls, giving him cornflakes in evaporated milk in my cupped hands. It is a messy procedure, but I always do it with new young animals, as the smell of the new order inextricably mixed up with that of food helps a tiny bewildered creature recognize who is going to look after it and be substitute mum, and is the beginning of trust, which is essential for any human–animal relationship.

He recognized that I was the source of food. Having discovered that the natives, after all, were friendly, he promptly decided that my sole function was to nurse him. If we did not cuddle him, he climbed us, telling us off soundly as he did so. On one memorable occasion when we were in our caravan he climbed Kenneth, who, wearing thin summer pyjamas, was making an early morning cup of tea.

The resulting yell caused us all to be regarded with extreme suspicion for the rest of our stay on that site, as it was a little difficult to explain that it had been caused by the kitten using him as a tree. Kym obviously felt the pain we endured was just punishment for ignoring him. He was blissfully unaware that he might not be wanted; or that we had other things to do. We had been created for his benefit. He was capable of leaping on us without warning from anywhere in the house, be it the top of the wardrobe, the top of a door, or even the curtain pelmets. It hurt.

It also upset our small daughter, who decided, embarrassingly and annoyingly at this stage, that she hated cats, and ran screaming from him every time he jumped. This made him, being Kym, even more determined to jump on her. He could not see why she fled from him, so that I spent a great deal of time in those first few weeks with a small girl cuddled against me on one side, and a very much smaller indignant kitten

curled on my lap, glaring at her, as I tried to reconcile the two of them. It needed as much work as the initial few days of a new puppy and kitten brought together.

Once she was converted she was his devoted servant, always ready to rescue him from his latest predicament.

His one aim in life, once he settled, was to brighten our days. There was always some piece of Kym mischief, or Kym misadventure to recount during an evening meal. He was extremely lively, extremely adventurous, and had enough curiosity for nineteen cats.

He also had double the number of cat lives and appeared to be anxious to lose every one of them.

He decided to get rid of his first life twenty-four hours after we acquired him. And being Kym, he did so as thoroughly as possible.

II

We were novices at pedigree kitten buying. It did not occur to us that one needed to know a great deal before starting out; the breeding might be too close so that the resulting kits were highly nervous and had some major fault; the kittens might be unhealthy.

Had I known more we would not have bought Kym. Which would have been very wise, but it would have deprived us of years of pleasure, it would not have given me half the experience with animals that has led to many of my books, and most certainly we would have missed a great character.

I did the same thing with a dog years later. He too was a very bad buy. In spite of that, he has given me invaluable experience, and is a terrific character.

So perhaps it is not always wise to be sensible! But that does not absolve breeders from responsibility. Ailing animals are very expensive pets, and not always lucky enough to go to an owner who is prepared to take enough trouble to keep them alive. Many are put down because ill health or disability is a nuisance—and an unlooked-for expense in veterinary fees and special diets, which is an enormous waste of the breeder's time and money.

Kym would feed only from my hand; and he ate very little. I thought, for the first day, that this was because he was pining for his mother. On the second day he refused to eat at all. His voice, though still loud, had a fretful overtone. I examined his sand box closely when I went to empty it. What I saw took us both to the vet, although he was not due for his inoculations till the next week.

The vet examined him.

'Take him straight back,' he said.

I looked at the kitten. He looked back at me. It was no use; the bond between us had been forged in those first few hours. I could not imagine what would happen to him if I did return him. Also he was a fierce little character, and I am not a giver-up.

I couldn't take him back.

'On your own head,' the vet said. 'He has worms. Masses of them. His mouth is covered with ulcers.' He opened it, and showed me. The whole of Kym's tongue and palate was hidden by yellow encrusted swellings. 'He has a sore throat. He has cat 'flu. He can't possibly eat with that mouth. I can't do much for him. He needs vitamins and antibiotics. He'll die on you. There's far too much wrong with him.'

He was not going to die on me.

And if I took him back to someone who had let him get into that condition before selling him, he undoubtedly would die, as they hadn't the knowledge to save his life. I hadn't much knowledge, but I obey instructions whether given by vet or doctor, feeling I have paid for advice and it's insane not to take it. And I would obey the instructions this vet gave me to the letter.

Kym was lying on the table, looking very small, very sick and very pathetic. His beautiful eyes were obscured by their third membrane, which the vet told me was a sure sign of worms; his coat had not recovered from the oil in the washing machine; his nose was running, and he was dribbling so much that his throat was soaked with saliva.

I held him for that first injection.

Enraged, he yelled. He had a pretty considerable voice.

His small paw struck angrily at the man who had inflicted such indignity on him. It looked like Tom Thumb defying a giant.

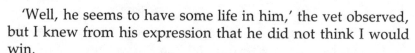

'Well, he seems to have some life in him,' the vet observed, but I knew from his expression that he did not think I would win.

I accept defeat with an old animal at the end of its life, when it is cruel and selfish to prolong pain, but I will not accept defeat with a young creature. I was going to fight. Every inch of the way, and the kitten was going to fight with me.

By the next day he was a very sick little cat. He had to have daily injections, and I knew every time I saw the vet's expression that he considered me a fool, throwing my money away on a useless cause. Which only made me more determined.

Kym was equally determined. He might be ill; he might feel awful, but there was one thing certain, and that was that as his mother wasn't here to comfort him, I had to do instead. No matter how he felt, he clawed his way up to me to lie in my lap, small head almost limp and lifeless against my hands, eyes staring into the fire at nothing.

Friends told one another it was pointless calling as I had become addicted to a kitten. As I was giving him five drops of glucose and water every fifteen minutes from an eye dropper I had bought from the chemist, I wasn't very attentive to conversation. My mind was on other things.

I rapidly became expert with the dropper.

While I was writing, Kym lay in my lap. While I was busy about the house, he lay in a small cardboard box, lined with a blanket under which was a hot-water bottle. As he wailed if I were not near him, I carried it with me, and he watched me make beds, and work around the house generally. I was determined he would not give up hope; once he himself determined to die, nothing I could do would stop him. He had to feel he was wanted. It wasn't easy, as I was strange to him, and during those first days there were moments when even I was sure I was going to lose. The vet never doubted it. He told me not to waste any more money, and to accept the inevitable.

My life revolved around glucose, water and the eye dropper.

A few drops, every quarter of an hour, fighting to keep him alive. Whatever happened now, he was not going to die on me, and every new day was an achievement. The children were upset, and I had rashly promised them that Kym wouldn't die. They knew promises were always kept.

Kym would live.

His feeble greeting each morning was reassurance to me that the struggle was not yet over.

At that time our lives were brightened every Wednesday and Friday by the visit of our greengrocer, Tom, who owned a horse and cart. He loathed lorries, and always said that when his horse died, he would die too. He only survived Prince by a very few months when at last the old horse went.

Tom was a countryman. His brother was a gamekeeper in Cumberland. Tom's visits to me, marked by cups of tea in summer and soup in winter, were always long talks on the habits of wild animals. He had hunted foxes; two men with guns and dogs, trying to keep the population from running riot. Two men on one hill on one Saturday killed seventy foxes, and there were more left to run. A vixen can have fifteen in a litter; if all survive, they will die of starvation anyway.

When Tom's horse had colic, Tom paid a boy to trot the horse around, while he drew the cart. He knew about animals; knew about horses, dogs and cats; knew many ways of fattening a pig, and had lived for a long time in the country himself. Goodness knows how he came to be a suburban greengrocer. He was a shy man, but he never could resist talking about country matters, or about racing, as he knew a great deal about both the breeding of racehorses and their form. Though I learned through him that a lot of horses don't run according to their form!

There had never been a small animal in our house. Tom laughed at our stick insects and recommended returning Ivanhoe to the pond. He now came in to get warm, and bent down to look at Kym, in his box by the fire, an old-fashioned kitchen stove with an oven beside it, and a vast metal guard to ensure safety.

'What's that? A weasel?'

'That' certainly didn't look much like a kitten. Kym was lying on his side, eyes closed, ribs barely moving. It was one of his worst days. I kept cleaning his nose and mouth, but the dribbling and discharge was continuous and he looked terrible. Tom turned him over.

'He's half dead,' he said. 'You'll never rear that. Better take it to the vet now. You're wasting your time.'

People are always telling me what I can't do. *You'll* never write a book. *You'll* never learn to drive. *You'll* never train a dog.

Little do they know. I'll show them.

'Want to bet?' I asked Tom, knowing his main weakness.

He took me on at once, but I would have liked to hedge that bet, as just for once I wasn't at all sure I was going to win it.

Luckily Kym had a tough ancestry. The day came when I arrived proudly at the vet with a clear-eyed kitten that had eaten solid food for the first time, and looked as if he would survive. By the end of the week he had lustrous fur, was racing round the house, and the vet had changed his opinion of me. He had thought me a fool. Now he knew I wasn't.

Tom paid his five shillings. We were neither of us reckless gamblers.

And then the fun began.

Kym now knew he was *my* cat. I had nursed him, cuddled him and forced food into him. I had been so determined that I had given him the will to live. I had never left him by day and had come down several times to feed and dose him each night. I had carried him upstairs when I went up, and he had never been separated from me while I was busy.

So he was now my shadow, as devoted as any dog. He followed me everywhere, yelling at the top of his voice if I dared to shut a door on him and leave him outside.

I thought it time to show him the garden. The days were warmer, and the earth box could be abandoned. But Kym hated the outside. He was very small, and sat there, complaining, because the wind shook the giant trees, and sobbed invisibly in their branches, so that they rose and swept across the sky, daunting him.

He hated the unseen fingers that ruffled his fur.

He raced to me, swarmed up me, sat on my shoulder, peered into my face, his eyes crossed, his voice excited, apparently declaiming in detail in a long monologue everything that had happened to him. It was so funny that I sometimes laughed, hurting his feelings beyond measure. He loathed being laughed at.

I don't like humanizing animals, but they undoubtedly communicate, and you can learn a lot of their language. My

present Alsatian has a special dance that she performs when her water bowl is empty. Kym had his means of communicating. He sat and willed the refrigerator or the pantry doors to open; he would rattle at the back door, yowling till I opened it; he sat in sink or bath, trying to get his tongue up the tap, if his water bowl were empty; and in the caravan he soon learned to tap the chain that kept the lids of the water carriers from getting lost. Each gesture had its own cry with it, so that he changed tones when he wanted different things.

His telling-me-about-the-world voice was extremely expressive, as if he were exclaiming and underlining, declaiming and commenting. In a strange place he used to reduce all of us to laughter as we could trace his progress by his voice, making sounds of astonishment, or delight, or giving a sudden yell for help as something enormous appeared on his horizon, which was always much more limited than ours.

He walked in a jungle when he was in long grass; in summer a tropical jungle, high above his head. Lie down at his level and the ground was humid, the air fetid. He learned to jump to a branch and sit where he could breathe more easily, out of the private forest that only the small beasts know.

Whenever anything bothered Kym, he climbed me. This was so painful that I developed an early warning system, listening for the anguished yowl that announced his coming. He was so very small. It might mean that there was an enormous nasty dog looking at him through the fence, vast tongue slavering as he panted hopefully, or a giant cat had invaded our territory, threatening him, or worse, chasing him.

None of the local established cats liked our Siamese. In his early days he was chivvied mercilessly. I sometimes thought they might have killed him if they had caught up with him, but luckily he could run very fast.

Meanwhile the garden was still unexplored territory and the earth box dominated both our lives. I kept trying to make him accept the outside. But he would only venture a few steps, crouched belly low against the ground, ears pricked, eyes wild, obviously a soldier going into enemy territory, needing all his senses alert. The least sound sent him scurrying to me, and the only way to prevent needlelike claws gripping my skin, leaving innumerable pinpricks in a traverse that showed where he had

climbed, was to be ready for him, to grab him fast, and to sit him on my shoulder.

He was also so lethal to stockings that I rarely wore a skirt at all. I live in slacks. It's cheaper with cats and dogs, and much more comfortable. Even with slacks, Kym's claws could still penetrate.

Neighbours, friends and tradesmen became resigned to seeing me open the front door with a small vociferous kitten sitting, like a witch's familiar, face against mine, doing his best to drown our conversation. He was even more successful in blotting out telephone calls. He hated the telephone. It was obviously ridiculous to him to see me talking away to that piece of plastic, with nobody there but him. Sure I could only be talking to him, he tried to make me look less absurd by answering everything I said before my caller could.

On one memorable occasion my husband phoned, asking me for the number of his passport as he was due to go on a trip abroad. I went to look, and left Kym sitting on the window sill beside the phone. At the other end of the line, Kenneth made some comment to his secretary. Kym recognized the voice, stuck an experimental paw into the receiver, bent his head and said 'Waugh' so clearly that my husband answered 'Hallo, fool.' Kym replied and they carried on an hilarious conversation until I came back, with me able to hear both sides. I only hoped his secretary had left the office. It may sound daft to talk to a cat on the telephone, but everyone who knew Kym had to admit that he was that sort of cat.

Kym and I soon started a battle of wills. Our first clash came one lovely sunny day when I was planting our new rockery with heathers. As fast as I put a plant in, Kym took it out and carried it in a triumphal march round the lawn. I captured him, replanted, and finally lost my temper and gave him a very hard tap across the paws.

He hissed at me and scratched, at which point I became mother cat and gave him a cuff on the ears. He recognized discipline at once. No mother animal allows her young to take liberties, and he knew now that I was boss. He came to my lap and curled up and licked my hand, and purred, a very sorry kitten. The rest of the heathers went in without trouble.

This did not always work.

He was the most persistent cat I have ever known, even for a Siamese. I now have two others, but they are nothing like as wilful as Kym. If I ignored him he leaned forward and tried to insert his paw into my mouth, presumably imagining that this would make me speak. Open mouths uttered words, and words meant a great deal to that particular cat. He loved them. He even understood some of them, like food, and garden, and come, but he was a very long time indeed learning to respect the one tiny word that is important to all animals, whether human or otherwise: *No!*

III

Kym learned the art of blackmail very early. If I denied him my lap, because I was busy, or denied him food, because it was not yet time, he went to attack what he obviously felt was our most cherished possession: our big armchair, which has a cover on it that is quite impossible for a small cat not to sharpen his claws on. The instant NO acknowledging that he had been noticed was all he wanted. Just attention. Sometimes he would sit there, paw raised, watching me, while I pretended not to see. He didn't attempt to scratch until I looked at him. At once he put his paw in position, attracting a yell of 'No. Bad cat. No.'

At this point, having gained his objective, he moved to the window sill, a very smug expression on his face. There he washed, ostentatiously, his attitude saying 'I never wanted to do it anyway.'

We never did cure him of using the carpet on the bottom stair as a scratching post. He had scratching blocks and scratching trees, but the bottom stair, when we were out, was a place where he could lie on his side, push with his hind paws and rake with his front paws. A frayed stair carpet on that bottom step was a major feature of the house while Kym was alive. We replaced it several times, but we never cured him. My present cats are angelic about scratching, always using the pads, and we have respectable carpets.

He also tore wallpaper, and if I punished him, by shaking and scolding, he rushed to the mantelpiece, leaped up, and quite deliberately pushed my ornaments on to the hearth,

watching in delight as they broke. He looked up gleefully, awaiting my reaction. He moved so fast that I never forestalled him and in the end we replaced all our ornaments with wooden ones that don't break when dropped. We still have them. I never dust them without being reminded of Kym, sitting on the mantelpiece, watching them fall. We never knew when he would indulge himself and try and smash my possessions, apparently to pay me out for thwarting him in some piece of wickedness he had just invented.

It was impossible to ignore him. If I shut him out of a room I soon discovered I couldn't stand the din he made, as he would not be quiet until I opened the door and let him in. He had an enormous voice which made a neighbour once quote to me a saying she had heard, that an ordinary cat will wake its owner, but a Siamese will wake the dead. She didn't like Siamese cats at all.

Nor could I leave him grounded, as even when he was fully grown, and weighed fourteen pounds, he would climb me, or leap me, almost knocking me backwards if he jumped while I was moving about and got his distance wrong.

He rode me while I peeled potatoes, commenting the whole time. He rode me while I made the beds. He sat on my shoulder, bellowing into my ear, varying his conversation with a swift lick that tickled horribly and always took me by surprise. He loved washing me and when he had finished his own toilet, which was meticulous and performed nightly in my lap around nine o'clock, he would wash both my hands and any part of my arms that was not covered, and then put a paw on my hand and laugh at me. This meant it was time to wash his tail, which I held for him as it had a habit of twitching out of his reach and annoying him. It was a particularly uncontrollable tail, it seemed, and did not always do what he wanted it to do.

He loved me to try and catch it so that he could twitch it away from me.

Kym's life outside the house was one long adventure. I often felt that he had the same tendencies as my small sons, who delighted to tell me how narrowly they had escaped death under the wheels of cars, bicycles, lorries, or by not falling out of the tallest tree in the world, which happened, very

125

conveniently, to be on the local playground, and a great temptation to adventurous children.

Kym's life obviously seemed to him just like that, as there were so many hazards. There was the road, which he learned to dash across at breakneck speed. I often wished he would confine himself to our back garden, but behind the houses on the other side there were fields, and there was a multitude of small animals.

There is an alley way between the houses opposite, ending in a stile. I can still see the remains of the fields as I write, but a new housing estate is obliterating our last wild space. Few people realized how wild those scanty acres were. I did not myself until I took to hunting for Kym in the long grass, where the cattle grazed.

There he found a country of his own; cuckoo flowers bloomed profusely in spring, and small mice hid as they heard his footsteps. Magpies nested in the tall tree, and yacked when they heard him coming. He watched all swift movement in the grasses. A weasel would appear, briefly, racing for cover, and vanish. Within moments the cat was busy with another clump of grass in which a mouse quivered. Not for long. Kym was a great mouser though he rarely killed them. He brought them home, proudly, and I took them from him, praised him, took him in, fed him, and returned the mouse to the field, hoping it would find its own way home. These were field mice, and no threat to us.

There were rabbits, which often lolloped down the road in the early morning, before the speeding cars arrived to scare them away. They sat in our garden.

Sometimes, when the grass was high in next door's back patch where their English setters roamed, the long ripe grass-seed ears hung invitingly over my fence. I would hear a sharp chik chik of anger from the cat, sitting in the window, eyes glaring, chattering his teeth in fury, as the rabbits stood on hind legs and pulled down the succulent seeds to eat. They were surprisingly long when they stood erect and neither Kym nor I moved until they had finished, though we stood there for different reasons.

Once they had gone I let him out, and he paced the lawn, sniffing at the ground where they had passed, plainly learning all about them.

Next door's tawny cat, Marmaduke, was a great rabbiter, and I thought Kym might prove the same. Kym's first real outdoor encounter with a wild rabbit occurred when he was small. We had a full-grown buck arrive in the garden and crouch under the plum tree, enjoying the shade. Kym had just gone outside. He was playing with a leaf, twisting and turning, whirling and twirling, in the elfin dance that always fascinated me so much that I forgot what I was doing and watched him enjoying his life as only a small child or an animal can, absorbed in the present, with no thought of the future and only random memories of the past.

He saw the rabbit just as the old buck saw him. He was a magnificent buck, full grown and very large. He sat up, his back to the cat, watching it over one shoulder with curious eyes. He had certainly never seen a Siamese cat before as at that time Kym was the only one in the district. He was now half grown, with long black paws, long black tail, a black mask, and crossed blue eyes that annoyed our doctor, who wanted the squint corrected. Those eyes were, many years later, to lead me to one of the oddest encounters of my life.

Kym saw the rabbit and sat, not sure what to make of this enormous beast. Not sure even if it were a rabbit, as those that came to nibble the grass ears were much smaller—probably this year's babies, half grown. This was Dad, immense, majestic, a rabbit to end all rabbits.

Dad knew about cats. He continued to look, ready to bound away if there was any threat from the much smaller animal at the other end of the lawn. Kym turned his back, and sat, apparently thinking. He washed one hind paw, very carefully, from end to end, sticking it at an angle into the air, examining it meticulously.

He peeped over his shoulder.

Rabbit, plainly mystified, was peeping over *his* shoulder.

Kym nibbled hastily at an itch, and swished his tail. Perhaps if he pretended Rabbit wasn't there, it would go away. It was his garden, after all. Rabbit turned his back again and gazed into space.

Kym washed the other leg.

Very slowly, as if unable to resist the temptation, he turned his head again, only to find that Rabbit had turned his head. Mesmerized, they stared at one another.

By now I had totally forgotten about housework, and had poured a cold drink and was sitting on the window sill to watch the outcome. Both animals continued to peer at one another at intervals for almost forty minutes. Neither moved from the spot on which he was firmly and safely anchored. It seemed as if this could go on all day. I was just reluctantly concluding that I really had better get on with my own affairs when both animals, as if given a signal, loped very slowly away in opposite directions.

Rabbit hopped in long slow bounds. Kym sneaked along, belly almost on the ground, until he came round the corner of the house, when he exploded into a run, raced in through the door, jumped to the table and then to my shoulder and launched into a long complicated involved monologue about what had been going on and how he had seen this enormous animal and it had sat there and had looked at him.

Try as I would, it was impossible not to feel he was giving a most explicit account of the goings-on out on the lawn. His voice rose and fell, soft, then loud, then exclamatory, until I was so helpless with laughter that he leaped off my shoulder on to the window sill and sat there, back to me, his tail lashing to and fro, absolutely furious with me because I had dared to laugh at him.

He found other things in the fields. There was a hare, and leverets, though luckily he never caught one. They were always well hidden but if I sat and watched the mother, I could usually see just where she had put her babies. They were always far apart. Then if one nest was raided, the others survived. The bound she made sideways off the nests was incredible, a vast leap which killed her scent, and foiled any dogs tracking her. Years later she found her way into *The Hare at Dark Hollow*, and on to 'Jackanory'.

There were moles and shrews and voles. There were birds. Kym loved bringing me presents. I became used to taking them from him and freeing any that were unharmed. He rarely did kill his prey, except for the moles, which were invariably dead. Perhaps they fought him; or perhaps he found them when they were already dying, due to the attentions of a mole-catcher.

I always put Kym indoors before freeing his catch. He invariably went out an hour later to see if it was there, where

he had left it. It never was. Those animals he did kill I found were almost always maimed; and I suspected the others were ill. He killed a one-legged blackbird, that was starvation thin; and a thrush which had a giant growth pushing the two parts of its beak wide open so that it could not have been able to feed for days. Other animals often had old injuries on them, so that I feel the cats, like other predators, cull, taking out the sickly creatures from the breeding cycle and improving the stock. For all that I dislike cat habits in that respect, one learns to live with it. It is a natural thing. If he caught a bird that was unharmed, I always put it high on our bird table, surrounded by a large quantity of wild birdfood. The presence of the other birds, coming for food, seemed to be a splendid antidote for shock. The bird invariably fed after about thirty minutes and then flew away.

The wise birds were never caught, as they soon knew our cat's progress. I used to say to friends who had called for coffee (after lunch, as the morning is always my working time at my typewriter), 'Just a minute. Cat's coming,' and I would go out of the room and let him in.

It was only when one of my closer friends got desperate and revealed that she and everyone else I knew regarded this as an uncanny and rather peculiar party trick, on a par with my witchlike habit of wearing Kym on my shoulder, that I realized how few people actually are aware of what is going on around them.

It was so obvious that I just couldn't see why they didn't know too.

Yet when I tried to explain I only added to their mystification.

The birds had told me.

The *birds*?

Birds are wonderful guardians for all wild things. I would hear those first angry notes of 'cat, cat, cat' in the far distance, across the fields. Kym had been hunting.

Then the calls came nearer. The magpies chickered in the big birch tree halfway down the twelve-acre field; the thrushes that nested in the thorn hedge passed on the call; the robin added his sharp little note of warning, as Kym approached the garden shed where Robin and his mate hid their babies; and then came

the yells from the thrushes in the laurel bush in the front garden opposite our own house.

Now my birds were yelling loud and furious, deafening me with their sounds. They were telling me, as plain as if they were speaking in my own language, that Kym had come round the corner of the house opposite, was in full view crossing the road, was coming up my garden path, was waiting by the front door.

CAT, CAT, CAT.

It couldn't be plainer.

Whenever he appeared, I came out and picked him up and took him in. If he were stalking birds on the lawn, I picked him up even more quickly. Within a very few weeks of the start of Kym's hunting life, cat and I were identified as one by the birds. If I appeared, Kym was almost certain to come too, either following me from the house, or racing to me from somewhere in the garden.

The warnings started, in time, as soon as I appeared, even if the cat were nowhere near. We were inseparable and I was obviously equally dangerous. In the same way a falconer, hunting often in the same place, finds the birds will shout, not when the hawk appears but when his van comes into view. It is soon useless hunting there; all the birds have vanished before the hawk is on his fist.

Our birds stayed put, so long as the cat did not appear in the tree.

They never yell now, as my two blue-point Siamese, Chia and Casey, exercise in a cage; a very large pen made for the dogs. I can't face the troubles we had with Kym with two of them. The birds ignore the dogs. I am no longer a threat, and no bird shouts at me.

Once Kym was inside he amused my guests by pacing the floor, eyes crossed, tail swishing, declaiming loudly with all the assurance of a born actor. Having informed us all of his adventures, he then jumped to my lap, and, with a deep sigh of content, turned himself around until he was comfortable, and proceeded to bath, washing delicately, inspecting each paw, and nibbling between the pads. Exhausted he curled up to sleep, first putting his paw firmly on my hand to make sure I couldn't knit. He hated knitting.

In the end, after nightly battles during which he pulled the wool off the needles, or teased at them until I dropped a stitch, I gave in, and became an ardent patron of St Michael instead. I never had liked knitting, but my mother and my mother-in-law both made me feel so guilty if I didn't indulge in this housewifely chore that I did try. My children sighed as they pulled on yet another garment that appeared to have been put together haphazardly, and rejoiced when I gave up.

I dressmade for a couple of years longer, until my daughter went to a party and came home and said rather wistfully, 'Can I have a proper dress from a shop before I go to another party?'

Thankfully I gave that up too. I could now write with an easy conscience. Kym approved of that as he could curl in my lap, or lie beside the typewriter, or sit in the cupboard and occasionally regale me with his latest bit of hot cat news.

By the time he was eight months old he was much more independent. But he still needed protection from Dusky, next door.

Dusky was an immense Persian who had regarded my garden as his for some years. He was a very dignified cat, and he was appalled when I imported a small screeching demon that didn't look like a proper cat, didn't sound like a proper cat, and seemingly didn't even smell like a proper cat. It was very easy for Dusky to be bold as he was twenty times the size of my kitten, and could see him off in seconds by fluffing his fur up to immense size, which was really tremendous as he had a very long coat. He then emitted an ear-splitting yowl.

What with Dusky howling and Kym yelling that Dusky was after him again and please come quick, it was very difficult to ignore the cats. Occasionally my kitten exploded into the kitchen through the open window instead of the door, landing on the kitchen table. Once I was making pastry and Kym landed in the bowl in a flurry of flour that didn't please either of us.

Even worse than Dusky was Beagle. This area has been dominated for a great many years by a succession of wandering beagles, probably all belonging to the same family, though I have never been quite sure of that. Each is allowed to wander as he chooses, let out in the morning to wreak mayhem, treeing cats, chasing other dogs, importuning in-season bitches,

trespassing in gardens where they eat the birds' food, and leaving unpleasant mementos on lawn or doorstep.

One of the least endearing habits they have is to chase cats. After all, they are bred for hunting, and hunt they will. The beagle that was contemporary with Kym chased little girls when he ran out of cats. But most of all he liked to make a detour that included our garden, so that he could chase Kym. No fence deterred him. He could climb over, or barge through, being a hefty little dog, and make a new gap. I like most dogs, but I grew to detest Beagle, all of them. No one has ever taught then NO.

Kym usually found a clear space to run home, but not always. He ran to trees. He was once marooned at the top of a telegraph pole. That was quite a morning, as there were men working on the next pole and they tried, very kindly, to get my kitten down.

He removed himself to the very tip of the pole and screamed. 'Being stolen!'

I ran out, armed with a plateful of fish.

'Don't touch that, it's vicious,' said a large man, sucking a long scratch on his hand.

I rattled the plate against the pole. Kym slipped down, sliding most of the way, emitting an agitated wail rather like a miniature air-raid siren. He landed on my shoulder where he became a melting, adoring thank-you-for-rescuing-me I-do-love-you purring cat, much to the men's amazement.

'He was frightened,' I explained with as much dignity as was possible with a plate of coley in one hand and a kitten rolling against my face, balanced on my shoulder, supported by the other hand.

The men were speechless as we walked away, Kym declaiming loudly, like a newsboy yelling Read All About It.

I never liked leaving Kym when I was out during the day. Something always went wrong. Once I came home and found him lying miserably in the lavender bush, with a strip of fur and skin about six inches long and an inch and half wide missing from between his shoulders. It was an injury that baffled me, and baffled our vet. It could have been done by a dog, but it was too regular. I suspected a vandal for years, until I happened to mention it to another veterinary friend. He had

seen a similar injury on a cat that had been run over by a car; something under the car had caught it on the back, and had made the same mark.

Apart from possible injuries, if I was going to the shops and Kym was in the garden he had his own way of ensuring that I didn't go it alone. A small shape would suddenly appear from the last house in the road that led to the village, and greet me with fervour. He had run through the gardens, invisible to me. He would them jump to my shoulder, to ride with me the rest of the way.

This was far from convenient, so that I had to go home, put Kym indoors and start out again. Neighbours who didn't know me must have thought me insane. But there is never any choice with a Siamese. If he wanted to ride my shoulder, he rode my shoulder. My present little male, Casey, won't be picked up unless he chooses, but Chia is a shoulder rider. She too gives me no choice.

I could argue with Kym all I liked. But back he came.

I had to devise a way to get him in, or I wasted a great deal of time hunting for him, looking under bushes and up trees and calling, which had no effect whatever, as if he didn't want to come, he didn't come.

I found out how to get him in by accident. He had a very mysterious habit of appearing the second I put food on his plate. I realized after much puzzling that it was an enamel plate and his quick ears caught the sound of fork or knife on metal.

Even then it didn't dawn on me that I could use this to advantage. One day I was beating eggs (for a cake) in a metal bowl. Kym appeared, eager, positive I had summoned him for food, and was so annoyed to find he was wrong that he tried to steal the eggs. I gave him a little taste of fish, and sent him out again, not realizing just why he had come in.

I started beating the eggs again and this time he came in even quicker, quite sure I had made a mistake and I really was making his dinner.

Thereafter, whenever we wanted Kym we beat a fork against a plate. The sound was enough to bring him at top speed, legs going so fast that they seemed to cross over as he ran. It was the only time he ever lost his dignity. Many distant neighbours must have wondered at the frequent tocsin sounds from our

garden, and so must those on caravan sites who were too far away to see the cat coming, summoned like the genie of the lamp by our din.

I often fed him tiny meals several times a day as it was more convenient to know he was safely shut indoors. This was particularly so when he grew up, since he made up for all that he had been made to suffer as a kitten by becoming Emperor of the road, insisting it was all his territory and beating up the neighbourhood cats, a habit that didn't really endear him to anyone, even though their pets had made his life a minor hell when he was small.

Kym's only defence as a kitten was to emit a fearsome yell, a weird screech that was enough to appal some visiting cat that thought he had an easy victim.

I soon discovered there is as much myth about the Siamese cat as there is about having babies. I was told they are exceptionally delicate (cats, not babies; they suffer from other peculiarities known to all the Jonahs who visit expectant mothers). The fragile Siamese rarely survives its first few weeks, so of course as soon as Kym was ill, everybody told me so. It is a delicate eater, only able to stomach things like chicken, turbot, halibut, and possibly steamed plaice.

If it should survive its youth, it is fierce, untamable, likely to scratch out the children's eyes, to ruin the furniture and to rip the curtains into shreds. It also makes an unpleasant, raucous, non-stop noise.

I love the noise. I was also sure I could tame a kitten. It is all a matter of training; some things you can teach a cat, but few people do try and train them. All my cats understand NO. And that has multiple uses. Chia and Casey also understand and respect OUT, used when they trespass in the pantry, or the room with our respectable chairs.

Kym survived his first illness.

He did make a noise, but he was extremely gentle, in spite of the apparent ferocity of his comments. We had daily games, most of which he invented. One of his favourites was to help make the beds. This meant bed-making took about five times as long as usual. The routine was unvarying. All animals and most humans love routine as it makes for order in a very disorderly world.

The games began with Kym sitting on the bed, eyes half closed, looking wicked, mumbling at me in an odd cross between a yowl and a purr, until I realized what he wanted and pushed my fist against his forehead. Back went his ears and he thrust his head hard against me. Just as I was beginning to tire of this part of the game, he rolled over, seized my fist in his mouth and covered it in tiny love nibbles, kicking against me with his hind legs, claws sheathed.

He held my arms firmly in his front paws, which were velvet soft against my skin. At first, while he was small, he sometimes became over-excited, and yelled in sudden frenzy and leaped clear. As he grew older he learned to control that, and the game ended with him nestled against me, crooning, delighting in contact, so that he rubbed his furry face against my cheek.

Only then could the bed-making proceed. Often I had to open up the blankets again, as he would either leap in from the opposite side of the bed and lie flat against the bed foot, or he would slip inside unseen and apparently vanish so that I searched the house for him until I saw that telltale hump, warm under the blankets, enjoying hiding while I sought.

Sometimes he merely leaped up and did a dervish dance, racing frenziedly round the bed, under the blanket, trying to catch my hand and pounce on it as I tucked in the bedding. I loathe bed-making, but Kym certainly livened up the process, and it usually ended in a wild romp as he chased off, and came back again to tease at anything I happened to hold in my hand.

He listened very anxiously for us to get up. He slept in the kitchen which was very warm, as we had an all-night fire there. His box was in the corner of the room, with an earth box against emergencies under the table. We never did know if he had emptied himself during the evening, and it seems to me absurd to trust to luck and then complain. The box is easy to clean and cats respect it. Kym never did make a mess anywhere in the house.

One day he was sick in the hall and this obviously worried him. I was having a bath. He came rushing upstairs, and stood on his hind legs and tried to hook me out of the water. At last, realizing he had something urgent to communicate and maybe needed to go outside, I went down, to be shown the mess on the floor. Once it was cleaned up he relaxed; I had done my

duty and could go back and finish my bath, while he went to sleep again. He had been eating grass, and I had brought him in before he had had time to get rid of it. Animals seem to use this as a cleansing habit. It's not a sign of diet deficiency or ill health. It may get rid of worms in wild animals.

Kym never bit, but he would not allow anyone to pick him up unless he chose. He perched high above them, watching them suspiciously, until he was sure they were friendly. My friends he always honoured by sitting on their laps, a pleasure not appreciated by non-cat-lovers, but Kym was blithely unaware of that.

Mary, who lives across the road, is allergic to cats. For some reason best known to Kym it was always her doorstep he chose to sun himself on, and her garden he used as a direct route to the field beyond. He had several adventures in it owing to his insistence in using it as a right of way.

On one occasion black cotton was strung to keep the birds off the crocuses, which were planted thickly, in large beautiful clumps, on either side of a small flight of stone steps that led down to the lawn. Black cotton must be invisible to cats, as Kym tripped, somersaulted in a totally undignified way, and landed on the grass, where he sat, washing furiously, to cover his embarrassment.

That did not cure him of using the garden. Other cats also made it their main path to the field, so that one day Mary met me and said, 'Have you seen a bald ginger cat anywhere? Kym fought him in my garden. Do come and look.'

It was impossible to believe any cat could have lost so much fur and not be bald, but when I looked somewhat anxiously at the various gingers round us, they all seemed intact. Kym had a bite on his shoulder. Within a few days this proved to be the first of the many abscesses that were to lead us to beat out a path to the vet's, and earn Kym the nickname of Battling Billy. We were soon only too well known, as those abscesses invariably needed lancing and injections of antibiotic to clear them up. Somehow Kym always got bitten in the sort of place that is impossible to see until it does go wrong and however carefully I examined him after a fight, I never could find anything other than scratches at first.

I sometimes suspected Kym of a misplaced sense of humour

as often after a fight that had sounded like the encounter of two spitting demons, yelling loudly enough to wake the dead, I would discover he had gone to earth either in Mary's garden (apparently bent on making her change her mind about cats, though he was going about it in quite the wrong way) or else somewhere in the road, not coming when he was called, staying away so long we decided that this was the end; he had fought to the death; or he had been run over; or he had been stolen. That is another thing that happens to Siamese cats, according to one's informers, though I suspect anyone trying to steal Kym would have had an exceptionally unpleasant few hours, and never have been able to stand him afterwards, as he rarely stopped 'talking'.

Just as we had given up all hope of ever seeing him again, he would appear with a wicked look in his eyes, greeting us fervently, surprised that we had been looking for him at all.

His favourite trick was to climb our apple tree, at the far end of the garden. There he would sit, pathetic, forlorn, *stuck*. Getting up was fine, his voice seemed to be telling us, but coming down was different. He sounded as if he were chiding us for being too slow, leaving him up there when he wanted to be down with us.

The children always rushed to his rescue when they were home, climbing the tree, handing him down gently to me, where he cuddled on my shoulder, so grateful to be safe again.

Then one day, after he had been rescued twice, the children all went out to tea. Strangely, he rarely climbed the tree when I was alone. I was talking on the telephone when I heard the anguished yowls and knew he was marooned again. There was nothing I could do about it at that moment.

I rang off, and rather unnervingly, the cries stopped. I wondered if he had fallen and, uncatlike, had damaged himself. I couldn't imagine any other reason for the silence as normally he yelled until someone came.

I went out into the garden.

There, swiftly, competently, as if he had done it a hundred times, as he probably had, was my little cat, coming down the apple tree. He saw me and froze, two inches from the ground, and began to shout again. I'm stuck, I'm stuck, I'm stuck.

I laughed so much that he was furious. He jumped the last

inches and stalked indoors and sat for the whole evening with his back to me, his tail swishing angrily at intervals. By bedtime he had forgiven me and was once more purring on my lap, helping me read.

This was a common and not very useful exercise, as his idea of help was to flip the pages back as I turned them over, sure that there was a much better way of dealing with yet another peculiar human activity. It took my attention away from him and annoyed him nearly as much as the telephone. My dogs peer with great interest at my book and sniff it before turning away in disgust. I often wonder what they make of human doings. An animal lives its life in an aura of constant and bewildering mystery conforming to rules it can never understand. It must feel as we would if isolated in a foreign country with unfamiliar etiquette and no interpreter, having to conform because we would be punished if we didn't.

Letter writing was even worse than reading books, from Kym's point of view, but it did hold more interesting possibilities. Pens could be played with. They could be carried away and hidden. They could be tapped to make interesting squiggles across the page. This was particularly rewarding as it invariably made me say something to him. Never mind that the something was said in anger. He wasn't being ignored. I knew he was there and had noticed him.

Pens could also be stalked and pounced at.

Papers, to Kym, were wonderful. They rustled. Christmas was the most exciting time in his life, when everyone had papers round them; tissues and golden paper that crinkled, and ribbons to tease, as well as baubles to knock off the Christmas tree. But failing Christmas every day, he settled for the newspaper.

That too rustled. It could be jumped at, when it tore with a satisfying rip and an equally satisfying roar of disapproval from Master, who at last was giving Kym attention. Also in the evening Kym liked to share his attentions between us and commuted from lap to lap, quite sure that his bulky purring weight was essential to human happiness.

He would lurk on the hearthrug, innocent. Watching. Then, just as our attention was focussed on anything but him he would leap.

He might land under the paper, purring, to lie in wait, occasionally reaching out his paw to tap the hand that turned the pages. He might land in the middle of it, disastrously. He might go right through it like a circus act. Whichever he did, the result was always very satisfying to him, and once the paper reader had stopped being angry, Kym was usually allowed to play the tunnel game.

The tunnel game was heaven and could go on for hours. Our boredom threshold was much lower than Kym's. He could wait endlessly by a minute hole in the garden expecting mice to materialize, occasionally poking a hopeful paw, sure that his wait would be rewarded, quite unaware that this particular hole was there for the clothes post to fit into.

The paper was set up on the floor in a tube, with a ping-pong ball at one end. Kym lurked under the sideboard, his tail end wagging from side to side, as he poised himself to pounce. A rush and a leap and a glorious rustle and he tapped the ball, which sped across the floor.

It was retrieved and set ready again and back under the sideboard he went, lurking there until we thought he had gone to sleep. Just as we relaxed, deciding to go on reading our books, he erupted like a small demon, flying through the tunnel and up over the furniture, until everyone but he was exhausted.

He had one other source of evening entertainment. Television usually baffled him, except for one programme. He adored Tony Hancock! Tony had a very large mouth—which he opened particularly wide as he talked. Kym spent the whole programme on top of the TV set trying to fish out Tony's tongue, which he must have thought was a mouse in a mousehole. By the time the programme ended we were usually hysterical, but not always because of its content. Sid James didn't produce the same effect!

A Fine Place for the Cat

MARGARET BONHAM

TWICE a week the green van came to the village; on the same two days Mrs Miller was up at half-past eight and leaning out of the sitting-room window. Her lank hair and her dirty and faded green casement curtains blew about in the wind, and out of the sitting-room window she leaned to watch the cats; for Mrs Miller, though she was indeed a fat slut and had no beauty and few virtues, felt strongly enough about cats to get out of her bed an hour or more early two days a week, winter and summer; and no other passion she was capable of had anything but the opposite effect.

Mrs Miller did not often or consciously look at the fish-man himself, and nor did any of the women who came out through their swinging gates with a dish in their hands and a leather purse. Mrs Miller watched the cats from her window, and the women, standing one or two at a time in the half-secure screen of the van's open doors, looked no higher than his hands weighing, than the herrings and mackerel, the scales and the lifting from the tray to their dish; more than capable he was of slipping a little herring from clean under their noses down to Mrs Rhys's Tab who yelled for it beside his boots. If his attention were distracted for a moment the women would shoo and scuff at Mrs Rhys's Tab with their squashed slippers, and Mrs Rhys's Tab would curl round to the other side of the fish-man's boots; and Mrs Miller would put out her tongue at the women from her window.

Neither Mrs Miller nor any of the women who came out to buy herrings and mackerel could have told you anything about the fish-man, except: he likes cats; medium tall he is, and thin;

140

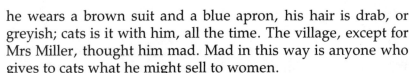

he wears a brown suit and a blue apron, his hair is drab, or greyish; cats is it with him, all the time. The village, except for Mrs Miller, thought him mad. Mad in this way is anyone who gives to cats what he might sell to women.

On Tuesdays and Fridays when the green van came to the village the tom cat from the Seven Stars waited on the stone pillar at the end of the bridge. Down from the driving-seat climbed the fish-man to open the doors at the back, and the Seven Stars' cat, already at his feet with its wide cheeks puffed wider, put one paw on his leg and opened its triangular mouth for the consummation of a whiting that the fish-man wedged into it, head and tail drooping on either side. The whiting and the Seven Stars' cat went off like a rocket into the yard of the inn; the fish-man, disinterested, weighed out plaice for the landlord. Beyond Mrs Miller's cottage, down the street, all the other cats waited at their gates.

All the other cats waited for the fish-man and their whiting, in the early morning sun, and the smell of breakfast and beeswax and the all-important smell of fish; in the cottages the children sat moving their mouths ringed with milk, and from her window Mrs Miller watched the fish-man drive past her from the Seven Stars to the other cottages, to the church gates; from the church gates back down the street, to stop last of all at her door. Though she did not like fish she ate it for dinner on Tuesdays and Fridays, in her parlour which was dirty and faded like the green casement curtains and had a dark circle on the buff wallpaper where she leaned back when she had finished, with her greasy head against the wall, a Woodbine in the corner of her mouth and her own cat Henry on her knees hooking fish-bones off the plate and chewing them one-sided on her stained cotton overall. He was an old cat; age after the fashion of age had taken away his good shape and by nature he was not intelligent; he did not even to Mrs Miller's eyes seem impressive, seem the sort of cat one would be proud to see sitting outside the gate waiting for the fish-man; but she was fond of him. The fish-man, looking at Henry teetering away behind a whiting, would say with an air of melancholy: 'Indeed it seems wrong for a cat to be old, Mrs Miller.' True, Mrs Miller thought; but she said: 'Well, fond of them you get, like.'

In the winter Henry died. Mrs Miller grieved over him and

refused the offer of a bastard kitten from the Seven Stars; but the fish-man's visits became meaningless talking of other people's cats and in time she began to think about getting another of her own. A great deal she thought about it, and saw herself with a beautiful and impressive cat like none of her neighbours', like no other cat in the village. The fish-man leaned on her gate in the snow and said: 'When will there be another Henry, now, Mrs Miller?' 'Maybe soon, now,' said Mrs Miller, looking remotely up at the dark trees laced white against the dark sky, behind his head. She took her two herrings on a plate and went flapping and crackling in her broken slippers up the snowy path and into her parlour to light the fire. She put the herrings on the rug beside her and sat on her heels pulling out from behind the coal-scuttle the crumpled paper in which Friday's cod had been wrapped. But when it was in the grate the word CATS looked at her between the bars and she pulled it out again and smoothed it on her knee, the front page of *The Times*. Feeling in her overall pocket for a bent cigarette, she read:

Pedigree female Siamese kitten for sale, 4 months; house-trained; 3½gns. carriage paid. Letchley, Elm House, Hastock, Shrops.

Mrs Miller, with an unlit Woodbine in the corner of her mouth, sat and stared at the empty grate, seeing in its crusted depths a firm picture of her front path and an elegant cat treading it like an heraldic creature and a tail like a dark gold ostrich plume waving against the snow. Mrs Miller had never seen a Siamese cat in her life. She got up from the hearthrug, leaving the herrings, and went to look for her wicked husband's typewriter, because she knew she had not the sort of handwriting in which to order a pedigree Siamese cat. It was a short letter and took her most of the morning. When it was finished she put a coat on top of her overall and went out and took some money from her Post-Office account and added some more from the housekeeping and bought postal orders for three and a half guineas. Then she stuck a stamp on the letter and went back and lit the fire.

'Well now, where is the new Henry, Mrs Miller?' said the fish-man on Friday, leaning on the white-edged gate; and Mrs Miller looked up at the trees and said: 'Coming any day now.

A new sort of cat I'm getting,' she said, staring up at the sky closing like a grey oyster-shell over the village; 'a valuable cat,' she said with a casual folding of her dirty overall round her neck against the cold wind. 'There's good news, Mrs Miller, indeed,' said the fish-man, 'a Persian cat, is it?' 'No,' said Mrs Miller, 'not an old Persian. Something different in the way of a cat it will be; not till it comes will you see what sort of a cat it is.' 'I hope it comes fast,' said the fish-man, 'for I can't wait to know.' 'Like enough by Tuesday,' said Mrs Miller. 'It's a she-cat,' she said over her shoulder as she flapped away up the path.

The letter came saying when the elegant new cat would arrive at the station. There was some furtive feeling in Mrs Miller that she must look impressive for such a cat's first view of her, and she put on her best blue costume and pearl earrings and the coat with a piece of fur, and combed her hair round her fingers and walked a mile through the snow to the station in black shoes with high heels. She sat half an hour in the waiting-room, for the train was late, but when it came in at last with the single carriage furred with a rim of smoky snow she shot into the luggage office and leaned against the counter like a lady while Mr Jones who did everything at the station brought in a bicycle and a wicker basket of hens and a smaller basket like someone's picnic lunch. Mr Jones put the smaller basket on the counter and it gave out a most appalling howl; a howl in a minor key it was, to make your blood run cold. 'God save us,' said Mr Jones, stepping back into the bicycle, 'what is in there, Mrs Miller?' 'A cat, it is,' said Mrs Miller uncertainly, and leaned forward to point out the label saying VALUABLE CAT tied to the handle. 'Indeed that is no cat,' said Mr Jones; 'cats mew. Let us have a look, now,' he said, and took hold of the strap with caution; but Mrs Miller, hypnotized by the howl, said quickly: 'No, Mr Jones, I will be taking it home with me now. What would we do if it got out?' Mr Jones shook his head and said: 'You should not be opening it at home with no man in the house; indeed, Mrs Miller, I should come and stand over it with the poker.' 'No poker will I have waved over my pedigree cat, Mr Jones,' said Mrs Miller, recovering her aplomb, 'and a cat it is for sure; I bought it out of the paper; it howls with fright from your old train.' And she picked up the basket firmly

and went out to the snowy road; by the time she got home to the cottage she was reconciled to such strangeness in a cat's voice and could not without difficulty wait to open the basket and see this elegant exotic creature that was to have dark-gold feathery fur and a tail like an ostrich plume.

So she put the basket on the parlour table before even she had taken off her coat, and undid the label and the strap and the catch and threw back the lid; and then reeling towards the fireplace she went with a melodramatic gesture like someone in a play, and cried: 'God help us!' knowing she had been sold for a fool and palmed off with some kind of monkey. Away went Mrs Miller's visions of long gold fur and golden plumes; such a sense of embarrassment she had now, thinking of what the fish-man would say, and the neighbours, and whether the creature would spring on her and howl, for she could see only the top half looking out of the basket. A creature it was for sure and not a cat, thought Mrs Miller; what cat has fur as flat as a skinned rabbit and a face as pointed as a piece of cheese and eyes as blue as china and squinting inwards to its nose? And what cat was called not Henry or Tab or Smut, but Tulan Caprian of Hastock? Mrs Miller spelt it out on the label. Disbelievingly she went on staring, and so did Tulan; disbelievingly she said 'Puss . . .?' and went back another step when Tulan climbed out of the basket on to the table; truly Mrs Miller would not have been surprised to see four green paws and a red tail with a fork on the end, and was hardly less taken aback by these thin legs like a Victorian dancer's in dark stockings and a tail no thicker, it seemed to Mrs Miller (who had not even now entirely given up thoughts of ostrich plumes), than a piece of tarred string. 'Well, God save us, delirious I must be,' she said to herself, and put the kettle on the fire with one eye on Tulan. Tulan sat on the table with that tail curled round those feet, and presently gave a tentative amiable howl. Mrs Miller, jumping at the tenor key, quickly took a plate of fish out of the cupboard and edged it on to the brown plush cloth. 'Well,' she said under her breath, 'one queer-looking monster you are and no mistake.' She backed away to the kitchen and made herself a cup of tea, which was not really what she wanted, but the Seven Stars was shut.

Alone in the parlour, in a shell of lamplight and firelight

away from the dark and snow outside, they spent the evening, Tulan confidently and Mrs Miller with a shocked distrust. Every time she looked at the azure squint, the dark thin legs, the dark-brown tail like a monkey's and the flat short fur the colour of pale oatmeal with a glitter like the sun on snow, she thought about what the neighbours would say and above all the fish-man to-morrow morning. Tulan sat in front of the fire with her dark pointed ears pricked up, turning the nearer one towards Mrs Miller when she sighed or muttered, as if in politeness to lose no word of what she said. This was unnerving; Mrs Miller fell silent and smoked a chain of bewildered cigarettes. At half-past nine she made herself another cup of tea, and Tulan for the first time jumped into her lap, curling dark feet under a pale swansdown breast, and purring. At half-past ten she could not be left alone and wild in the kitchen or the parlour for the night. She slept on Mrs Miller's bed.

Because of the fish-man the alarm clock was set for a quarter-past eight. Mrs Miller woke to see Tulan square in her line of vision and six inches from her eyes. She recoiled and got out of bed. At once she thought of the fish-man and wished she were safe in solitude, his visit past; but she said to herself: 'I will have to get it over, and a nuisance it will be; indeed, he is sure to laugh at the creature; but I will get it over and out of the way.' She put on her clothes and her messy faded overall, and went down with Tulan to the kitchen.

When the fire was lit she slopped into the parlour and looked out of the window. There the green van stood outside the Seven Stars, and the black tom cat (a cat to reassure you after the what-you-will chewing the table-cloth fringe behind your back) was galloping off with his whiting between the red and snowy pillars of the yard entrance. All down the street the green van went, stopping and selling fish to the women who came out with white dishes and strawberry noses into the cold, stopping and giving fish to the fine ordinary cats that mewed as cats should and rubbed their properly furred and covered flanks aginst the fish-man's boots; down the street it went to the church gates, watched with growing misgiving by Mrs Miller from behind her stained and faded green curtains, turned round, and drove back to her cottage. Mrs Miller looked despairingly at Tulan, picked

up the enamel dish and went out of the blistered door.

'Well, Mrs Miller, now,' said the fish-man with his hand on the gate, 'will the grand new cat be here yet?'

Mrs Miller looked up at the trees. 'Well,' she said repressively, 'arrived it has for sure; but indeed it's not the sort of cat I expected. It's a great wonder to me,' she said with a rush, preparing him for the worst, 'that it passes for a cat at all.'

'Very sad that is, Mrs Miller, now, if it's not what you hoped,' said the fish-man, 'but perhaps it's only she will not be feeling herself after the journey.'

'Oh, no,' said Mrs Miller on a round note, thinking of the parlour table-cloth, 'she is feeling herself all right; her looks it is that are not like a proper cat's at all.' She tapped her fingers on the enamel dish and stared up at the trees in silence, but the fish-man was looking over her shoulder at the door. He looked past her at the cottage and the open door, and cried with such an air of surprise that she was startled. 'Why, Mrs Miller,' he cried, 'why, she's a beauty!' Mrs Miller turned round and saw Tulan, seeming very small, treading with her dark-legged dancer's step up the snowy path, with her dark ears pointed to the breath of fish, her dark thin tail like a question mark up from the pale thin line of her back; Mrs Miller looked at her and saw with a shock that she was a beauty indeed. Now all the other cats seemed gross and without shape. But she said nothing, only stared at Tulan and tapped her fingers on the enamel dish; and Tulan trod up to the fish-man and gave her urgent howl.

The fish-man was enchanted; he took her up in his arms and said: 'Why, Mrs Miller, this is the greatest beauty of a cat I've seen in a lifetime, for sure. God save us, Mrs Miller,' he said, 'were you telling me you were disappointed in a cat like this? What sort of cat is it called, now?' 'It's a Siamese cat,' said Mrs Miller, caught out in the wrong opinion and a little cross, 'and a big cat I thought it would be with a great tail like feathers.' 'So help me,' said the fish-man, 'will you look at the blue eyes? What would you want with a lot of fur and no bones? Losing her to me you will be, Mrs Miller, if she's not the cat you wanted.'

'Well, I do want her,' said Mrs Miller quickly; 'it's getting used to her is a matter of time.' She looked at Tulan and then at the fish-man, and in a moment she laughed; meeting the fish-man's eyes over Tulan's head like two people in a film over the head of a reconciling child, for the first time Mrs Miller impaled him with a direct stare and saw that his eyes were as blue as the cat's; and for his part the fish-man thought the cat's eyes were not more blue than hers. Tulan breathed fish over his shoulder, and howled. 'Well, Mrs Miller,' he said, and turned to the van, 'we will see what the beautiful cat would like.' He picked up a whiting by its tail and held it over Tulan who embraced it like a monkey, and hanging on by claws and teeth was lowered through the air to the ground. Mrs Miller and the fish-man stood in the snow and watched the whiting disappear faster than you could believe.

With Tulan there was no doubt the fish-man was a success. 'What does your husband say to such a cat, now?' he said suddenly. Mrs Miller opened her eyes as startled as if Tulan had asked instead: she had not believed him capable of talking about anything but cats and fish and the weather. 'That I couldn't tell you,' she said, 'for he's not here.' 'In the Forces he would be, I expect,' said the fish-man; and Mrs Miller said: 'Very likely, indeed, if they are not too particular; three years it is since he set eyes on me and I would be sorry if I saw him again.' 'That's a sad thing for you, Mrs Miller,' said the fish-man, 'and grieved I am to hear it, but we all make mistakes.' Mrs Miller looked at the high trees, and after a pause she said: 'Well, I will be going in now.' 'Well, you will take another little fish for the beautiful cat,' said the fish-man, leaning over Tulan in passionate admiration and slapping a whiting as large as a dogfish on to Mrs Miller's enamel dish, 'and on Friday I will be seeing the cat again. There is something to look forward to, Mrs Miller,' he said, standing with his elbow on the gate, watching both of them go up the path, Mrs Miller scrunching and scuffing in her broken slippers and Tulan prancing behind howling and flipping up her back legs. Both he and Mrs Miller, with one mind, had forgotten the two herrings that Mrs Miller had come out to buy for her dinner.

Having accepted Tulan, Mrs Miller found that it meant what might almost be called hard work. Tulan's passion was inevitably for the front line. She could not be forgotten for hours at a time and satisfied with a stroke and a plate of fish; she would be talked to incessantly, and carried her side of the conversation with a positive conviction; she would not be left alone. Mrs Miller found herself playing exacting games on the stairs, playing bending three feet from the ground to be patted on both temples, playing with balls of paper for Tulan to fly somersaulting round the room without touching the floor. Soon, since Tulan howled when she was left, Mrs Miller began to take her out shopping in the village, held in a fold of her coat. The village people, disapproving, called her 'Mrs Miller's monkey'. Now Tulan slept in bed with her head against Mrs Miller's neck on the pillow, and Mrs Miller put on extra face cream for Tulan to lick off. She was an unsentimental, affectionate slut of a creature and Tulan's company suited her down to the ground; the next best thing she was to the right man, and even then less trouble.

Longer and longer the fish-man stayed leaning over the gate on Tuesdays and Fridays, talking to both of them; his gifts to Tulan inflated so in size that indeed Mrs Miller would not have been surprised to see him drag a shark out of his van any moment. 'I am thinking I will have to have a cat like this for myself, Mrs Miller,' he said, 'for seeing her twice a week is not enough.' Mrs Miller leaned her elbow on the rotting gatepost and looked over his head. 'What would your wife think of that?' she said, and the fish-man watched Tulan with a whiting as big as herself and said: 'There is no wife in my house and never has been.' 'Then who looks after you?' said Mrs Miller, and he said: 'Why for sure, I look after myself. There is no worry for me in not having things as they should be,' he said, 'for a cat or two and plenty to eat and a good fire is enough.' 'That's right indeed,' said Mrs Miller, stooping to run her finger between Tulan's ears. She looked up at him with her greasy hair falling in her eyes and smirked to show her white teeth. 'Enough for anyone, for sure,' she said.

The snow melted and Tulan grew a shade larger and sometimes the fish-man stayed talking for an hour or more; when Tulan was too full of fish to howl for more she would sit on his shoulder and wash her Oriental face, and Mrs Miller would prop herself against the still-rotting gatepost which creaked on and off under her considerable weight, and they would talk cats till their throats were dry. This was something for the

148

village to gossip about under its breath in the shops, how long the green van stayed outside the cottage; but never more than a yard from it went Mrs Miller and the fish-man, so there was no surmise of absence to add interest, and for her part Mrs Miller was secure in herself and cared not a straw what was said. Now when she looked up over the fish-man's head at the tall line of trees on the hill they were dark with the red colour of advancing spring. 'This sort of weather I would like to be going on holiday,' she said to the fish-man; and the fish-man said quickly, as if he had been waiting: 'Would you like a little drive in the van, now?'

Mrs Miller went on staring at the trees in silence; at last she said: 'Indeed, that would be a nice change; where is it you will be going from here?' 'Pleased I would be to take you anywhere you want,' said the fish-man, 'but if you would like it we could take Tulan to see my cats. Not a very good house, mine is, but she would be welcome.' 'That would be a change for Tulan too,' said Mrs Miller, looking at him carefully and seeming pleased with what she saw. She went flapping up the damp path into the kitchen, and put on her coat, and took eighteen and ninepence out of the teapot on the shelf and her Post Office Savings book from the chaos behind the mangle, and snapped them into a dirty handbag, and went out and shut the door behind her. The fish-man leaned on the gate, and Tulan sat on his shoulder beginning to howl for more whiting, for the first lot was an hour past and she had room again. 'She will not have been in a motor before, I expect,' said the fish-man, and swung her down on to his arm. 'Well there, is everything ready, then?' he said, looking at Mrs Miller; and Mrs Miller said: 'For sure everything is ready, now,' and shut the gate with a bang that broke the post. Mrs Miller knew, and the fish-man knew, that she would not come back to the cottage again except to settle her affairs; but they said nothing.

'There is a fine place for the beautiful cat,' said the fish-man, and he put the speechless Tulan into the back of the van with all the sprats and whiting and herrings, and shut the doors.

'A fine place indeed,' said Mrs Miller, and sitting beside him in the front, on a torn fishy cushion, she watched Tulan through the little window while they drove past the Seven Stars and out of the village.

149

The Blue Flag

KAY HILL

CHANGE of fortune, calculated by the second hand of a watch, measurable within the span of a schoolroom ruler, and with no more apparent reason behind it than the senseless ferocity of lightning, can plunge a racing stable, without warning, into disaster. Yet it is hard to believe even on the sworn evidence of a group of reputedly intelligent and certainly honest people, that one insignificant creature, described in the dictionary as a small domestic carnivorous quadruped, preying on mice, etc., persecuted by dogs, and credited with nine lives, could by any means, not excluding clairvoyance, foretell the future in such a way as to restore the fortunes of an entire establishment.

Every racing stable is, of course, a hot-bed of superstition; and it is not surprising that those of the National Hunt, faced with the added hazards of fences, hurdles and rough weather, are worse than most. Magpies, funerals, even a choked carburettor in the horsebox engine on the way to a meeting, are seized on by the stable lads as an excuse for the peculiar failure on that day of the horses under their charge.

The trainer perhaps knows better. Old Dasman, for instance, may have learned so much about racing that he is no longer genuine, except on those rare occasions when he is in the mood; or the bay mare, having lost a bit of speed with age, is only capable of winning a three-mile 'chase if the pace is slow enough to suit her. The best must therefore be made of the materials at hand, and there is always the possibility—with luck—of being able to place them to win a race.

There are times, however, when even a trainer feels that

the blows of fate come from an agency beyond his control. The normal first-night nerves and hasty tempers, part of the rehearsal for every race meeting, turn into an abnormal dread. The feeling spreads throughout the yard; even when the horses are safely fed, watered, and bedded down, with every imaginable peril accounted for, the evening inspection is faced with foreboding of fresh disaster.

With this fear in mind, and the last round completed, Donald Forster stood in Chantry's empty box listening, as if, when hands and eyes had told him that all was well, a sound outside the contented rhythm of the evening feed would give warning to his overstrung nerves of some undreamed-of trouble. A mouse rustled and squeaked in the straw under his feet and beyond the circle of light cast by the stable lamp in his hand, his shadow rose huge and distorted across the hayrack.

There was little use, he thought, in standing here brooding. It would have been far better to have gone out with Nan; mixed with a crowd, and tried to force the memory out of his mind. Not that there was much chance of that, when the race conjured itself up in front of his eyes, like a newsreel played again and again, to a sickened audience.

He could see them now, coming into the straight: Chantry and the favourite clear of the field with two fences to go. The favourite off the bit and under pressure, while Mike, the young jockey on Chantry, sat there with a double handful. A voice on the stands behind exclaimed, as if in torment: 'Three miles of bloody agony.' Owning the favourite was evidently no consolation.

With this confirmation of his opinion that Chantry was a certainty, Donald found his glasses shaking, and clouding over in his hands.

He heard the guard-rail crack as the favourite took off; saw her, as his vision cleared, burst the fence into a shower of birch twigs, crumple on to her knees on the landing side, and struggle in the churned-up mud to recover her foothold; while Chantry, completing the arc of a perfect jump, his white blaze showing clearly for a moment against the dark background of the fence, pitched into her as she rolled back exhausted under his feet.

There was a confusion of horses and jockeys—then the terrible stillness, the frantic waving of a flag down at the jump,

the certainty of disaster; and the crowd, fickle, and suddenly hateful, cheered home the winner past the post.

Across the yard, the darkened house suddenly blazed into light, flooding the wet cobblestones into a cheerful oblong path and jerking Donald back into reality. Nan was back; and by the sounds from the kitchen had evidently brought someone home with her. All the better, he thought, if she had. Anything to prevent him taking it out of her as he had been doing for the past week. The very things he loved in her seemed to bring out this cruelty. Her courage and honesty, her refusal to talk over or rake up the past; even the changeling look in her face that had baffled and fascinated him from the first, as if she knew, and drew strength from, some world which he could never enter. Yet there was nothing fluid or indefinite about those features, whose bone formation was so perfect that his un-skilled hand had drawn recognizable sketches of her, on blotting paper and telephone pads, on the backs of race cards and on envelopes; haunted as he had been by that quality which still eluded him.

Old Lady Galtres, that worldly old bird, had nearly hit the nail on the head last summer at the tennis party.

'I love to see Nan in disguise,' she had said, 'in a little cotton frock, with a ribbon round her hair, and eyes like the serpent of the Nile.' She was somewhere near the truth—getting warm.

'Hang it all,' he thought, 'if I go on like this, I will start believing in leprechauns and seal men and the whole Irish bag of tricks!'

Picking up his lamp and closing the door of the box behind him, he crossed over to the house and, pausing for a moment, dazzled by the light in the kitchen, he was surprised to see that Nan was alone in the room.

She was kneeling on the hearthrug, talking and laughing, with her dark hair falling in a sweep across her face. Looking up into her eyes from the basket which enthroned it was a white kitten.

'A *white* kitten,' he said, suddenly furious. 'What the devil are you doing with that?'

'It's not white,' she answered, 'it's a Siamese, with a pedigree that even you could approve of.'

'The perfect moment to bring a thing like that on to the

place,' he said, 'with a head lad as superstitious as blazes about cats, and things as they are with us just now. Its life will be short and sweet if Shover sees it. You know what he does with every white kitten born in this yard—the bucket.'

'Its life will be sweet,' said Nan with certainty, 'and its eyes are the colour of the winner's flag. The tide has turned, Donald—I'm never wrong. Our luck is coming in with Minette.'

'Good Lord,' he said, 'are even the cats French-bred these days?'

'She's bred to stay,' said Nan, 'and her namesake had good racing connections; she was the sister of Charles the Second, and described as "the Queen of a thousand fêtes"; so the kitten should know how to celebrate a winner.'

The thing was sitting up in its basket now, looking round the room and not at all afraid. Donald stared into the incredible blue of its eyes and, as he held its gaze, the extraordinary feeling came to him that this was a glance of recognition

between people who had met before. Suddenly it shut its eyes and, opening its mouth, uttered a harsh mournful, drawn-out cry; as if, thought Donald, a tugboat had borrowed the *Queen Mary's* siren.

'The thing's hungry,' he said. 'It probably lives on caviare. For heaven's sake get it something to eat, and if you *must* raid the place for every delicacy we possess—get it done now. I'm going down to fetch Martha back from the Women's Institute.'

Nan sighed with relief as the door slammed behind him. She was, to tell the truth, a little appalled by her new responsibility. Where were the silken cushions, the deep carpets, and the luxury which should have made a background for this exotic creature? All she had to offer was a shabby room, with a cold, tiled floor and horse blankets thrown over the chairs; and outside, all the perils of the stable yard, with, above all— Shover.

Picking up a torch, she went into the larder, examining the shelves for something appetizing. A tin of sardines, another of steak, a little cream—surely it would relish one of these. She arranged them separately in small dishes and carried them with ceremony back into the room. A sound of crackling met her ears. The kitchen table was a litter of water biscuits and ration cheese. Enjoying a plebeian meal in shameless gluttony, the distinguished guest greeted her warmly then, topping up its supper with a drink of cold water from the dog's dish, climbed back into the basket, curled one sooty paw over its face, with what even then Nan suspected of being calculated appeal, and fell fast asleep.

The sight of such innocence, guileless or not, led Nan into a mistake for which she was to suffer, on and off, during the years of a short lifetime. Picking up the basket, with the kitten sleeping, she carried it up to her bedroom.

Four hours of sleep are hardly enough for any human being and certainly too little for an irate husband.

Aware of a coming and going round her pillow, of an ecstatic purring, and a gentle but relentlessly insistent paw easing the bedclothes from her face, Nan accepted defeat. Stretched out full length beside her in the bed, with its head under her chin, the little tyrant settled down to a night of luxury.

154

When daylight came the room was empty, and the window into the garden wide open.

Nan tore downstairs, struggling into her dressing-gown as she ran. 'If it's that cat you're after,' said Martha, with all the familiarity of service to two generations, 'you needn't bother yourself. It's on the garden wall having its breakfast with the stable cats, and what with it howling to come in and howling to go out, I've been working in a draught fit to starve me.'

'But it doesn't *have* that sort of breakfast,' said Nan. 'It eats quite different food from the yard cats.'

'It's having it now,' said Martha, 'and a fair job it was making of it the last time I saw it. Go and look for yourself.'

Nan slammed the front door and went out into the sodden morning of early spring, making her way round the house to the garden wall joining the kitchen window.

The stable cats were sitting at a respectful distance from their bowl of bread and milk. Nigger, the battered old tom, with his chewed ear, and nose moulded into an aristocratic Roman from repeated rat bites, was stretching out a timid paw towards his dish. A cantankerous snarl greeted his every movement and, before Nan had time to move, Minette, gulping bread and milk between her complaints, shot out a black-gloved fashion model's arm and pinned Nigger's paw down on to his chosen titbit, spattering his startled face with the only meal of the day.

'Well,' said Martha when the thief was carried safely back into the house, which it seemed to regard as a building specially constructed for a delightful escape act, 'what did I tell you? There's no need to bother your head about such as that. It'll take care of itself, and the rest of us too, unless I'm mistaken.'

'Martha,' said Nan, 'you're an angel.'

'If I am,' grumbled Martha, 'it's with standing here, getting frozen to death, and not with any nice feelings I have towards that one. Just you wait till Shover sees it. He'll soon put it straight.'

Shover, whose real name was forgotten or perhaps unknown (to such an extent that a lifelong friend, on ringing up the stables and asking for Mr Richardson, had been told that no one of that name worked there), was supposed to have

acquired the nickname through being, in his early youth, chauffeur to a duke.

Stable boys scurrying about the yard trailing straw on the newly-swept concrete, or riding out with their knees under their chins in imitation of their heroes of the Flat, were reprimanded with the unanswerable retort: 'The Duke would have had something to say about that.' There was apparently no detail of stable management that the duke had not observed, and there was little doubt that, according to Shover, he must have spent every waking hour firmly planted, like a gnarled old oak tree, in the middle of the stable courtyard.

Whether or not the duke existed, Shover had been instructed at some time to spare neither himself nor his underlings. A short, thick-set man, with dark eyes and the quick step of a horseman, he had never been seen to wear an overcoat, to smile in a moment of victory, or to complain of defeat.

Minette met Shover on the fourth day. The never-to-be-forgotten moment was witnessed by Donald, helpless with laughter, and conscious of a growing respect for the indomitable will-power of the little cat.

Shover had dismounted and was leading Steel Train, the pride of his heart, into the stables after morning work. Crouched in the box door, a blue stare of obstinacy seeming to dominate her entire body, Minette had no intention of giving way. Shover advanced relentlessly, in a juggernaut procession of whiplash heels and clattering feet until the horse, sensing something new in his experience, hesitated for a moment then, trembling slightly, picked his way step by step over the cat and plunged with a snort of terror through the doorway into safety.

The attraction of the stables for Minette, following this victory, was so potent that for a time Nan thought her companionship was lost; only to find it renewed and increased with a delicate understanding that no stranger was allowed to witness.

Donald, to Nan's amusement, was granted an entirely different treatment. His commanding roars for silence, fortified by thumps on the table, or on a fleeing rump, were received with simulated terror. Discipline was only apparently restored; since the culprit, invisible and mute, was waiting for the slightest sign of relaxation on his face, or in the tone of his voice.

'That cat,' said Donald one morning after the usual scene, 'is a

Victorian miss—except that she believes in being heard and not seen.'

He was instantly rewarded by a faint cajoling sound from beneath his favourite chair; followed by a slight movement, which revealed a pair of eyes offering a languishing upward glance, worthy of a slave girl to an Eastern prince.

'She adores you,' said Nan, 'in a perfectly shameless way. I wait on her hand and foot, prepare all her food, wash her dishes, open and shut doors, put up with her bullying, and yet when strangers are here, she ignores me and shows off with you. What makes it worse is when people say: "Are Siamese cats *really* quite different from ordinary cats, and dog-like in their devotion?" One answers: "Yes, they are very devoted in a subtle undog-like way," only to find oneself stared through by indifferent and sometimes baleful eyes.'

'I am not taken in,' said Donald, 'I caught you both off guard the other night when I was making the racing entries. The cat has an iron will, she is undefeatable—that is the clue to her character. She does things when and how she pleases.'

He had, on the night in question, looked across the lamp-lit room to see Nan curled up in her chair, absorbed in a book. The cat, silent, falling in with her mood, had stretched a light paw across her arm, sharing in the very turning of the pages. Nan glanced down for a moment, smiled, and was answered by a peculiar crooning note which Donald had never before heard in Minette's repertoire; used as he was to the steady clamour, like the tolling of a bell, with which she greeted the first stirring of the household in the mornings. As he watched, the pair had exchanged a look which went beyond words, then settled down again into silence.

'Do you know what they are saying about her in the stables?' asked Donald slowly, as if he had at last made up his mind to reveal something of the utmost importance. 'That whichever box that cat patronizes produces a winner within a fortnight. I know it's crazy. She is obviously just changing her hunting ground—but add it up.'

'Dasman won first,' said Nan, 'then the grey mare.'

'Minette was in Dasman's box. I saw her myself,' said Donald. 'After he won, she crossed the yard to the grey mare. Dasman won twice more, but that's beside the point. The mare

won the first time out—she wasn't ready, but there was that mix-up at the open ditch, which left her nothing to do. Following that, the cat went next door to the four-year-old, and he came out and won that hurdle as he liked.'

'Where is she now?' asked Nan, as if she already knew the answer.

'She has been in Steel Train's box exactly a fortnight. Not only that, she goes to sleep on his back—and how a creature with claws like a pterodactyl climbs on to a fit thoroughbred without meeting a sudden and violent death, I don't know. The horse adores her; he breathes in over her, like a vacuum cleaner, until every hair on her back stands on end, and all she does is to purr. Shover knows about it too. I caught him making a bed of hay for her the other day, to keep her in the box. He was talking away, saying: "Whoa pet—steady now," as if he were half scared of her. The lads call her Min. of Ag. and Fish. and every one of them, including the entire village, believes that the horse is a certainty tomorrow in the Hunter Chase. I haven't told you before,' added Donald, 'but I will tell you now. Steel Train is a hell of a horse: an Aintree horse next year, if all goes well. There is another thing; it's only a short journey to the course, but I am taking no risks. Shover and I are packing up to go with the horse tonight—that means you can't be there to lead him in. I must have someone here in charge when we are both away.'

'That's all right,' said Nan. 'I would be torn in two anyway. Minette's kittens should arrive on Sunday. Just think of it—a Siamese for every horse in the yard.'

'Ye gods,' said Donald.

When the clatter of departure had long died down, Nan lay in bed vainly trying to sleep, or at least to draw to her, in the stillness of the night, that certainty which often came to her before some big event in her life.

Moonlight streamed through the open window in a shaft of pale comfortless light; and from a box across the yard she could hear the restless stamping of a horse.

There was a rustle in the leaves of the tree outside, a soft thud, and an unearthly transfigured cat, phosphorescent and sinuous like a mackerel in a summer sea, trod delicately down the moonlight on to the bed. Without a sound or a greeting it curled into the security of Nan's encircling arm, as if fear itself

had no power within that ring.

Morning brought to Nan the feeling that she and Minette were walking down a dark tunnel towards a blaze of light. Each in her way occupied herself with trivial duties, as if to ward off the appointed hour. Minette, tearing up pieces of the Racing Calendar, transformed her basket into a semblance of Epsom Downs on Derby Day. Nan, taking up her gardening tools, started weeding the bed near the front door, within earshot of the house. The grass, warmed by spring sunshine, gave off a scent of crushed turf, bringing the race-course sharply to her memory.

She could picture the hills behind, with their scurrying cloud shadows leading far away into the lost distances of the Roman Wall, forming an amphitheatre for the colour and noise of a race meeting. Her favourite place on the rails from which she could stretch out her hand and touch the horses as they went down past the judges' box was remote from the cheerful racket of the bookmakers and the paddock.

Donald would ride past, grave, absorbed, mature beyond his years, unconscious of her presence. Like a Spaniard, she thought—a matador; for, like a bull-fighter, he was preparing for extreme physical exertion, in which the brain played a lightning part, and the weighing and balancing of an animal's pace and endurance were a measure of his skill. Beyond that lay the possibility of disablement, and the risk of death.

The sunlight faded from the garden and a chill, reminiscent of autumn, rose from the ground, as cold as the apprehension in her heart. Slowly gathering up the weeds from the path, dreading the return to the house, Nan was suddenly aware of a complete relaxation of tension. She stood for a moment listening, and far away, beyond the village, she heard the steady repeated hooting of a horn, increasing in volume and reinforced by the rumbling of a heavy vehicle on the road. Sidelights gleamed in the gateway, and as Nan ran to the driver's cabin and caught sight of Shover's face, expressionless and unsmiling, she knew for certain that the winner had come home. She followed man and horse across the yard and stood rolling bandages, as Shover ran his hands over Steel Train's precious legs.

'Clean as glass,' he said. 'He could have gone round again. Wouldn't have blown a candle out when I led him in. I got away as soon as I could—you make a lot of false friends with a winner like this—and left the Boss to stay on till the end. And he wasn't half celebrating, I can tell you. He rode a good race, first over the first fence to get out of trouble, and then settled down nicely. That young captain feller on Dobson's horse set off at five-furlong pace—all hell and no notion; and took a whole lot more with him. Going up the hill, Steel Train and the favourite were lying fourth, with the field beginning to string out a bit, and by the time they came round the first time, the captain and all his lot that had been out in front, had come back to them, and a few had fallen. There were one or two loose horses bothering them, but they cleared off when they came past the paddock. Going up the hill the second time round, the Boss moved into third place, and when they started to come down towards the wood, the leaders turned the tap on good and proper; there were just the three of them then, with the rest strung out in a race on their own. Coming out of the dip he must have given the horse a breather. I had no glasses, so I couldn't see if he was tiring or not, it gave me a bit of a turn. A chap behind me started to yell: 'Come on my beauty—it's Steel Train coming like a train,' and the next thing he'd jumped the last fence two lengths clear, and was increasing the lead, till he passed the post with his ears pricked.'

'I think you are to be congratulated,' said Nan, 'on all the work you've put into it, and your belief in him, after the knocks we've taken. Perhaps,' she added, teasing him, 'a cat had something to do with it too.'

'The best ratter we've ever had on the place,' said Shover reluctantly. 'Show her one in the bottom of a corn bin, and she'll dive in and chase it that fast, she fair laps it.'

A faint sound attracted their attention to a corner of the box. Advancing with a stable lamp, Shover pulled away some straw with a fork, and stood back aghast.

Relaxed in the shameless ecstasy of motherhood, gazing up with fearless pride, Minette revealed a row of coal-black kittens nestling like piglets along her flanks.

'Well!' said Shover sternly, allowing the faint smile reserved for new-born foals to soften his features for a moment. 'The Duke would have known how to deal with that lot. He'd never have stood for a day like this, ending in a catastrophe.'

The Story of Webster

P. G. WODEHOUSE

'CATS are not dogs!'

There is only one place where you can hear good things like that thrown off quite casually in the general run of conversation, and that is the bar parlour of the 'Angler's Rest'. It was there, as we sat grouped about the fire, that a thoughtful Pint of Bitter had made the statement just recorded.

Although the talk up to this point had been dealing with Einstein's Theory of Relativity, we readily adjusted our minds to cope with the new topic. Regular attendance at the nightly sessions over which Mr Mulliner presides with such unfailing dignity and geniality tends to produce mental nimbleness. In our little circle I have known an argument on the Final Destination of the Soul to change inside forty seconds into one concerning the best method of preserving the juiciness of bacon fat.

'Cats', proceeded the Pint of Bitter, 'are selfish. A man waits on a cat hand and foot for weeks, humouring its lightest whim, and then it goes and leaves him flat because it has found a place down the road where the fish is more frequent.'

'What I've got against cats', said a Lemon Sour, speaking feelingly, as one brooding on a private grievance, 'is their unreliability. They lack candour and are not square shooters. You get your cat and you call him Thomas or George, as the case may be. So far, so good. Then one morning you wake up and find six kittens in the hat-box and you have to reopen the whole matter, approaching it from an entirely different angle.'

'If you want to know what's the trouble with cats,' said a red-

161

faced man with glassy eyes, who had been rapping on the table for his fourth whisky, 'they've got no tact. That's what's the trouble with them. I remember a friend of mine had a cat. Made quite a pet of that cat, he did. And what occurred? What was the outcome? One night he came home rather late and was feeling for the keyhole with his corkscrew; and, believe me or not, his cat selected that precise moment to jump on the back of his neck out of a tree. No tact.'

Mr Mulliner shook his head.

'I grant you all this,' he said, 'but still, in my opinion, you have not got to the root of the matter. The real objection to the great majority of cats is their insufferable air of superiority. Cats, as a class, have never completely got over the snootiness caused by the fact that in Ancient Egypt they were worshipped as gods. This makes them too prone to set themselves up as critics and censors of the frail and erring human beings whose lot they share. They stare rebukingly. They view with concern. And on a sensitive man this often has the worst effects, inducing an inferiority complex of the gravest kind. It is odd that the conversation should have taken this turn,' said Mr Mulliner, sipping his hot Scotch and lemon, 'for I was thinking only this afternoon of the rather strange case of my cousin Edward's son, Lancelot.'

'I knew a cat—' began a Small Bass.

My cousin Edward's son, Lancelot (said Mr. Mulliner) was, at the time of which I speak, a comely youth of some twenty-five summers. Orphaned at an early age, he had been brought up in the home of his Uncle Theodore, the saintly Dean of Bolsover; and it was a great shock to that good man when Lancelot, on attaining his majority, wrote from London to inform him that he had taken a studio in Bott Street, Chelsea, and proposed to remain in the metropolis and become an artist.

The Dean's opinion of artists was low. As a prominent member of the Bolsover Watch Committee, it had recently been his distasteful duty to be present at a private showing of the super-super-film, *Palettes of Passion*; and he replied to his nephew's communication with a vibrant letter in which he emphasized the grievous pain it gave him to think that one of his flesh and blood should deliberately be embarking on a career which must inevitably lead sooner or later to the painting of Russian princesses lying on divans in the semi-nude with their arms round tame jaguars. He urged Lancelot to return and become a curate while there was yet time.

But Lancelot was firm. He deplored the rift between himself and a relative whom he had always respected; but he was dashed if he meant to go back to an environment where his individuality had been stifled and his soul confined in chains. And for four years there was silence between uncle and nephew.

During these years Lancelot had made progress in his chosen profession. At the time at which this story opens, his prospects seemed bright. He was painting the portrait of Brenda, only daughter of Mr and Mrs B. B. Carberry-Pirbright, of 11 Maxton Square, South Kensington, which meant thirty pounds in his sock on delivery. He had learned to cook eggs and bacon. He had practically mastered the ukulele. And, in addition, he was engaged to be married to a fearless young *vers libre* poetess of the name of Gladys Bingley, better known as The Sweet Singer of Garbidge Mews, Fulham—a charming girl who looked like a pen-wiper.

It seemed to Lancelot that life was very full and beautiful. He lived joyously in the present, giving no thought to the past.

But how true it is that the past is inextricably mixed up with the present and that we can never tell when it may spring some delayed bomb beneath our feet. One afternoon, as he sat making a few small alterations to the portrait of Brenda Carberry-Pirbright, his fiancée entered.

12 He had been expecting her to call, for today she was going off for a three weeks' holiday to the South of France, and she had promised to look in on her way to the station. He laid down his brush and gazed at her with a yearning affection, thinking for the thousandth time time how he worshipped every spot of ink on her nose. Standing there in the doorway with her bobbed hair sticking out in every direction like a golliwog's, she made a picture that seemed to speak to his very depths.

'Hullo, Reptile!' he said lovingly.

'What ho, Worm!' said Gladys, maidenly devotion shining through the monocle which she wore in her left eye. 'I can stay just half an hour.'

'Oh, well, half an hour soon passes,' said Lancelot. 'What's that you've got there?'

'A letter, ass. What did you think it was?'

'Where did you get it?'

'I found the postman outside.'

Lancelot took the envelope from her and examined it.

'Gosh!' he said.

'What's the matter?'

'It's from my Uncle Theodore.'

'I didn't know you had an Uncle Theodore.'

'Of course I have. I've had him for years.'

'What's he writing to you about?'

'If you'll kindly keep quiet for two seconds, if you know how,' said Lancelot, 'I'll tell you.'

And in a clear voice which, like that of all the Mulliners, however distant from the main branch, was beautifully modulated, he read as follows:

> *The Deanery,*
> *Bolsover, Wilts.*

My dear Lancelot,

As you have, no doubt, already learned from your *Church Times*, I have been offered and have accepted the vacant Bishopric of Bongo-Bongo, in West Africa. I sail immediately to take up my new duties, which I trust will be blessed.

In these circumstances it becomes necessary for me to find a good home for my cat Webster. It is, alas, out of the question that he should accompany me, as the rigours of the climate and the lack of essential comforts might well sap a constitution which has never been robust.

I am dispatching him, therefore, to your address, my dear boy, in a straw-lined hamper, in the full confidence that you will prove a kindly and conscientious host.

With cordial good wishes,

Your affectionate uncle,

THEODORE BONGO-BONGO

For some moments after he had finished reading this communication, a thoughtful silence prevailed in the studio.

Finally Gladys spoke.

'Of all the nerve!' she said. 'I wouldn't do it.'

'Why not?'

'What do you want with a cat?'

Lancelot reflected.

'It is true,' he said, 'that, given a free hand, I would prefer not to have my studio turned into a cattery or cat-bin. But consider the special circumstances. Relations between Uncle Theodore and self have for the last few years been a bit strained. In fact, you might say we had definitely parted brass-rags. It looks to me as if he were coming round. I should describe this letter as more or less what you might call an olive-branch. If I lush this cat up satisfactorily, shall I not be in a position later on to make a swift touch?'

'He is rich, this bean?' said Gladys, interested.

'Extremely.'

'Then', said Gladys, 'consider my objections withdrawn. A good stout cheque from a grateful cat-fancier would un-doubtedly come in very handy. We might be able to get married this year.'

'Exactly,' said Lancelot. 'A pretty loathsome prospect, of course; but still, as we've arranged to do it, the sooner we get it over, the better, what?'

'Absolutely.'

'Then that's settled. I accept custody of cat.'

'It's the only thing to do,' said Gladys. 'Meanwhile, can you lend me a comb? Have you such a thing in your bedroom?'

'What do you want with a comb?'

'I got some soup in my hair at lunch. I won't be a minute.'

She hurried out, and Lancelot, taking up the letter again, found that he had omitted to read a continuation of it on the back page.

It was to the following effect:

PS. In establishing Webster in your home, I am actuated by another motive than the simple desire to see to it that my faithful friend and companion is adequately provided for.

From both a moral and an educative standpoint, I am convinced that Webster's society will prove of inestimable

165

value to you. His advent, indeed, I venture to hope, will be a turning-point in your life. Thrown, as you must be, incessantly among loose and immoral Bohemians, you will find in this cat an example of upright conduct which cannot but act as an antidote to the poison cup of temptation which is, no doubt, hourly pressed to your lips.

PPS. Cream only at midday, and fish not more than three times a week.

He was reading these words for the second time, when the front doorbell rang and he found a man on the steps with a hamper. A discreet mew from within revealed its contents, and Lancelot, carrying it into the studio, cut the strings.

'Hi!' he bellowed, going to the door.

'What's up?' shrieked his betrothed from above.

'The cat's come.'

'All right. I'll be down in a jiffy.'

Lancelot returned to the studio.

'What ho, Webster!' he said cheerily. 'How's the boy?'

The cat did not reply. It was sitting with bent head, performing that wash and brush up which a journey by rail renders so necessary.

In order to facilitate these toilet operations, it had raised its left leg and was holding it rigidly in the air. And there flashed into Lancelot's mind an old superstition handed on to him, for what it was worth, by one of the nurses of his infancy. If, this woman had said, you creep up to a cat when its leg is in the air and give it a pull, then you make a wish and your wish comes true in thirty days.

It was a pretty fancy, and it seemed to Lancelot that the theory might as well be put to the test. He advanced warily, therefore, and was in the act of extending his fingers for the pull, when Webster, lowering the leg, turned and raised his eyes.

He looked at Lancelot. And suddenly with sickening force there came to Lancelot the realization of the unpardonable liberty he had been about to take.

Until this moment, though the postscript to his uncle's letter should have warned him, Lancelot Mulliner had had no suspicion of what manner of cat this was that he had taken into

his home. Now, for the first time, he saw him steadily and saw him whole.

Webster was very large and very black and very composed. He conveyed the impression of being a cat of deep reserves. Descendant of a long line of ecclesiastical ancestors who had conducted their decorous courtships beneath the shadow of cathedrals and on the back walls of bishops' palaces, he had that exquisite poise which one sees in high dignitaries of the Church. His eyes were clear and steady, and seemed to pierce to the very roots of the young man's soul, filling him with a sense of guilt.

Once, long ago, in his hot childhood, Lancelot, spending his summer holidays at the deanery, had been so far carried away by ginger-beer and original sin as to plug a senior canon in the leg with his air-gun—only to discover, on turning, that a visiting archdeacon had been a spectator of the entire incident from his immediate rear. As he had felt then, when meeting the archdeacon's eye, so did he feel now as Webster's gaze played silently upon him.

Webster, it is true, had not actually raised his eyebrows. But this, Lancelot felt, was simply because he hadn't any.

He backed, blushing.

'Sorry!' he muttered.

There was a pause. Webster continued his steady scrutiny. Lancelot edged towards the door.

'Er—excuse me—just a moment . . .' he mumbled. And, sidling from the room, he ran distractedly upstairs.

'I say,' said Lancelot.

'Now what?' asked Gladys.

'Have you finished with the mirror?'

'Why?'

'Well, I—er—I thought', said Lancelot, 'that I might as well have a shave.'

The girl looked at him, astonished.

'Shave? Why, you shaved only the day before yesterday.'

'I know. But, all the same . . . I mean to say, it seems only respectful. That cat, I mean.'

'What about him?'

'Well, he seems to expect it, somehow. Nothing actually said, don't you know, but you could tell by his manner. I

thought a quick shave and perhaps a change into my blue serge suit—'

'He's probably thirsty. Why don't you give him some milk?'

'Could one, do you think?' said Lancelot doubtful. 'I mean, I hardly seem to know him well enough.' He paused. 'I say, old girl,' he went on, with a touch of hesitation.

'Hullo?'

'I know you won't mind my mentioning it, but you've got a few spots of ink on your nose.'

'Of course I have. I always have spots of ink on my nose.'

'Well . . . you don't think . . . a quick scrub with a bit of pumice-stone . . . I mean to say, you know how important first impressions are . . . .'

The girl stared.

'Lancelot Mulliner,' she said, 'if you think I'm going to skin my nose to the bone just to please a mangy cat—'

'Sh!' cried Lancelot, in agony.

'Here, let me go down and look at him,' said Gladys petulantly.

As they re-entered the studio, Webster was gazing with an air of quiet distaste at an illustration from *La Vie Parisienne* which adorned one of the walls. Lancelot tore it down hastily.

Gladys looked at Webster in an unfriendly way.

'So that's the blighter!'

'Sh!'

'If you want to know what I think,' said Gladys, 'that cat's been living too high. Doing himself a dashed sight too well. You'd better cut his rations down a bit.'

In substance, her criticism was not unjustified. Certainly, there was about Webster more than a suspicion of *embonpoint*. He had that air of portly well-being which we associate with those who dwell in cathedral closes. But Lancelot winced uncomfortably. He had so hoped that Gladys would make a good impression, and here she was, starting right off by saying the tactless thing.

He longed to explain to Webster that it was only her way; that in the Bohemian circles of which she was such an ornament genial chaff of a personal order was accepted and, indeed, relished. But it was too late. The mischief had been done. Webster turned in a pointed manner and withdrew silently behind the chesterfield.

Gladys, all unconscious, was making preparations for departure.

'Well, bung-oh,' she said lightly. 'See you in three weeks. I suppose you and that cat'll both be out on the tiles the moment my back's turned.'

'Please! Please!' moaned Lancelot. 'Please!'

He had caught sight of the tip of a black tail protruding from behind the chesterfield. It was twitching slightly, and Lancelot could read it like a book. With a sickening sense of dismay, he knew that Webster had formed a snap judgement of his fiancée and condemned her as frivolous and unworthy.

It was some ten days later that Bernard Worple, the neo-Vorticist sculptor, lunching at the Puce Ptarmigan, ran into Rodney Scollop, the powerful young surrealist. And after talking for a while of their art:

'What's all this I hear about Lancelot Mulliner?' asked Worple. 'There's a wild story going about that he was seen shaved in the middle of the week. Nothing in it, I suppose?'

Scollop looked grave. He had been on the point of mentioning Lancelot himself, for he loved the lad and was deeply exercised about him.

'It is perfectly true,' he said.

'It sounds incredible.'

Scollop leaned forward. His fine face was troubled.

'Shall I tell you something, Worple?'

'What?'

'I know for an absolute fact', said Scollop, 'that Lancelot Mulliner now shaves every morning.'

Worple pushed aside the spaghetti which he was wreathing about him and through the gap stared at this companion.

'Every morning?'

'Every single morning. I looked in on him myself the other day, and there he was, neatly dressed in blue serge and shaved to the core. And, what is more, I got the distinct impression that he had used talcum powder afterwards.'

'You don't mean that!'

'I do. And shall I tell you something else? There was a book lying open on the table. He tried to hide it, but he wasn't quick enough. It was one of those etiquette books!'

'An etiquette book!'

'*Polite Behaviour*, by Constance, Lady Bodbank.'

Worple unwound a stray tendril of spaghetti from about his left ear. He was deeply agitated. Like Scollop, he loved Lancelot.

'He'll be dressing for dinner next!' he exclaimed.

'I have every reason to believe', said Scollop gravely, 'that he does dress for dinner. At any rate, a man closely resembling him was seen furtively buying three stiff collars and a black tie at Hope Brothers in the King's Road last Tuesday.'

Worple pushed his chair back, and rose. His manner was determined.

'Scollop,' he said, 'we are friends of Mulliner's, you and I. It is evident from what you tell me that subversive influences are at work and that never has he needed our friendship more. Shall we not go round and see him immediately?'

'It was what I was about to suggest myself,' said Rodney Scollop.

Twenty minutes later they were in Lancelot's studio, and with a significant glance Scollop drew his companion's notice to their host's appearance. Lancelot Mulliner was neatly, even foppishly, dressed in blue serge with creases down the trouser-legs, and his chin, Worple saw with a pang, gleamed smoothly in the afternoon light.

At the sight of his friends' cigars, Lancelot exhibited unmistakable concern.

'You don't mind throwing those away, I'm sure,' he said pleadingly.

Rodney Scollop drew himself up a little haughtily.

'And since when', he asked, 'have the best fourpenny cigars in Chelsea not been good enough for you?'

Lancelot hastened to soothe him.

'It isn't me,' he exclaimed. 'It's Webster. My cat. I happen to know he objects to tobacco smoke. I had to give up my pipe in deference to his views.'

Bernard Worple snorted.

'Are you trying to tell us', he sneered, 'that Lancelot Mulliner allows himself to be dictated to by a blasted cat?'

'Hush!' cried Lancelot, trembling. 'If you knew how he disapproves of strong language!'

'Where is this cat?' asked Rodney Scollop. 'Is that the

animal?' he said, pointing out of the window to where, in the yard, a tough-looking Tom with tattered ears stood mewing in a hard-boiled way out of the corner of its mouth.

'Good heavens, no!' said Lancelot. 'That is an alley cat which comes round here from time to time to lunch at the dustbin. Webster is quite different. Webster has a natural dignity and repose of manner. Webster is a cat who prides himself on always being well turned out and whose high principles and lofty ideals shine from his eyes like beacon fires. . . .' And then suddenly, with an abrupt change of manner, Lancelot broke down and in a low voice added: 'Curse him! Curse him! Curse him! Curse him!'

Worple looked at Scollop. Scollop looked at Worple.

'Come, old man,' said Scollop, laying a gentle hand on Lancelot's bowed shoulder. 'We are your friends. Confide in us.'

'Tell us all,' said Worple. 'What's the matter?'

Lancelot uttered a bitter, mirthless laugh.

'You want to know what's the matter? Listen, then. I'm cat-pecked!'

'Cat-pecked?'

'You've heard of men being hen-pecked, haven't you?' said Lancelot with a touch of irritation. 'Well, I'm cat-pecked.'

And in broken accents he told his story. He sketched the history of his association with Webster from the latter's first entry into the studio. Confident now that the animal was not within earshot, he unbosomed himself without reserve.

'It's something in the beast's eye,' he said in a shaking voice. 'Something hypnotic. He casts a spell upon me. He gazes at me and disapproves. Little by little, bit by bit, I am degenerating under his influence from a wholesome, self-respecting artist into . . . well, I don't know what you call it. Suffice it to say that I have given up smoking, that I have ceased to wear carpet slippers and go about without a collar, that I never dream of sitting down to my frugal evening meal without dressing, and'—he choked—'I have sold my ukulele.'

'Not that!' said Worple, paling.

'Yes,' said Lancelot. 'I felt he considered it frivolous.'

There was a long silence.

'Mulliner,' said Scollop, 'this is more serious than I had supposed. We must brood upon your case.'

'It may be possible', said Worple, 'to find a way out.'

Lancelot shook his head hopelessly..

'There is no way out. I have explored every avenue. The only thing that could possibly free me from this intolerable bondage would be if once—just once—I could catch that cat unbending. If once—merely once—it would lapse in my presence from its austere dignity for but a single instant, I feel that the spell would be broken. But what hope is there of that?' cried Lancelot passionately. 'You were pointing just now to that alley cat in the yard. There stands one who has strained every nerve and spared no effort to break down Webster's inhuman self-control. I have heard that animal say things to him which you would think no cat with red blood in its veins would suffer for an instant. And Webster merely looks at him like a Suffragan Bishop eyeing an erring choirboy and turns his head and falls into a refreshing sleep.'

He broke off with a dry sob. Worple, always an optimist,

attempted in his kindly way to minimize the tragedy.

'Ah, well,' he said. 'It's bad, of course, but still, I suppose there is no actual harm in shaving and dressing for dinner and so on. Many great artists . . . Whistler, for example—'

'Wait!' cried Lancelot. 'You have not heard the worst.'

He rose feverishly, and, going to the easel, disclosed the portrait of Brenda Carberry-Pirbright.

'Take a look at that,' he said, 'and tell me what you think of her.'

His two friends surveyed the face before them in silence. Miss Carberry-Pirbright was a young woman of prim and glacial aspect. One sought in vain for her reasons for wanting to have her portrait painted. It would be a most unpleasant thing to have about any house.

Scollop broke the silence.

'Friend of yours?'

'I can't stand the sight of her,' said Lancelot vehemently.

'Then', said Scollop, 'I may speak frankly. I think she's a pill.'

'A blister,' said Worple.

'A boil and a disease,' said Scollop, summing up.

Lancelot laughed hackingly.

'You have described her to a nicety. She stands for everything most alien to my artist soul. She gives me a pain in the neck. I'm going to marry her.'

'What!' cried Scollop.

'But you're going to marry Gladys Bingley,' said Worple.

'Webster thinks not,' said Lancelot bitterly. 'At their first meeting he weighed Gladys in the balance and found her wanting. And the moment he saw Brenda Carberry-Pirbright he stuck his tail up at right angles, uttered a cordial gargle, and rubbed his head against her leg. Then turning, he looked at me. I could read that glance. I knew what was in his mind. From that moment he has been doing everything in his power to arrange the match.'

'But, Mulliner,' said Worple, always eager to point out the bright side, 'why should this girl want to marry a wretched, scrubby, hard-up footler like you? Have courage, Mulliner. It is simply a question of time before you repel and sicken her.'

Lancelot shook his head.

173

'No,' he said. 'You speak like a true friend, Worple, but you do not understand. Old Ma Carberry-Pirbright, this exhibit's mother, who chaperones her at the sittings, discovered at an early date my relationship to my Uncle Theodore, who, as you know, has got it in gobs. She knows well enough that some day I shall be a rich man. She used to know my Uncle Theodore when he was Vicar of St Botolph's in Knightsbridge, and from the very first she assumed towards me the repellent chumminess of an old family friend. She was always trying to lure me to her At Homes, her Sunday luncheons, her little dinners. Once she actually suggested that I should escort her and her beastly daughter to the Royal Academy.'

He laughed bitterly. The mordant witticisms of Lancelot Mulliner at the expense of the Royal Academy were quoted from Tite Street in the south to Holland Park in the north and eastward as far as Bloomsbury.

'To all these overtures', resumed Lancelot, 'I remained firmly unresponsive. My attitude was from the start one of frigid aloofness. I did not actually say in so many words that I would rather be dead in a ditch than at one of her At Homes, but my manner indicated it. And I was just beginning to think I had choked her off when in crashed Webster and upset everything. Do you know how many times I have been to that infernal house in the last week? Five. Webster seemed to wish it. I tell you, I am a lost man.'

He buried his face in his hands. Scollop touched Worple on the arm, and together the two men stole silently out.

'Bad!' said Worple.

'Very bad,' said Scollop.

'It seems incredible.'

'Oh, no. Cases of this kind are, alas, by no means un-common among those who, like Mulliner, possess to a marked degree the highly-strung, ultra-sensitive artistic temperament. A friend of mine, a rhythmical interior decorator, once rashly consented to put his aunt's parrot up at his studio while she was away visiting friends in the north of England. She was a woman of strong evangelical views, which the bird had imbibed from her. It had a way of putting its head on one side, making a noise like someone drawing a cork from a bottle, and asking my friend if he was saved. To cut a long story short, I

174

happened to call on him a month later and he had installed a harmonium in his studio and was singing hymns, ancient and modern, in a rich tenor, while the parrot, standing on one leg on its perch, took the bass. A very sad affair. We were all much upset about it.'

Worple shuddered.

'You appal me, Scollop! Is there nothing we can do?'

Rodney Scollop considered for a moment.

'We might wire Gladys Bingley to come home at once. She might possibly reason with the unhappy man. A woman's gentle influence. . . . Yes, we could do that. Look in at the post office on your way home and send Gladys a telegram. I'll owe you for my half of it.'

In the studio they had left, Lancelot Mulliner was staring dumbly at a black shape which had just entered the room. He had the appearance of a man with his back to the wall.

'No!' he was crying. 'No! I'm dashed if I do!'

Webster continued to look at him.

'Why should I?' demanded Lancelot weakly.

Webster's gaze did not flicker.

'Oh, all right,' said Lancelot sullenly.

He passed from the room with leaden feet, and, proceeding upstairs, changed into morning clothes and a top hat. Then, with a gardenia in his buttonhole, he made his way to 11 Maxton Square, where Mrs. Carberry-Pirbright was giving one of her intimate little teas ('just a few friends') to meet Clara Throckmorton Stooge, authoress of *A Strong Man's Kiss.*

Gladys Bingley was lunching at her hotel in Antibes when Worple's telegram arrived. It occasioned her the gravest concern.

Exactly what it was all about she was unable to gather, for emotion had made Bernard Worple rather incoherent. There were moments, reading it, when she fancied that Lancelot had met with a serious accident; others when the solution seemed to be that he had sprained his brain to such an extent that rival lunatic asylums were competing eagerly for his custom; others, again, when Worple appeared to be suggesting that he had gone into partnership with his cat to start a harem. But one fact emerged clearly. Her loved one was in serious trouble of some

kind, and his best friends were agreed that only her immediate return could save him.

Gladys did not hesitate. Within half an hour of the receipt of the telegram she had packed her trunk, removed a piece of asparagus from her right eyebrow, and was negotiating for accommodation on the first train going north.

Arriving in London, her first impulse was to go straight to Lancelot. But a natural feminine curiosity urged her, before doing so, to call upon Bernard Worple and have light thrown on some of the more abstruse passages in the telegram.

Worple, in his capacity of author, may have tended towards obscurity, but, when confining himself to the spoken word, he told a plain story well and clearly. Five minutes of his society enabled Gladys to obtain a firm grasp on the salient facts, and there appeared on her face that grim, tight-lipped expression which is seen only on the faces of fiancées who have come back from a short holiday to discover that their dear one has been straying in their absence from the straight and narrow path.

'Brenda Carberry-Pirbright, eh?' said Gladys, with ominous calm. 'I'll give him Brenda Carberry-Pirbright! My gosh, if one can't go off to Antibes for the merest breather without having one's betrothed getting it up his nose and starting to act like a Mormon Elder, it begins to look a pretty tough world for a girl.'

Kind-hearted Bernard Worple did his best.

'I blame the cat,' he said. 'Lancelot, to my mind, is more sinned against than sinning. I consider him to be acting under undue influence or duress.'

'How like a man!' said Gladys. 'Shoving it all off on to an innocent cat!'

'Lancelot says it has a sort of something in its eye.'

'Well, when I meet Lancelot,' said Gladys, 'he'll find that I have a sort of something in my eye.'

She went out, breathing flame quietly through her nostrils. Worple, saddened, heaved a sigh and resumed his neo-Vorticist sculpting.

It was some five minutes later that Gladys, passing through Maxton Square on her way to Bott Street, stopped suddenly in her tracks. The sight she had seen was enough to make any fiancée do so.

Along the pavement leading to No. 11 two figures were advancing. Or three, if you counted a morose-looking dog of a semi-dachshund nature which preceded them, attached to a leash. One of the figures was that of Lancelot Mulliner, natty in grey herringbone tweed and a new Homburg hat. It was he who held the leash. The other Gladys recognized from the portrait which she had seen on Lancelot's easel as that modern Du Barry, that notorious wrecker of homes and breaker-up of love-nests, Brenda Carberry-Pirbright.

The next moment they had mounted the steps of No. 11, and had gone in to tea, possibly with a little music.

It was perhaps an hour and a half later that Lancelot, having wrenched himself with difficulty from the lair of the Philistines, sped homeward in a swift taxi. As always after an extended *tête-à-tête* with Miss Carberry-Pirbright, he felt dazed and bewildered, as if he had been swimming in a sea of glue and had swallowed a great deal of it. All he could think of clearly was that he wanted a drink and that the materials for the drink were in the cupboard behind the chesterfield of his studio.

He paid the cab and charged in with his tongue rattling dryly against his front teeth. And there before him was Gladys Bingley, whom he had supposed far, far away.

'You!' exclaimed Lancelot.

'Yes, me!' said Gladys.

Her long vigil had not helped to restore the girl's equanimity. Since arriving at the studio she had had leisure to tap her foot three thousand, one hundred and forty-two times on the carpet, and the number of bitter smiles which had flitted across her face was nine hundred and eleven. She was about ready for the battle of the century.

She rose and faced him, all the woman in her flashing from her eyes.

'Well, you Casanova!' she said.

'You who?' said Lancelot.

'Don't you say "Yoo-hoo!" to me!' cried Gladys. 'Keep that for your Brenda Carberry-Pirbright. Yes, I know all about it, Lancelot Don Juan Henry the Eighth Mulliner! I saw you with her just now. I hear that you and she are inseparable. Bernard

Worple says you said you were going to marry her.'

'You mustn't believe everything a neo-Vorticist sculptor tells you,' quavered Lancelot.

'I'll bet you're going back to dinner there tonight,' said Gladys.

She had spoken at a venture, basing the charge purely on a possessive cock of the head which she had noticed in Brenda Carberry-Pirbright at their recent encounter. There, she had said to herself at the time, had gone a girl who was about to invite—or had just invited—Lancelot Mulliner to dine quietly and take her to the pictures afterwards. But the shot went home. Lancelot hung his head.

'There was some talk of it,' he admitted.

'Ah!' exclaimed Gladys.

Lancelot's eyes were haggard.

'I don't want to go,' he pleaded. 'Honestly, I don't. But Webster insists.'

'Webster!'

'Yes, Webster. If I attempt to evade the appointment, he will sit in front of me and look at me.'

'Tchah!'

'Well, he will. Ask him for yourself.'

Gladys tapped her foot six times in rapid succession on the carpet, bringing the total to three thousand, one hundred and forty-eight. Her manner had changed and was now dangerously calm.

'Lancelot Mulliner,' she said, 'you have your choice. Me, on the one hand, Brenda Carberry-Pirbright on the other. I offer you a home where you will be able to smoke in bed, spill the ashes on the floor, wear pyjamas and carpet slippers all day and shave only on Sunday mornings. From her, what have you to hope? A house in South Kensington—possibly the Brompton Road—probably with her mother living with you. A life that will be one long round of stiff collars and tight shoes, of morning coats and top hats.'

Lancelot quivered, but she went on remorselessly.

'You will be at home on alternate Thursdays, and will be expected to hand the cucumber sandwiches. Every day you will air the dog, till you become a confirmed dog-airer. You will dine out in Bayswater and go for the summer to

Bournemouth or Dinard. Choose well, Lancelot Mulliner! I will leave you to think it over. But one last word. If by seven-thirty on the dot you have not presented yourself at 6a Garbidge Mews ready to take me out to dinner at the Ham and Beef, I shall know what to think and shall act accordingly.'

And brushing the cigarette ashes from her chin, the girl strode haughtily from the room.

'Gladys!' cried Lancelot.

But she had gone.

For some minutes Lancelot Mulliner remained where he was, stunned. Then, insistently, there came to him the recollection that he had not had that drink. He rushed to the cupboard and produced the bottle. He uncorked it, and was pouring out a lavish stream, when a movement on the floor below him attracted his attention.

Webster was standing there, looking up at him. And in his eyes was that familiar expression of quiet rebuke.

'Scarcely what I have been accustomed to at the Deanery,' he seemed to be saying.

Lancelot stood paralysed. The feeling of being bound hand and foot, of being caught in a snare from which there was no escape, had become more poignant than ever. The bottle fell from his nerveless fingers and rolled across the floor, spilling its contents in an amber river, but he was too heavy in spirit to notice it. With a gesture such as Job might have made on discovering a new boil, he crossed to the window and stood looking moodily out.

Then, turning with a sigh, he looked at Webster again—and, looking, stood spellbound.

The spectacle which he beheld was of a kind to stun a stronger man than Lancelot Mulliner. At first, he shrank from believing his eyes. Then, slowly, came the realization that what he saw was no mere figment of a disordered imagination. This unbelievable thing was actually happening.

Webster sat crouched upon the floor beside the widening pool of whisky. But it was not horror and disgust that had caused him to crouch. He was crouched because, crouching, he could get nearer to the stuff and obtain crisper action. His tongue was moving in and out like a piston.

179

And then abruptly, for one fleeting instant, he stopped lapping and glanced up at Lancelot, and across his face there flitted a quick smile—so genial, so intimate, so full of jovial camaraderie, that the young man found himself automatically smiling back, and not only smiling but winking. And in answer to that wink Webster winked too—a whole-hearted, roguish wink that said as plainly as if he had spoken the words:

'How long has this been going on?'

Then with a slight hiccough he turned back to the task of getting his drink before it soaked into the floor.

Into the murky soul of Lancelot Mulliner there poured a sudden flood of sunshine. It was as if a great burden had been lifted from his shoulders. The intolerable obsession of the last two weeks had ceased to oppress him, and he felt a free man. At the eleventh hour the reprieve had come. Webster, that seeming pillar of austere virtue, was one of the boys, after all. Never again would Lancelot quail beneath his eye. He had the goods on him.

Webster, like the stag at eve, had now drunk his fill. He had left the pool of alcohol and was walking round in slow, meditative circles. From time to time he mewed tentatively, as if he were trying to say 'British Constitution'. His failure to articulate the syllables appeared to tickle him, for at the end of each attempt he would utter a slow, amused chuckle. It was about this moment that he suddenly broke into a rhythmic dance, not unlike the old Saraband.

It was an interesting spectacle, and at any other time Lancelot would have watched it raptly. But now he was busy at his desk, writing a brief note to Mrs Carberry-Pirbright, the burden of which was that if she thought he was coming within a mile of her foul house that night or any other night she had vastly underrated the dodging powers of Lancelot Mulliner.

And what of Webster? The Demon Rum now had him in an iron grip. A lifetime of abstinence had rendered him a ready victim to the fatal fluid. He had now reached the stage when geniality gives way to belligerence. The rather foolish smile had gone from his face, and in its stead there lowered a fighting frown. For a few moments he stood on his hind legs, looking about him for a suitable adversary: then, losing all vestiges of self-control, he ran five times round the room at a high rate

of speed and, falling foul of a small footstool, attacked it with the utmost ferocity, sparing neither tooth nor claw.

But Lancelot did not see him. Lancelot was not there. Lancelot was out in Bott Street, hailing a cab.

'6a Garbidge Mews, Fulham,' said Lancelot to the driver.

Trouble Everywhere

DOREEN TOVEY

S UGIEH came into season for the first time in September, while we were in Scotland and she was once more staying with the Smiths. We were afraid she might. According to the book it could happen with a precocious Siamese as early as four months, and as Sugieh was by this time seven months old and so precocious it made you want to spit, it was obvious she was saving her efforts for a special occasion.

With the aid of James she staged it magnificently. She uttered her first call in the middle of a dinner party and scared everybody, including herself, nearly out of their wits. The Smiths, realizing what was happening, had hardly finished assuring the more nervous guests that she was not going mad when she called again, louder than before. Whereupon, they told us, their eyes glazing slightly at the memory, James, hearing her voice through the mists of sleep and forgetting for the moment that he was no longer the cat he had been, had leapt gallantly out of the gramophone and tried to make love to her on the hearthrug, and Sugieh had shinned up the standard lamp in alarm and brought it down in the cutlets.

It said much for the Smiths that, even after that, we still remained friends. They wouldn't even let us pay for the lamp. They did warn us, though, that Sugieh was what they termed an exceptional caller. Eventually they had had to lock her in their spare room, and though James was allowed to visit her whenever he liked and within a couple of days had succeeded in persuading her that there were other things in life besides love—she emerged, they said, as placidly as if it had never

182

happened, drank a jug of milk to cool her throat and went happily off with him to dig holes in the garden—while it lasted they had been quite unable to hear themselves speak.

It was quite a while before we heard her ourselves. After that first effort she went so long without calling again that in fact we began to get suspicious. Those moonlit October nights when she had refused to come in and we had gone to bed without her, lying awake worrying about foxes and badgers until, around midnight, she would come tearing up the stairs bellowing that she hadn't any idea of the time and why on earth hadn't we *called* her? Had she perhaps gone innocently into the woods and been pounced on, even as she opened her mouth for her first tremulous call, by some feline Don Juan? Or had she—which was much more likely, knowing Sugieh—kept her love pangs to herself and gone deliberately off to look for a tom, realizing from her experience with the Smiths that if she let out one squeal while we were around we would lock her up and spoil all the fun?

Sugieh knew, but she wasn't telling. As the weeks wore on and we eyed her more and more suspiciously—there was no doubt at all that she was getting plumper, though that *might* have been because she was growing out of kittenhood—all she did was smirk coyly and stretch so that we could get a better look. When we asked her sternly what she had been up to, she half-closed her eyes and gave a faint, ecstatic squawk.

Christmas drew nearer, Sugieh still hadn't called, and eventually there was no doubt at all in our minds. While up the lane Father Adams rubbed his hands and prepared gleefully for Mimi's happy event, we shook our heads reproachfully at Sugieh and prepared to conceal her shame.

As it happened we were all wrong. Mimi, to Father Adam's chagrin, had a false pregnancy and produced no kittens at all while Sugieh, tickled pink at the way she had fooled us, came triumphantly into season on Christmas Day, roaring like a lion. It seemed that social occasions had that effect on her. After a feed of turkey—never shall I forget the look of awe on her face when she saw a turkey for the first time; you could see her mentally writing off those pheasants on the spot—a run in the woods to see if there were any more turkeys up there, and a brisk game of snakes and ladders which she won by sweeping

all the counters on the floor, she suddenly threw herself on her back and burst into song. My brother-in-law looked at her in alarm and asked what was wrong. Mindful that there were children present I looked at him meaningly and said Nothing. She got like that sometimes, when she was Excited. Our nine-year-old twin nephews, looking at each other in horror, promptly put aside their snakes and ladders and explained that she was making *that* noise because she wanted a husband.

The Smiths were right about her being an exceptional caller. Sugieh had always had a powerful voice, even for a Siamese, and her love song was excruciating. By day she followed us round the house screaming and throwing herself hopefully on her back every time we looked at her. At night she thumped round in the spare room, yelling more furiously than ever because, unable to stand the racket at such close quarters, we refused to let her come to bed with us. By dawn on the morning after Boxing Day we could stand it no longer. Charles, loudly damning all Siamese to perdition, took her down and shut her in the bathroom.

Ours is an old place and the bathroom is not only on the ground floor but separated from the original part of the cottage by a two-foot-thick stone wall. When after a while the screams, now mercifully faint, stopped altogether we told ourselves smugly that Sugieh was no fool; she knew when we had her beaten. For the first time in two days we prepared to get some sleep.

A split second later the father and mother of all cat fights started up in the garden, and we nearly went through the roof. 'Sugieh!' I screeched, barely touching ground as I leapt out of bed and down the stairs. 'Quick!' urged Charles—stopping nevertheless to put on his slippers and belt his dressing-gown before pelting after me.

Sugieh was quite safe. She had not, as by this time we suspected her of being perfectly capable of doing, gone through the ventilator or prised the window open with a crowbar. She was sitting in the bathroom window like the queen of a medieval tourney, squinting with smug delight while outside two lusty knights battled for her favours in the polyanthus.

She stayed in season for a week and each night, with

unfailing regularity, there was a cat fight outside the bathroom window. A fortnight later she began calling again. We had intended waiting until she was a year old before having her mated, but it was more than flesh and blood could stand. At eleven months Sugieh, with great enthusiasm, became a bride.

She was mated—the maiden lady's tom being in our opinion too flat-faced, and Ajax being unromantically laid up with an abscess in his ear—to a cat called Rikki, at a Siamese stud farm forty miles away. Rikki's owners said she was one of the most forward cats they had ever seen. She was also, they said, the loudest. Normally it took about four days to make sure that young queens, who were often nervous, were properly mated, but on the evening of the second day they 'phoned to say there was no doubt at all about Sugieh and would we please fetch her as soon as possible because she was disturbing all the other cats while Rikki, far from being the triumphant male, was padding round his enclosure with a haunted look on his face and jumping every time he heard her voice.

At least, we thought, as we drove wearily home that night with Sugieh in the back still sobbing hysterically for her beloved husband—his owners had told us to keep her indoors for a couple of days or, love-him-forever or not, she might console herself with the farmyard tom and still have mongrel kittens—at least after *this* was over we should have some peace.

We were always forecasting things like that about Sugieh, and we were always wrong. After the noisiest marriage in the history of the cat kennels Sugieh embarked on a pregnancy which couldn't have been more involved if she'd read a doctor's book. First, after two days of dewy-eyed dreaming about Rikki—she couldn't waste any more time than that; she only had nine weeks to get everything in—she developed Morning Sickness. Either that or she was suddenly overcome with shame at the thought of her scandalous behaviour at the kennels. The result was, anyway, that she went completely off her food, sat around looking frail and swaying slightly with closed eyes—and finally, with a temperature of 104, had to be driven dramatically through a snowstorm for streptomycin injections.

No sooner did we get her over that—'When you love animals

185

they make you their slaves,' said the vet gazing sentimentally into her sad blue eyes, but even he couldn't have anticipated the scene when, suddenly recovering her appetite in the middle of the night, she insisted on being fed with crab paste on Charles's pillow—she developed a passion for jam tarts. They had to be jam tarts, though she never ate the jam; and they had to be stolen. If we gave her one she retched realistically, shook her back leg at it and walked away. Left alone, however, she would clear a plateful in a day, stealing them from the pantry and carrying them off to the bathroom, where she carefully ate the pastry rims and left the middles on the floor and Charles absent-mindedly trod them all over the house.

Fired, we imagined, by a desire that her kittens should all be Seal Points like Rikki—a real Yul Brynner of a cat he had been, with massive black shoulders and a wicked, wedge-shaped head—she also drank more coffee then it seemed possible a cat could hold, and, for some unfathomable reason, took to chewing paper; a habit which, the day she ate Charles's Aunt Ethel's telegram, landed us in serious trouble.

Charles's Aunt Ethel, when she decided to stay with members of the family, always announced her impending arrival by telegram; that way the family had no chance to get out of it. In our case, as we lived, as she was always telling us, at the back of beyond, the telegram also contained the time of the train so that Charles could drive over to the station and collect her.

When, therefore, she appeared dramatically on the doorstep one cold wet night, looking grimly at us over the top of her streaming pince-nez and announcing that not only had she Waited in Vain for a whole hour at the junction but the taxi she had then been Forced to Take had broken down at the end of the lane (it always did for strangers; Fred Ferry had no intention of taxing his springs on our potholes if he could help it), it was obvious that we were for it.

She wouldn't believe we hadn't had the telegram. She had Sent It, she said, and that was that. It didn't help, either, when Charles rang the post office—rather irately, to impress Aunt Ethel—and asked what the devil they'd done with it. The postmaster, who was a man of spirit, said what the devil did

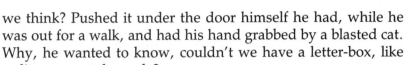

we think? Pushed it under the door himself he had, while he was out for a walk, and had his hand grabbed by a blasted cat. Why, he wanted to know, couldn't we have a letter-box, like ordinary normal people?

We did have a letter-box. It was, as the regular postman knew, in the kitchen door. Charles had transferred it from the front door after Blondin nearly decapitated himself one day through sticking his head nosily through the flap and not being able to get it back. If the telegram had been put by mistake under the front door, Charles told the astonished postmaster, only one thing could have happened. Our cat must have eaten it.

She had. While she watched strategically from the top of the stairs and Aunt Ethel dramatically waited for an explanation at the bottom we found the incriminating evidence—a soggy, well-chewed corner of the envelope—under the hall chair.

What happened then was little short of miraculous. Aunt Ethel was just about to storm out in high dudgeon—she had never liked our animals very much since the day Blondin light-heartedly deposited a small, warm trickle down her neck while she was dozing in a chair and this, she informed us icily, was the Last Straw—when Sugieh got up and lumbered slowly down the stairs.

By this time she had a figure like a pear-drop, though up till now it didn't seem to have inconvenienced her very much. Only the previous week she had gone across the garden so fast after a bird she had run into a cloche and cut her nose. Not seriously; just enough to send her even more cross-eyed than usual for a few days looking at the scar. She still, too, climbed trees like the wind without any apparent ill-effect on anybody except Charles who groaned and clutched his head every time she banged her—we hoped—valuable cargo of kittens against a branch.

Now, to our utter astonishment, she crept wearily down-stairs as if she could hardly drag herself along, looked Aunt Ethel pathetically in the eye and said 'Waaah!'

Maybe her discomfort was genuine. Maybe it was the result of eating that orange envelope. At any rate we had no more trouble that visit. By night Aunt Ethel slept with Sugieh cradled in her compassionate arms. By day she nursed her on her lap, tenderly stroking her ears and telling her what wicked owners she had, to let the poor little darling be taken advantage of like that.

The poor little darling, wallowing in sympathy as only a Siamese can, acquiesced soulfully in everything she said. To listen to her she had never ever wanted to get married, and we had dragged her down to Dorset by the hair of her innocent little head.

We didn't care. For the first time in months—what was more with Sugieh *and* Aunt Ethel in the house—we had a little peace.

ENTER FOUR GLADIATORS

Sugieh had her kittens at the end of March. After a harrowing evening trying to persuade her to have them in a cardboard box lined with newspaper, as recommended by the cat book, while she just as persistently kept getting out of it and marching upstairs flat-eared with indignation at the very idea, they were born just after midnight. On our bed—otherwise, she said, she wouldn't have them at all—while Charles and I sat either side of her, cat book in hand, anxiously awaiting complications.

There were none. Except for the fact that the last one to arrive was half the size of the other three—and that, as Charles pointed out to her, was entirely her own fault; he had warned her often enough about rushing up those trees—everything went off quietly, efficiently and speedily.

It was the last time anything was to go off quietly in our house for a long time to come. The next morning we awoke to the depressing discovery that Sugieh, who never did anything by halves, had decided to become the Perfect Mother.

That, while it lasted, was purgatory. For the first few days she hardly left the kittens for a moment. When she wanted food she stood at the top of the stairs and shouted. When we took it up to her she was either back in her basket feeding them as though they were delicate lilies about to fade before her very eyes, or pacing anxiously up and down like a commercial traveller with a train to catch.

The kittens weren't much help either. The only time we did persuade her to come down with us for a while she had hardly had time to cross her eyes at Shorty in the old familiar way

before there was a piercing wail from above and she was off up the stairs two at a time shouting look what happened when she left them for a Moment. Now they were being Kidnapped!

Nobody outside a lunatic asylum would have wanted to kidnap that lot, and well she knew it. From the moment they solemnly opened one eye each, days before they should have done, and leered forth at the world like a lot of piratical Fu Manchus it was obvious that they were up to no good. It gave the act a wonderful fillip, though. Much better than the perfect mother, Sugieh was now the perfect mother defending her children from the kidnappers.

Nobody was free from suspicion on this score. When the Rector came to tea she no longer sat on his knee and shed affectionate hairs on his best black trousers. She stayed in the hall giving him sinister looks round the door. When the butcher's boy arrived, instead of running out ahead of everybody else to have a private word about the liver, she glared at him from the window bawling One step Nearer and she'd call the Police.

When the police did come, in the shape of P.C. McNab bearing a summons for Charles who had not surprisingly driven into town one morning in a coma and left the car under a no-parking sign for two hours, she kicked up such a fuss we weren't at all surprised to see McNab bring out his notebook as soon as he got out into the lane and make an entry that undoubtedly related to breaches of the peace. And when Aunt Ethel came for the weekend specially to see the kittens and we brought them downstairs thinking she, at any rate, would be all right because she was a friend of Sugieh's, Sugieh nearly went mad.

One after another, as fast as she could, she grabbed the kittens by the scruff of the neck and rushed them dramatically back to the spare room. At bedtime every night for the past year she had complained loudly and bitterly that the spare room was a Vile Prison and she might just as well be Marie Antoinette. Now, it seemed, it was the only place in the world where her kittens were safe. When Aunt Ethel followed apologetically after her with the basket and an odd kitten she had found on the stairs Sugieh, standing bravely on guard in the doorway, growled at her so realistically with her tail

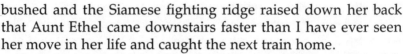

bushed and the Siamese fighting ridge raised down her back that Aunt Ethel came downstairs faster than I have ever seen her move in her life and caught the next train home.

Even Sugieh, I think realized she had overdone it that time. Either that or she was tired of playing at perfect mothers. The next morning, anyway, she dumped the kittens in bed with us at seven o'clock as nonchalantly as if she had never heard of kidnappers, went off into the woods and didn't come back until nine. From then on she made it perfectly clear that they were as much our responsibility as hers.

We have since often wondered whether being dropped on their heads as often as those kittens were in the next few weeks had any connection with the way they grew up. Every morning at least one of them went down with a thump as Sugieh leapt madly on to the bed, stuffing kittens into my arms as fast as she could, and though we wouldn't have gone as far as Sugieh and said that that one was Spoiled—she never bothered to pick up the one she had dropped; just looked at him in annoyance and went off to get another—or it was obvious that it couldn't have done them much good. It was significant, too, that the one who got dropped on his head more often than anybody else was Solomon.

Everybody who knows him has, at some time or other, asked us why on earth we called him Solomon. The answer is that it was his mother's idea of a joke. Knowing full well that we planned to keep a tom out of her first litter as a show cat and to call him—rather brightly, we thought—Solomon Seal, she obligingly produced three toms to give us a choice, watched with intense interest for a couple of weeks as, cat book in hand, we went over their points and debated which we should have—and finally had the biggest laugh of her life when it turned out there was only one we could keep. The one we had written off at the start because he had big feet, ears like a bat and brains to match. All the rest, including the diminutive queen, were Blues.

Solomon, in addition to his other faults, had spotted whiskers. Long before the dusky smudges appeared on his nose and paws to warn us that he was ours for life we had been able to distinguish him from the others by this peculiarity. 'Like an orchid,' said Aunt Ethel, tenderly retrieving him from the coal bucket on her next visit, after she and Sugieh had made it up and Sugieh, dumping her squirming, screeching family into Aunt Ethel's lap by way of a peace-offering, had dropped him overboard as usual. Like bamboo would have been nearer the truth. I have never seen a cat who looked so much like Popski in my life. Bamboo or orchid, it was by his whiskers we recognized him as the one who always fed lying down.

We nearly had a fit the first time we saw it—three kittens feeding away for dear life and standing, to get a better grip, on the fourth, who appeared to be unconscious. After we had dragged him out three times to give him air, however, only to find that within a few minutes he had disappeared once more beneath the scrum, we began to get suspicious. When we lifted the top layer of kittens and had a look our suspicions were confirmed. While the others squealed and clawed and battled for position on top, the one with the big feet and spotted whiskers lay blissfully underneath, on his back, with the whole bottom row to himself.

The result of his uninterrupted meals was, of course, that he soon became the biggest kitten of the lot and it was because of this, and the fact that he was Sugieh's favourite, that he was always being dropped.

When she felt like showing off—and it did, though we hated to admit it, make a charming picture—it was always Solomon that she carted down the lane, smirking blandly over his fat white head at the applause. As, however, the outing was essentially in the nature of a film star pushing her offspring round Hyde Park for the benefit of the photographers she usually dropped him on the path as soon as she got back and left him for us to put away. Sometimes she came over the wall and dropped him in the ditch. Invariably she dropped him when she tried some awkward manoeuvre like leaping on to the bed. As he grew bigger she dropped him more and more. When she carried him upstairs his fat white body bumped solidly against every stair. Aunt Ethel, trying fruitlessly to wrest him from Sugieh's grasp on one such occasion, forecast darkly that he would grow up not quite right in the head. She couldn't go wrong there, of course. No Siamese is ever right in the head. Nevertheless it was odd that when Solomon did grow up he had even more peculiarities than an ordinary

Siamese—including an overwhelming desire to be dragged round by the scruff of his neck.

It was incredible, seeing that once Sugieh stopped being the perfect mother she acted more as if she needed a course in child care, how those kittens survived. When they wanted washing she washed them so hard they nearly shot out of their skins. When they annoyed her she bit them so hard they screamed for mercy. All except Solomon, who bit her back and then, when she chased him, rolled over and waved his four black socks so disarmingly that he got an extra feed while the others weren't looking.

She had no idea of diet at all. At four weeks old, when according to the book we were supposed to start weaning them on to a patent milk food, she said it wasn't good for them and drank it herself. At six weeks, when we were practically going round the bend because—acting no doubt on her instructions —they shut their eyes and mouths firmly the moment they as much as saw a saucer and we despaired of ever weaning them at all, we found her upstairs one morning surreptitiously feeding them with large lumps of rabbit from her own breakfast and watching proudly while they fought over it like tigers.

She knew quite well that it was wrong. When we lectured her about their delicate stomachs she sat with her eyes down, looked at us from under her eyelashes and said it was Solomon. It may well have been, at that. Solomon, who was the one we had worried about most over this feeding business because he was such a big kitten and how he was managing on nothing but his mother's milk we had dared not think, was at that moment standing knee-deep in the middle of the rabbit bowl slurping it back like spaghetti. Solomon, at any rate, was the one chosen—not from malice but because she thought he was so wonderful we couldn't resist him—to bear the blame for everything from then on.

When she stole one of Charles's best yellow socks and showed the delighted kittens how to chew holes up and down the leg till it looked like a colander it was Solomon—when the reaction set in and she realized what she'd done—who was detailed to bring us the remains while the rest sat in trepidation on the landing, ready to run.

When we went to the cinema one night and foolishly left

them on our bed because it was cold and they looked so appealing cuddled together on the eiderdown it was Solomon —the rest, led by Sugieh, bolted under the bed the minute they heard us coming up the stairs—who was left in small, solitary splendour to explain the row of holes across the top of a brand-new blanket. He had a job doing that. There was only one cat whose mouth would have fitted those round wet holes—and she was flat on her stomach under the bed, pretending she was part of the carpet. There was only one cat, too, strong enough to turn back the bedspread and eiderdown and pull the blanket out. Solomon listened, his big bat ears wide with horror, while we told him who she was, what she was, and what we were going to do to her when we caught her. Something obviously had to be done in a hurry if he was going to save Mum from the tanning of her life—and on the spur of the moment he did it. As I held the blanket up, wailing that it was absolutely useless, he bounced forward, his eyes bright with inspiration, and wiggled a fat black paw through one of the holes. That, he said, was the game they had been playing before we came in. That was the very reason Mum had chewed the holes, and it was terrific fun. Why didn't we have a go?

We were always suckers for that little black pansy face. We did. Within a few seconds the bed was an hilarious mass of kittens charging gleefully up and down the eiderdown and poking paws at us through the blanket while Sugieh, reappearing as if by magic once she knew the danger was past, grabbed Solomon by the scruff of the neck and dropped him light-heartedly off the pillow as a reward.

It wasn't the only reward she gave him. I nearly fainted on the spot when after supper that night he marched proudly into the living room with his spotted whiskers sprouting on one side as exuberantly as a gorse bush—and the other side completely bare. He was only eight weeks old then and we thought they had dropped out as a result of eating too much rabbit. We didn't know Siamese mothers sometimes did that to their favourite kittens when they were particularly pleased with them.

The vet told us that—rather shortly, we thought, seeing that he was supposed to like Siamese cats—at half past eleven that night.

Heathcliff

LLOYD ALEXANDER

WHERE he came from, and the circumstances under which Heathcliff passed the first years of his life, I do not know. He arrived fully grown; mature, neither very young nor very old. Whether he had been a lost cat, an enterprising one who decided to shift for himself, abandoned, or simply neglected by a former owner, I never ascertained. He could have been called a blue Persian, although more grey than otherwise, and his hair a little shorter than the ideal. He had style nevertheless. And undeniable blood lines— whose they were remained a mystery. Since Persians are not ordinarily brought up in the humblest environments, he might even have enjoyed opulence at one time, but he gave the impression that his past was a subject better left unmentioned.

One afternoon at the end of winter, I happened to see Rabbit playing on the lawn with a strange cat. I went out to investigate and the newcomer took refuge in a hydrangea bush. Most cats do not approach humans recklessly. The possibility of concealed weapons, clods or sticks, tends to make them reserved. Homeless cats in particular—with some justification, unfortunately—consider humans their natural enemies. Much ceremony must be observed, and a number of diplomatic feelers put out before establishing a state of truce. Heathcliff went through the preliminaries with dispatch. He emerged from his bush, circled me a few times and finally came to rub his head against my legs, and allow me a closer look at him.

He was a cat for a melodrama. Faded and rainwashed, his sideburns jutted out from his massive head and his tail fluttered like a bundle of old clothes on a stick. A patched

muffler of a frill hung at his throat and his bushy hindquarters took the shape of a pair of riding-breeches. His long hair gave him a deceptive stoutness; when I stroked him I found little flesh and a great prominence of bones.

The two cats were on such good terms, racing and stalking each other, that I at first imagined Heathcliff to be a friend from the club on a brief social call. Instead, I noticed he hung around the lawn all afternoon, evidently without other engagements. At meal times he presented himself at the kitchen door with Rabbit.

I had no intention of adopting a new cat. I had grown so fond of Rabbit over the past year that taking in another seemed like treason. Rabbit entirely suited my needs and I hadn't yet realized that a cat addict's wants are infinitely expandable. But I couldn't refuse him a meal. The sight of Rabbit, gobbling meat at his usual place on the drainboard, was so evidently distressing to him that, disregarding Janine's warning, I put some meat on a saucer and carried it to the porch.

Until then, I had never heard of the contract under which a man who feeds a cat once is obliged to continue the practice as long as they both shall live. Heathcliff knew the law better than I and insisted on having it carried out to the letter. He disappeared at nightfall, but next morning I found him on the porch waiting for breakfast. With his pompous, owlish glance and ragged tail he reminded me of an unemployed actor who, by bluff and brass, has made his way into a restaurant a little before the other diners; and waits at an empty table, napkin under chin, trying to look as if he intended to pay and wondering how soon before he is turned out. When he saw me, he rolled over on his back and began to purr loudly. I gave him a saucer of milk.

I met him at every turn after that. Our house has three doors—front, side, and a kitchen door at the back, and Heathcliff seemed to be at every one. If I went out by the front, he tried to slip past into the living-room; if I left by the side, he popped out from behind one of the porch columns; at the kitchen, he hung spread-eagled from the screen. Anywhere else, as soon as he caught sight or scent of me, he ran as fast as he could, moustachios flying, to beg admittance to the house.

I resigned myself to feeding him but I was still unconvinced I should let him in. So was Rabbit. Although Heathcliff was the only cat for whom he showed any immediate affection, Rabbit never permitted him to take complete liberty. If Heathcliff tried to make his way into the cellar, via the private entrance, Rabbit blocked the window and warned him off with upraised paws. Sometimes Heathcliff managed to slip by and Rabbit pursued him around the barrels and packing-cases and expelled him before he had a chance to discover the way upstairs. Elsewhere, Rabbit defended his property by methods not always in the best traditions of sportsmanship.

The roof of the tool-shed near the house made an excellent watch-tower and Rabbit customarily sunned himself there at certain times of day. He had discovered a means of climbing to the roof, taking a paw-hold on one of the narrow window-sills and carefully swinging himself over the eaves. Heathcliff decided it would be pleasant to share that spot with Rabbit, but he hadn't learned the special manoeuvres necessary to reach it. He tried to scale the wall directly. Never an agile cat, Heathcliff reminded me of a man wearing an Inverness cape, blundering up the side of a sheer cliff. He did pretty well in spite of it, and got as far as the eaves. But he hadn't mastered Rabbit's trick of swinging over and he dangled in mid-air, gripping the edge of the roof with his claws. Rabbit, watching the whole procedure, finally got up and swatted Heathcliff. The latter lost his hold and plopped to the ground. Each time he reappeared at the eaves, Rabbit pushed him off again until Heathcliff abandoned the idea.

On another occasion, Heathcliff must have been guilty of some breach of etiquette and Rabbit chased him up the maple tree. While Heathcliff paced angrily along a branch, Rabbit waited below, ready to pounce. He kept him up there until supper-time.

Aside from a few disagreements, their relations were most cordial and I thought I should hire Heathcliff to be Rabbit's assistant and help with the outside work. I converted the old dog house into a cat's cottage, but Heathcliff declined to use it. He did agree to live in the tool-shed. Grudgingly, for he had his mind set on something better: his goal nothing less than a position, with full honours and emoluments, in the house.

Heathcliff was always a cat for plots, intrigues and grandiose

schemes. During his first week, he exploited every possibility. He tried to make himself invisible and walk into the living-room behind Rabbit. The few times that Rabbit mewed for direct admittance instead of coming up through the cellar, Heathcliff pushed in front of him, to get first crack at the opening door. Otherwise, he simply sat on the porch and yelled.

His admittance, despite his careful planning, came about by accident. Late one night, a frantic chirping woke me up. From the window I could see a vague shape flitting around the mulberry trees. The noise was so desperate that I ran outside without bothering to dress. I found Heathcliff pursuing a fledgling robin. Although too young to fly efficiently, the little bird was giving the cat a difficult time, fluttering, staying constantly on the move. Usually a young, healthy bird can fly circles around a cat. I knew in this case the odds favoured the cat, so I caught Heathcliff and picked him up. Since the tool-shed had a sizeable hole at the bottom of the door, I was sure Heathcliff would return to his unfinished business as soon as I went away. And he could escape from the cellar with no trouble. In my pyjamas, too chilly to spend any more time in thought, I carried Heathcliff into the house and locked him in the kitchen. Afterwards, I returned to the lawn, got hold of the little bird, put it on a branch of the mulberry and went back to bed.

I neglected to mention the incident to Janine and her surprise the next morning on entering the kitchen was only matched by that of Rabbit. When he came in for his breakfast, the unexpected sight of Heathcliff indoors—happily drinking a saucer of milk—floored him. Rabbit leaped immediately into a Halloween position, spat and chased the intruder into the living-room. Heathcliff took refuge under the sofa and would not be moved.

In disgust, Rabbit ate quickly and went to his office. Heathcliff stayed in or near his sanctuary for the rest of the day. That evening, as I sat reading in the living-room, Heathcliff came out and jumped on my lap, as if it had been his custom for years. I had acquired a second cat.

Two cats can live as cheaply as one, and their owner has twice as much fun. At first, I wondered what problems might arise

from keeping two complete toms under the same roof—I didn't believe in neutering cats at the time, and full males are notoriously bad-tempered at close quarters with each other. But aside from Rabbit's hasty reaction that first morning, their relationship continued, and nothing more serious than friendly scuffles ever occurred. The cats worked out their own arrangements and divided up the house and grounds like two potentates.

As if by agreement, Rabbit continued to exercise full authority over the outside; Heathcliff appropriated all indoors as his special province. After his long struggle to become a house-cat, I suppose he didn't want to risk being shut out again, and for a long time he rarely went farther than the porch.

He was particularly fond of the window-sill in my workroom. The sun shone there most of the day and he could relax in absolute idle luxury, his immense tail curled around him, watching me at work over my writing-table. He also patronized the living-room sofa and, of course, the bed.

Nothing dislodged him, once he had made up his mind, except the vacuum cleaner. Any other time, when we wanted him to move, we had to pick him up bodily and make the transfer ourselves. But the roar of the cleaner terrified him. As soon as he heard it, he bolted for cover as far as possible from the noise. Rabbit must have laughed secretly; mechanical contrivances disturbed him not at all, and he played boldly with the electric cord while Heathcliff trembled under the sofa.

Another area which held great fascination for him was the kitchen. It had taken him no time to discover that this particular spot was the source and fountain-head of all his delectable plates of meat and saucers of milk. He felt a proprietary interest in it and liked to make sure everything was being conducted as it should, that meals appeared in quantity and on time. He liked to peep into the refrigerator and risked having his head shut in by the closing door. He also climbed to the top of the stove, discontinuing the practice after he singed his tail.

At every sound of rattling dishes from the kitchen, he went immediately and stationed himself in the middle of the floor— no matter to him whether he got tripped over or had his tail stepped on. At the sight of his plate being filled, he began a kind of Indian war-dance, mewing, strutting in circles and

shaking his preposterous sideburns.

In the beginning, whenever we fed him, he gulped his food so quickly that occasionally I had to take away his dish to give him time to swallow what he had in his mouth. Rabbit was a methodical eater, very neat about keeping food on his plate, not exactly slow, but thorough; but Heathcliff ploughed into a portion of meat and gravy, tipping over the dish in his anxiety. Later, when he realized that meals were to be a permanent feature of his life, he stopped taking such a desperate view of them and ate more slowly; lingering over each mouthful, sniffing, and licking his whiskers. Rabbit, by comparison, could have eaten twice as much in the same length of time.

Heathcliff also instituted the midnight snack in our house. Previously, we fed Rabbit twice a day: milk and cat food in the morning, sometimes with the addition of a raw egg; ground horsemeat or liver at six in the evening. After Heathcliff had been living with us a short while, he began drifting into the kitchen late at night, making questioning sounds at the refrigerator. He found me an easy mark, for I always responded to his suggestions by giving him a titbit. When Rabbit discovered that things were being served at this unexpected hour, he also became an enthusiastic supporter of the third meal, and the midnight snack soon turned into a full-scale banquet. Janine and I even came to participate, eating sandwiches and drinking coffee while we waited for the cats to finish.

After the dishes had been cleared away, and the two cats assured that this was positively our last appearance in the roles of *maîtres d'hôtel*, Rabbit sauntered off to his club and Heathcliff wrapped up his tail for the night.

Their sleeping arrangements followed the plot of the comic opera in which two unsuspecting lodgers share the same room at different times. Although Rabbit had made no extended tours since Christmas and stuck more or less close to the house during the cold weather, the arrival of summer drew him irresistibly to the outside world. There were too many crickets, young mice, tree toads and other small nocturnal creatures circulating throughout the premises for a cat of his temperament to waste time in idle repose.

Heathcliff, on the other hand, must have seen enough of that

sort of thing in his past life, for he preferred to spend the nights in bed. He took up Rabbit's old stand, stretched across my feet.

My wife claims that I am a restless sleeper. I deny but cannot disprove it. I do suffer from a mild insomnia, and admit to a great deal of preliminary tossing and turning. Heathcliff accepted my habits without complaint. As I shifted from left side to right, stomach to back, drawing my feet up and down, he rode out the storm, gripping the sheets with his claws like a man hanging on a life raft. Once or twice, he would give a reproachful whimper when the going got too rough; but I always discovered him in the same spot next morning.

By dawn, the time at which Heathcliff usually began to arouse himself, Rabbit came in for a pre-breakfast nap. Rabbit jumped on to the bed, taking over the warm area left by Heathcliff, while the latter yawned, stretched, tested out his claws on the rug and washed himself leisurely. If Heathcliff decided to take a few minutes' extra snooze, Rabbit simply curled up on top of him.

Their schedules also overlapped a bit at various times throughout the day. At meals, of course. But a certain hour just before nightfall found both animals alert, unoccupied with serious business and ready for lawn sports. Without fail, Rabbit would appear at a corner of the tool-shed and give a peculiar bell-like call.

Heathcliff usually waited in the open kitchen window, perched on the sill, listening for the signal. He had overcome much of his fear of being locked out, and he answered Rabbit willingly. He leaped to the ground, warmed up with a few preliminary passes and the athletic competition began.

The programme consisted of a combination bill, including mixtures of boxing, fencing, ju-jitsu, French *savate*, and Graeco-Roman wrestling.

The styles of the two cats were noticeably different. Rabbit, a swordsman, moved quickly to the attack, thrusting out a paw or darting in for quick nips at his opponent's ears and neck. His short, glossy coat, smooth as an acrobat's tights, made him appear no more than a flash of brown and white as he turned somersaults, whirled about, or stopped short in his tracks only to race off again a moment later.

Meanwhile, Heathcliff imitated the Lion of Lucerne, reclin-

ing in a defensive posture on his side. His shaggy blue mane awry, his yellow eyes watching every pirouette, he awaited a chance to seize the dancing Rabbit in his paws. Heathcliff was a body-punching in-fighter; if Rabbit missed his timing, the blue cat enveloped him, gripping him in a fuzzy half-nelson applied from the front. Sometimes he snatched the initiative from Rabbit and went blustering after him with a great show of fireworks.

They put on such realistic performances I feared that one of them might be hurt; but they invariably came out ruffled and unwounded. As far as I could determine, the various matches ended in a draw.

They continued skirmishing until after sundown; as I watched them in the dusk, the common shrubbery turned easily to a wilder vegetation and my two friends to ghostly tigers stalking one another relentlessly through a more primitive world.

It became obvious, in the following weeks, that Heathcliff was my personal cat. I could hardly go from one room to the next without having him follow me; if I left him on the bed or napping on his window-sill and went elsewhere in the house, I would shortly hear a thump and a few moments later the big bushy cat would stalk up behind me. When I bent down to pat him, he rolled over gleefully—one of his favourite gestures of affection. Unlike Rabbit, he enjoyed being carried and let me pick him up willingly. He rested his enormous head on a spot just below my collar-bone while his tail draped over my arm like an old blue shawl.

For my part, I was always pleased to see him. My fondness for Rabbit had not diminished, but I admit it flattered me to find a cat who took such an interest in my company. With the fine weather, Rabbit's outside duties increased and most of a day would pass before we got even a momentary glimpse of him in the house. Heathcliff, however, was usually at hand whether I felt in a cat-patting mood or not. He seemed to know that sooner or later I would come around to him, and he wanted to be on the spot.

But flattery and waiting on humans are not a cat's strong suits. Even in the house Heathcliff could be as aloof as if he

were miles away. At times, perhaps to teach me not to take him for granted, he would refuse to have any dealings with me whatsoever. As I tried to stroke him, he would pull himself up indignantly and dash away as if I had tried to assassinate him. Normally, he would allow me an amount of friendly teasing, disarranging his ruff or nipping the end of his mighty tail with my fingers; in a bad temper, he gave a low growl and his upraised, unsheathed paws indicated that he was in no frame of mind for trifling. Fortunately, such occasions were rare, and afterwards he made up for them by louder purrs and still more enthusiastic rolling.

I have no idea what causes an animal to single out one person in a family, to choose irrevocably one individual as a constant companion and thoroughly exclude all others. When he had time, Rabbit shared his favours impartially; glad to see my wife and glad to see me. If purring or kneading seemed in order, he supplied enough to go around. Never shy with strangers, he treated visitors politely and sometimes could be induced to play with children.

Heathcliff stayed only by my side and he had a definite aversion to guests. Although he never ran away from them, he shook his sideburns disdainfully if anyone but myself tried to pat him. In company, he would crouch at my feet, or on my lap, blinking his yellow eyes furiously. If I happened to converse with more than usual interest, he would push hard against me, poking a little with his claws to remind me of his presence. Or else frown balefully—a terrible, vengeful scowl that actually frightened the wife of a friend of mine. As a result, he never enjoyed half the popularity of the debonair Rabbit. People who got to know him, over a period of time, came to appreciate his personality; but others frequently asked why I tolerated such a disagreeable cat.

Heathcliff's favouritism and partiality for me even made Janine criticize him on occasion. She felt, justifiably, that she had introduced me to cats and that I still hadn't emerged from the novice stage. It reasonably followed that she, if anyone, should enjoy a slight priority in Heathcliff's attentions. She certainly deserved it, for she saw to his material welfare more that I did, feeding him, changing his sand box when he demanded it, and removing the uncomfortable knots which I

was too clumsy to separate from his fur.

Heathcliff, in fact, profited by his disinterest. In trying to win him over, Janine bribed him with extra servings and special treats.

He fully realized that Janine held supreme sway over the kitchen. He asked her, not me, for his meals, shaking his head and practically pointing at his dish. If she was late in preparing his midnight snack his method of alerting her followed a lengthy pattern. Rabbit showed his desires by simply jumping to the drainboard. Heathcliff preferred a more indirect approach. First he would scratch the rug—an unfailing means of getting my wife's attention; then he would make several false starts in the direction of the kitchen. By this time, Janine was expected to follow him. If she hesitated, or stopped in the middle of the living-room, he would return, circle around her and lead off again. Sometimes, to tease him, she pretended she didn't understand what he meant. Then Heathcliff redoubled his scratching and his movements towards the kitchen became more urgent. Finally, when she relented, he led the way, dancing triumphantly in front of her.

When he finished, he lodged himself on my lap and had nothing more to do with Janine for the rest of the evening.

Despite his affection for me, Heathcliff considered I had shortcomings. He took steps to correct them, and showed the same persistence he had used in trying to enter the house. I never realized any of my habits were unreasonable, but they appeared so in Heathcliff's eyes and he never missed an opportunity to set me on the right path.

He objected, first, to my irregular schedule. At the time, I was working as a free-lance writer and also had assignments to do some translations. Since my days were my own and I could organize myself as I pleased, I kept late hours and followed a very flexible time-table. I would start some time in the evening and continue until twelve or one, getting up next morning at eight. But more often I would keep on long past my usual quitting hour, in which case I slept almost to noon. After lunch, I would begin again and spend the rest of my afternoon at my writing-table. Depending on how the work was going, everything became subject to change without notice. I might work through an entire afternoon, evening and night, eating when I felt like it and sometimes not at all. My wife had disapproved of this ever since our marriage, but it took the perseverance of Heathcliff to make me revise my habits.

To begin with, I did everything backward as far as he was concerned. In contrast to Rabbit, Heathcliff was a day-time cat. An early riser, he would breakfast as soon as he could persuade my wife to prepare it. Fortified with milk and cat food, he felt in a mood for exercise and early morning recreation. Although he never budged, no matter how much I tossed him about during the night, I was fair game whenever I slept late in the mornings. After his breakfast, he always returned to the bedroom to see what I was doing; and if I made the slightest move in my sleep, he would leap to the bed and pounce on me, grappling my feet through the covers or racing back and forth across my stomach. If I appeared determined to ignore his advances, he would reluctantly curl up with me for a while only to start again; but the shock of a large tom-cat bouncing on my chest was usually enough to awaken me for good. He kept up the practice until, in self-defence, I began working at six in the morning and starting to bed a little earlier.

Not content with this, he also disrupted my afternoons. Heathcliff was a firm believer in the afternoon nap: his time was half past three, and the place my lap. I could do little with him sprawled over my knees and he looked so comfortable that I began to think he didn't have such a bad idea. So Heathcliff and I came to take an hour off together.

Gradually, I reversed my original programme, working through the day and taking meals at normal human hours. I accomplished just as much, and made both Janine and Heathcliff considerably happier.

On one point, however, Heathcliff and I could reach no compromise: my violin. I had taken up the instrument as a hobby and means of relaxation. Like every amateur, I some-times carried my avocation to extremes, sawing and scraping until I felt more exhausted than relaxed. But I practised religiously an hour a day, starting after supper.

I can't believe the vibrations of the notes themselves hurt the cat's ears, for Rabbit never objected. But Heathcliff could not

tolerate the noise. He found the instrument personally disagreeable, and worse: a violent, active detestation which he took no pains to conceal. If he were with me when I started tuning up, he would come over, whimpering, trying to coax me to put away the fiddle by rubbing against my legs and arching his back to be patted. If this didn't work, he suggested a game. Since I practised in my workroom, Heathcliff could always find some crumpled paper to knock around. He would bring it to the middle of the floor, swat it back and forth, and cast inviting glances in my direction. Finally, when all else failed, he took direct action. Balancing himself on his hind feet, he reached up and sank his claws into my knees. The more I played, the harder he scratched, yowling and growling at the same time. I tried practising with a mute, but he liked that no better.

It did no good to turn him out of the room. Much as he hated the violin, he came to the workroom whenever he heard it, running from the kitchen, the bedroom, no matter where he happened to be at the moment. In the summer, with the windows open, he could hear the fiddle outside and would interrupt his activities on the lawn to come in and register his protests.

As usual, I surrendered to him and cut my practice sessions short. If my wife had him to thank for putting me on a respectable schedule, I'm sure the neighbours were equally gratified by his effect on my musical ambitions.

Cats make an impression on us which we fortify and elaborate with our own imaginations. It is no crime, and we love them all the more because of it. But I have never met a cat who produced such a variety of effects as Heathcliff. At first, with his shabby fur and preposterous swagger, he reminded me of Mr Micawber. Or a confidence man, a hoaxer and humbug. With his air of mystery, his long meditations on the windowsill, he turned easily into a romantic poet. I also found resemblances to a philosopher, an out-at-elbows aristocrat, or a weary old reprobate.

But, at bottom, for me he was always Heathcliff. I saw too much wildness in him, with his brooding, gypsy-like aspect,

ever to put a great deal of credence in the other roles. Although I had been reading *Wuthering Heights* when he came, and its characters were immediately in my mind, I think I would have recalled that name in any case as the only one possible.

Heathcliff turned the book topsy-turvy for me. As a joke, I would read certain portions of it to my wife, emphasizing the name whenever it appeared in the text. The effect was even more remarkable when Heathcliff himself happened to be with us.

I would find something like, '. . . *he is a dark-skinned gypsy in aspect, in dress and manners a gentleman: that is, as much a gentleman as many a country squire: rather slovenly, perhaps, yet not looking amiss with his negligence, because he has an erect and handsome figure; and rather morose'*.

Meanwhile, our own Heathcliff would blink his yellow owl's eyes as if he approved.

What began as amusement has continued in spite of me. To this day, I cannot read the passage, '*his basilisk eyes were nearly quenched . . . his lips sealed in an expression of unspeakable sadness . . .*' or, '*Mr Heathcliff, grim and saturnine'*, without thinking of my good friend.

But I do not feel it has spoiled the book. It has merely given me an unusual approach to the work of Emily Brontë.

The Cat that Walked by Himself

RUDYARD KIPLING

THIS befell and behappened and became and was, O, my Best Beloved, when the tame animals were wild. The Dog was wild, and the Horse was wild, and the Cow was wild, and the Sheep was wild, and the Pig was wild—as wild as could be—and they walked in the wet wild woods by their wild lones, but the wildest of all the wild animals was the Cat. He walked by himself, and all places were alike to him.

Of course the Man was wild too. He was dreadfully wild. He didn't even begin to be tame till he met the Woman and she did not like living in his wild ways. She picked out a nice dry cave, instead of a heap of wet leaves, to lie down in, and she strewed clean sand on the floor, and she lit a nice fire of wood at the back of the cave, and she hung a dried Wild Horse skin, tail down, across the opening of the cave, and she said: 'Wipe your feet when you come in, and now we'll keep house.'

That night, Best Beloved, they ate Wild Sheep roasted on the hot stones and flavoured with wild garlic and wild pepper, and Wild Duck stuffed with wild rice, and wild fenugreek and wild coriander, and marrowbones of Wild Oxen, and wild cherries and wild granadillas. Then the Man went to sleep in front of the fire ever so happy, but the Woman sat up, combing. She took the bone of the shoulder of mutton, the big flat blade bone, and she looked at the wonderful marks on it, and she threw more wood on the fire and she made a magic. She made the first Singing Magic in the world.

Out in the wet wild woods all the wild animals gathered together where they could see the light of the fire a long way

off, and they wondered what it meant.

Then Wild Horse stamped with his foot and said: 'O, my friends and my enemies, why have the Man and the Woman made that great light in that great cave, and what harm will it do us?'

Wild Dog lifted up his nose and smelled the smell of the roast mutton and said: 'I will go up and see and look and stay: for I think it is good. Cat, come with me.'

'Nenni,' said the Cat. 'I am the Cat who walks by himself, and all places are alike to me. I will not come.'

'Then we will never be friends again,' said Wild Dog, and he trotted off to the cave.

But when he had gone a little way, the Cat said to himself: 'All places are alike to me. Why should I not go too and see and look and come away?' So he slipped after Wild Dog softly, very softly, and hid himself where he could hear everything.

When Wild Dog reached the mouth of the cave he lifted up the dried Horse skin with his nose a little bit and sniffed the beautiful smell of the roast mutton, and the Woman heard him and laughed and said: 'Here comes the first wild thing out of the wild woods. What do you want?'

Wild Dog said: 'O, my enemy and wife of my enemy, what is this that smells so good in the wild woods?'

Then the Woman picked up a roasted mutton bone and threw it to Wild Dog and said: 'Wild thing out of the wild woods, taste and try.' Wild Dog gnawed the bone and it was more delicious than anything he had ever tasted, and he said: 'O, my enemy and wife of my enemy, give me another.'

The Woman said: 'Wild thing out of the wild woods, help my Man to hunt through the day and guard this cave at night and I will give you as many roast bones as you need.'

'Ah!' said the Cat listening, 'this is a very wise Woman, but she is not so wise as I am.'

Wild Dog crawled into the cave and laid his head on the Woman's lap and said: 'O, my friend and wife of my friend, I will help your Man to hunt through the day, and at night I will guard your cave.'

'Ah!' said the Cat listening, 'that is a very foolish Dog.' And he went back through the wet wild woods waving his tail and walking by his wild lone. But he never told anybody.

When the Man woke up he said: 'What is Wild Dog doing here?' And the Woman said: 'His name is not Wild Dog anymore, but the First Friend because he will be our friend for always and always and always. Take him with you when you go hunting.'

Next night the Woman cut great green armfuls of fresh grass from the water meadows and dried it before the fire so that it smelled like new-mown hay, and she sat at the mouth of the cave and plaited a halter out of horsehide, and she looked at the shoulder of mutton bone—at the big broad blade bone— and she made a magic. She made the second Singing Magic in the world.

Out in the wild woods all the wild animals wondered what had happened to Wild Dog, and at last Wild Horse stamped with his foot and said: 'I will go and see why Wild Dog has not returned. Cat, come with me.'

'Nenni,' said the Cat. 'I am the Cat who walks by himself, and all places are alike to me. I will not come.' But all the same he followed Wild Horse softly, very softly, and hid himself where he could hear everything.

When the Woman heard Wild Horse tripping and stumbling on his long mane she laughed and said: 'Here comes the second wild thing out of the wild woods. What do you want?'

Wild Horse said: 'O, my enemy and wife of my enemy, where is Wild Dog?'

The Woman laughed and picked up the blade bone and looked at it and said: 'Wild thing out of the wild woods, you did not come here for Wild Dog, but for the sake of this good grass.'

And Wild Horse, tripping and stumbling on his long mane, said: 'That is true, give it to me to eat.'

The Woman said: 'Wild thing out of the wild woods, bend your wild head and wear what I give you and you shall eat the wonderful grass three times a day.'

'Ah,' said the Cat listening, 'this is a clever Woman, but she is not so clever as I am.'

Wild Horse bent his wild head and the Woman slipped the plaited hide halter over it, and Wild Horse breathed on the woman's feet and said: 'O, my mistress and wife of my master,

210

I will be your servant for the sake of the wonderful grass.'

'Ah,' said the Cat listening, 'that is a very foolish Horse.' And he went back through the wet wild woods, waving his wild tail and walking by his wild lone.

When the Man and the Dog came back from hunting, the Man said: 'What is Wild Horse doing here?' And the Woman said: 'His name is not Wild Horse anymore, but the First Servant because he will carry us from place to place for always and always and always. Take him with you when you go hunting.'

Next day, holding her wild head high that her wild horns should not catch in the wild trees, Wild Cow came up to the cave, and the Cat followed and hid himself just the same as before; and everything happened just the same as before; and the Cat said the same things as before, and when Wild Cow had promised to give her milk to the Woman every day in exchange for the wonderful grass, the Cat went back through the wet wild woods walking by his lone just the same as before.

And when the Man and the Horse and the Dog came home from hunting and asked the same questions, same as before, the Woman said: 'Her name is not Wild Cow anymore, but the Giver of Good Things. She will give us the warm white milk for always and always and always, and I will take care of her while you three go hunting.'

Next day the Cat waited to see if any other wild thing would go up to the cave, but no one moved, so the Cat walked there by himself, and he saw the Woman milking the Cow, and he saw the light of the fire in the cave, and he smelled the smell of the warm white milk.

Cat said: 'O, my enemy and wife of my enemy, where did Wild Cow go?'

The Woman laughed and said: 'Wild thing out of the wild woods, go back to the woods again, for I have braided up my hair and I have put away the blade bone, and we have no more need of either friends or servants in our cave.'

Cat said: 'I am not a friend and I am not a servant. I am the Cat who walks by himself and I want to come into your cave.'

The Woman said: 'Then why did you not come with First Friend on the first night?'

Cat grew very angry and said: 'Has Wild Dog told tales of me?'

Then the Woman laughed and said: 'You are the Cat who walks by himself and all places are alike to you. You are neither a friend nor a servant. You have said it yourself. Go away and walk by yourself in all places alike.'

Then the Cat pretended to be sorry and said: 'Must I never come into the cave? Must I never sit by the warm fire? Must I never drink the warm white milk? You are very wise and very beautiful. You should not be cruel even to a Cat.'

Then the Woman said: 'I knew I was wise but I did not know I was beautiful. So I will make a bargain with you. If ever I say one word in your praise you may come into the cave.'

'And if you say two words in my praise?' said the Cat.

'I never shall,' said the Woman, 'but if I say two words you may sit by the fire in the cave.'

'And if you say three words?' said the Cat.

'I never shall,' said the Woman, 'but if I do you may drink the warm white milk three times a day for always and always and always.'

Then the Cat arched his back and said: 'Now let the curtain at the mouth of the cave, and the fire at the back of the cave, and the milk pots that stand beside the fire remember what my enemy and the wife of my enemy has said.' And he went away through the wet wild woods waving his wild tail and walking by his wild lone.

That night when the Man and the Horse and the Dog came home from hunting, the Woman did not tell them of the bargain she had made because she was afraid that they might not like it.

Cat went far and far away and hid himself in the wet wild woods by his wild lone for a long time till the Woman forgot all about him. Only the Bat—the little upside-down Bat—that hung inside the cave knew where Cat hid, and every evening he would fly to Cat with the news.

One evening the Bat said: 'There is a Baby in the cave. He is new and pink and fat and small, and the Woman is very fond of him.'

'Ah,' said the Cat listening, 'but what is the Baby fond of?'

'He is fond of things that are soft and tickle,' said the Bat.

212

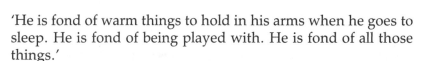

'He is fond of warm things to hold in his arms when he goes to sleep. He is fond of being played with. He is fond of all those things.'

'Ah,' said the Cat, 'then my time has come.'

Next night Cat walked through the wet wild woods and hid very near the cave till morning time. The woman was very busy cooking, and the Baby cried and interrupted; so she carried him outside the cave and gave him a handful of pebbles to play with. But still the Baby cried.

Then the Cat put out his paddy-paw and patted the Baby on the cheek, and it cooed; and the Cat rubbed against its fat knees and tickled it under its fat chin with his tail. And the Baby laughed; and the Woman heard him and smiled.

Then the Bat—the little upside-down Bat—that hung in the mouth of the cave said: 'O, my hostess and wife of my host and mother of my host, a wild thing from the wild woods is most beautifully playing with your Baby.'

'A blessing on that wild thing whoever he may be,' said the Woman straightening her back, 'for I was a busy Woman this morning and he has done me a service.'

That very minute and second, Best Beloved, the dried horse-skin curtain that was stretched tail-down at the mouth of the cave fell down—So!—because it remembered the bargain, and when the Woman went to pick it up—lo and behold!—the Cat was sitting quite comfy inside the cave.

'O, my enemy and wife of my enemy and mother of my enemy,' said the Cat, 'it is I, for you have spoken a word in my praise, and now I can sit within the cave for always and always and always. But still I am the Cat who walks by himself and all places are alike to me.'

The Woman was very angry and shut her lips tight and took up her spinning wheel and began to spin.

But the Baby cried because the Cat had gone away, and the Woman could not hush him for he struggled and kicked and grew black in the face.

'O, my enemy and wife of my enemy and mother of my enemy,' said the Cat, 'take a strand of the thread that you are spinning and tie it to your spindle wheel and drag it on the

floor and I will show you a magic that shall make your Baby laugh as loudly as he is now crying.'

'I will do so,' said the Woman, 'because I am at my wits' end, but I will not thank you for it.'

She tied the thread to the little pot spindle wheel and drew it across the floor and the Cat ran after it and patted it with his paws, and rolled head over heels, and tossed it backward over his shoulder, and chased it between his hind legs, and pretended to lose it, and pounced down upon it again till the Baby laughed as loudly as he had been crying, and scrambled after the Cat and frolicked all over the cave till he grew tired and settled down to sleep with the Cat in his arms.

'Now,' said the Cat, 'I will sing the Baby a song that shall keep him asleep for an hour.' And he began to purr loud and low, low and loud, till the Baby fell fast asleep. The Woman smiled as she looked down upon the two of them and said: 'That was wonderfully done. Surely you are very clever, O, Cat.'

That very minute and second, Best Beloved, the smoke of the fire at the back of the cave came down in clouds from the roof because it remembered the bargain, and when it had cleared away—lo and behold!—the Cat was sitting, quite comfy, close to the fire.

'O, my enemy and wife of my enemy and mother of my enemy,' said the Cat, 'it is I, for you have spoken a second word in my praise, and now I can sit by the warm fire at the back of the cave for always and always and always. But still I am the Cat who walks by himself and all places are alike to me.'

Then the Woman was very, very angry and let down her hair and put more wood on the fire and brought out the broad blade bone of the shoulder of mutton and began to make a magic that should prevent her from saying a third word in praise of the Cat. It was not a Singing Magic, Best Beloved, it was a Still Magic; and by and by the cave grew so still that a little we-wee Mouse crept out of a corner and ran across the floor.

'O, my enemy and wife of my enemy and mother of my enemy,' said the Cat, 'is that little Mouse part of your magic?'

'No,' said the Woman, and she dropped the blade bone and jumped upon a footstool in front of the fire and braided up her hair very quick for fear that the Mouse should run up it.

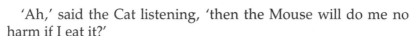

'Ah,' said the Cat listening, 'then the Mouse will do me no harm if I eat it?'

'No,' said the Woman, braiding up her hair, 'eat it quick and I will always be grateful to you.'

Cat made one jump and caught the little Mouse, and the Woman said: 'A hundred thanks to you, O, Cat. Even the First Friend is not quick enough to catch little Mice as you have done. You must be very wise.'

That very moment and second, O, Best Beloved, the milk pot that stood by the fire cracked in two pieces—So!—because it remembered the bargain, and when the Woman jumped down from the footstool—lo and behold!—the Cat was lapping up the warm white milk that lay in one of the broken pieces.

'O, my enemy and wife of my enemy and mother of my enemy,' said the Cat, 'it is I, for you have spoken three words in my praise, and now I can drink the warm white milk three times a day for always and always and always. But *still* I am the Cat who walks by himself and all places are alike to me.'

Then the Woman laughed and set him a bowl of the warm white milk and said: 'O, Cat, you are as clever as a Man, but remember that the bargain was not made with the Man or the Dog, and I do not know what they will do when they come home.'

'What is that to me?' said the Cat. 'If I have my place by the fire and my milk three times a day I do not care what the Man or the Dog can do.'

That evening when the Man and the Dog came into the cave the Woman told them all the story of the bargain, and the Man said: 'Yes, but he has not made a bargain with me or with all proper Men after me.' And he took off his two leather boots and he took up his little stone ax (that makes three) and he fetched a piece of wood and a hatchet (that is five altogether), and he set them out in a row and he said: 'Now we will make a bargain. If you do not catch Mice when you are in the cave, for always and always and always, I will throw these five things at you whenever I see you, and so shall all proper Men do after me.'

'Ah,' said the Woman listening. 'This is a very clever Cat, but he is not so clever as my Man.'

The Cat counted the five things (and they looked very knobby) and he said: 'I will catch Mice when I am in the cave for always and always and always: but still I am the Cat that walks by himself and all places are alike to me.'

'Not when I am near,' said the Man. 'If you had not said that I would have put all these things away (for always and always and always), but now I am going to throw my two boots and my little stone ax (that makes three) at you whenever I meet you, and so shall all proper Men do after me.'

Then the Dog said: 'Wait a minute. He has not made a bargain with me.' And he sat down and growled dreadfully and showed all his teeth and said: 'If you are not kind to the Baby while I am in the cave for always and always and always I will chase you till I catch you, and when I catch you I will bite you, and so shall all proper Dogs do after me.'

'Ah,' said the Woman listening. 'This is a very clever Cat, but he is not so clever as the Dog.'

Cat counted the Dog's teeth (and they looked very pointed) and he said: 'I will be kind to the Baby while I am in the cave as long as he does not pull my tail too hard for always and always and always. But still I am the Cat that walks by himself and all places are alike to me.'

'Not when I am near,' said the Dog. 'If you had not said that I would have shut my mouth for always and always and always, but now I am going to chase you up a tree whenever I meet you, and so shall all proper Dogs do after me.'

Then the Man threw his two boots and his little stone ax (that makes three) at the Cat, and the Cat ran out of the cave and the Dog chased him up a tree, and from that day to this, Best Beloved, three proper Men out of five will always throw things at a Cat whenever they meet him, and all proper Dogs will chase him up a tree. But the Cat keeps his side of the bargain too. He will kill Mice and he will be kind to Babies when he is in the house, as long as they do not pull his tail too hard. But when he has done that, and between times, he is the Cat that walks by himself and all places are alike to him, and if you look out at nights you can see him waving his wild tail and walking by his wild lone—just the same as before.

A Ship of Solace

ELEANOR MORDAUNT

THE cat stands alone, distinct—out-individualizing every individual. 'Let us agree with the world in general that a cat has nine lives,' pursued Charlotte; 'and that this cat has nine different individualities to its nine different lives—that makes fourteen people on board this ship that really count, the cat being half.'

When Charlotte talks in that way she reminds me of Plato—of course, she is not so deep, but she is just as mystifying and convincing. 'For instance, when a man, by feeling, hearing, or perceiving a thing by any of the senses, knows what it is that thus strikes the senses, and at the same time imagines to himself another thing (independent of that knowledge, by virtue of a quite different knowledge), do we not justly say that the man remembers the thing that comes into his mind?' Charlotte has heard that cats have nine lives; she feels that there can be no individuality without life; she perceives that the ship's cat has individuality to a striking degree, and (independent of that knowledge, by virtue of a quite different knowledge—namely, a woman's genius for jumping at conclusions) argues that the cat is fully the equal of the nine other individuals on board this ship. The line of argument is distinctly Charlotte, notwithstanding that the sentences between the inverted commas are to be found in the 'Phaedo'.

And yet, after all, even without the wisdom of the ages to support her line of argument, she is right. There are many men—of sorts—on board, but there is only one cat, and *such* a cat! She is always spoken of as 'he', in spite of the fact that on the return voyage last trip she brought in the world a family of kittens, during a most unholy gale off Cape Horn; though the Captain tells me that she treated them with the barest toleration, 'being such an arrant scoundrel, such a hard case, that he is a deal more like a boy than a girl'.

But the ship's cat is not only more like a 'he' than a 'she', it has also more of the characteristics of a dog than any cat I ever met before, the chief of them being its unswerving and undivided devotion to the Captain; and that in spite of being teased and tormented, and, worst of all, laughed at, in a way that would alienate most cats' affections for ever.

We—that is, the cat and the Captain—keep cocks and hens on board, which during the fine weather parade the decks in the most exasperatingly consequential manner. Still, they are popularly supposed to be held within certain bounds, these bounds being the delight of the cat. Let the Lord of the Harem lead his train of wives up on to the poop-deck and he pays dearly for his temerity. 'Boy' does not at once take matters into his own hands, but if the Captain is below will deliberately walk down the companion and into his cabin, stare him in the face for a moment, and then make his exit, walking backwards, and with weird emphatic mews entreating him to come and witness the scandal that is disgracing 'their' ship. Even then he awaits orders, at the side of his master, up on the poop-deck, the whole of his muscular little body, with its precise tiger-like markings, tense and rigid, the pupils of his clear green eyes contracted to mere pin-points by the intensity of his feelings as he watches, not the intruders, but the eye of his god. Then suddenly, without a word, some electric current seems to pass between them, his back arches, he crouches a little, ready for a spring, so ready that he is off, like a bolt from a tightly strung catapult, almost before the words 'At 'em, Boy!' are out of the Captain's mouth.

For a moment the cock may face him—feathers ruffled, beak agape, wings spread—but it is only for the moment, during which his hysterical female belongings are scattering, Boy's one care being that they shall not go over the rail. Then comes their lord's turn, and he is harried on all sides, the furred fury that attacks him appearing a mere blurred mist of many cats, so swiftly does he circle and leap and dart, scratch and spit. The cock's wings are spread as a protection, no longer in defiance, his erstwhile brilliant and erect comb becomes pale and flaccid, his curving tail feathers, that but a moment before would not have disgraced a Field-Marshal's hat, trail on the deck. With ducking head he runs to and fro, then suddenly throws all pretence of dignity to the winds, flings out his long ungainly legs and hurtles over the break of the poop after his departing fair, who are fleeing to their own quarters in the midships, with their tails blown over their heads like inverted crinolines.

To see Boy play ball with a piece of cork is a truly wonderful study in curves and intensest vitality. He crouches just about three yards from his master, the pupils of his eyes expanded till they look like black wells, with the merest rim of green, his tail beating the deck with a regular circular movement.

'Ready, Boy!' cries the Captain, and he stiffens himself with a joyous quiver which runs through the whole of the lithe little body, in which every atom of life is gathered for the spring; it is for the time a matter of life and death, and his whole being is aflame with ardour; there is he himself, and the cork, and, incidentally, the man who throws—nothing else, and no one else in the whole of the wide world.

'Now!' The cork is flung and Boy springs, stretched to his full length, then gathered to a ball in mid air, with front paws upraised like a cricketer's hands, full a yard from the deck, catches the cork between his white-stockinged feet, and rolls on the deck, kicking at it in a perfect transport of delight with his hind-feet.

But if he misses? Ah, that is another matter. Supposing we are too well-mannered to laugh, he simply appears oblivious of the bauble having been thrown at all, but walks the deck a little, goes up to it in a leisurely fashion, sniffs as if to say, 'What in the world can this be?' looks at his master—'a game, eh?' and finally picking it up, deposits it at his feet, asking, as an obviously new idea, that it shall be thrown. But if anyone, other than his master, has laughed, the game is over for the day, and off goes his Highness in a fit of sulks, which is, in its intensity, another sign of how great a mistake his real sex has been, for women seldom sulk: they usually have too much to say on any matter which annoys them.

At such times as this he delights in getting into the most dangerous positions, on the taffrail, or up on the boats, with

219

the air of one who says to himself: 'I'll give them a good fright for once, and they'll be sorry for this levity, then they'll wish they hadn't.'

'Come down out of that!' shouts the Captain. But Boy merely cocks an eye at him and does not budge an inch, till his master stoops for a coil of rope, when he is off like a flash to a safer position, for he knows quite well that he is not allowed in certain places, even though the ship is, so to speak, his own.

When a sheep has been killed the fresh meat is hung just below the boats on the main-deck, and draws Boy like a magnet, though nothing on earth would tempt him to help himself. But if we are all on the poop-deck, including him, of course, for he hates solitude, and the Captain so much as takes his knife out of his pocket, he mews wildly and trembles all over with excitement. There is an example of self-control! He wants it terribly; so terribly that he is almost mad with excitement at the prospect of even the merest morsel. He could help himself easily any hour of the day or night; yet he never does so. Now, tell me, is morality a matter of the soul, which is allowed to the inveterate drunkard, the irreclaimable thief, and is yet denied to Boy? In the saloon it is the same: the Captain has only to pick up his cap and the cat is rubbing himself against his legs mewing, 'Meat, meat, meat—meat—*please*, dear.'

Yet it is not merely cupboard love, for however warm the saloon fire, however wet the deck, however rainy and stormy the weather, if the Captain is up on deck, there the cat must be also. Sometimes his courage will half fail him, and he will wait to see if his idol has not merely gone up to take a look at the weather and then return again; but he cannot rest, and after a moment or so of anxious watching he throws comfort to the winds and is off, not to return to the warmth and light till his master returns too. A few nights ago he was caught by a heavy sea and washed backwards and forwards over the deck, hopelessly, helplessly, till he was secured by the mate and brought to the saloon, a dejected wisp of misery, to be washed in fresh water and dried by the fire. But even then he could not rest; his eyes, as he lay on my lap, were for ever on the door, and he was off again before he was one-half dry.

It is not even as though he has an easy time with his idol, for he is always getting his tail and ears pulled, and his little toes pinched, though he but seldom retaliates with claw or tooth, while if he does he is so bitterly ashamed of himself that it is really heart-breaking to see his utter dejection.

When first we came on board, Boy regarded us with the utmost suspicion; perhaps we reminded him of his own sex, or perhaps it was sheer dislike of petticoats fluttering aboard *his* ship. But since that first night, when Charlotte was so ill, all this has changed. While the Captain made poultices, Boy was constantly in and out, clambering on to the bunk, and clamouring strenuously for notice and explanations, for puss is feminine enough in this—he will know the why and wherefore of everything. And now, having found that we are tolerated, to say the least of it, by his master, he tolerates us too, and will make himself quite at home on my knee, occasionally even placing two soft little front-paws on my chest, and inviting me amicably to rub noses. But this is only when he cannot sit on his master's knee, which he infinitely prefers, uncomfortable as it always looks, and must be, with no nice warm spread of dress for him to repose on.

Particularly Cats

DORIS LESSING

I CAME to live in a house in cat country. The houses are old and they have narrow gardens with walls. Through our back windows show a dozen walls one way, a dozen walls the other, of all sizes and levels. Trees, grass, bushes. There is a little theatre that has roofs at various heights. Cats thrive here. There are always cats on the walls, roofs, and in the gardens, living a complicated secret life, like the neighbourhood lives of children that go on according to unimagined private rules the grown-ups never guess at.

I knew there would be a cat in the house. Just as one knows, if a house is too large people will come and live in it, so certain houses must have cats. But for a while I repelled the various cats that came sniffing around to see what sort of a place it was.

During the whole of that dreadful winter of 1962, the garden and the roof over the back verandah were visited by an old black-and-white tom. He sat in the slushy snow on the roof; he prowled over the frozen ground; when the back door was briefly opened, he sat just outside, looking into the warmth. He was most unbeautiful, with a white patch over one eye, a torn ear, and a jaw always a little open and drooling. But he was not a stray. He had a good home in the street, and why he didn't stay there, no one seemed able to say.

That winter was further education into the extraordinary voluntary endurances of the English.

These houses are mostly L.C.C. owned, and by the first week of the cold, the pipes had burst and frozen, and people were waterless. The system stayed frozen. The authorities opened a main on the street corner, and for weeks the women of the street made journeys to fetch water in jugs and cans along pavements heaped with feet of icy slush, in their house slippers. The slippers were for warmth. The slush and ice were not cleared off the pavement. They drew water from the tap, which broke down several times, and said there had been no hot water but what they boiled on the stove for one week, two weeks—then three, four and five weeks. There was, of course, no hot water for baths. When asked why they didn't complain, since after all they paid rent, they paid for water hot and cold, they replied the L.C.C. knew about their pipes, but did not do anything. The L.C.C. had pointed out there was a cold spell; they agreed with this diagnosis. Their voices were lugubrious, but they were deeply fulfilled, as this nation is when suffering entirely avoidable acts of God.

In the shop at the corner an old man, a middle-aged woman and a small child spent the days of that winter. The shop was chilled colder even than the below-zero weather nature was ordaining, by the refrigeration units; the door was always open into the iced snowdrifts outside the shop. There was no heating at all. The old man got pleurisy and went to hospital for two months. Permanently weakened, he had to sell the shop that spring. The child sat on the cement floor and cried steadily from the cold, and was slapped by its mother who stood behind the counter in a light wool dress, man's socks and a thin cardigan, saying how awful it all was, while her eyes and nose ran and her fingers swelled into chilblains. The old man next door who works as a market porter slipped on the ice outside his front door, hurt his back, and was for weeks on unemploy- ment pay. In that house, which held nine or ten people, including two children, there was one bar of electric fire to fight the cold. Three people went to hospital, one with pneumonia.

And the pipes stayed burst, sealed in jagged stalactites of ice; the pavements remained ice slides; and the authorities did nothing. In middle-class streets, of course, snow was cleared as it fell, and the authorities responded to angry citizens demanding their rights and threatening lawsuits. In our area, people suffered it out until the spring.

Surrounded by human beings as winterbound as if they were cave dwellers of ten thousand years ago, the peculiarities of an

223

old tomcat who chose an icy roof to spend its nights on lost their force.

In the middle of that winter, friends were offered a kitten. Friends of theirs had a Siamese cat, and she had a litter by a street cat. The hybrid kittens were being given away. Their flat is minute, and they both worked all day; but when they saw the kitten, they could not resist. During its first weekend it was fed on tinned lobster soup and chicken mousse, and it disrupted their much-married nights because it had to sleep under the chin, or at least, somewhere against the flesh, of H., the man. S., his wife, announced on the telephone that she was losing the affections of her husband to a cat, just like the wife in Colette's tale. On Monday they went off to work leaving the kitten by itself, and when they came home it was crying and sad, having been alone all day. They said they were bringing it to us. They did.

The kitten was six weeks old. It was enchanting, a delicate fairy-tale cat, whose Siamese genes showed in the shape of the face, ears, tail, and the subtle lines of its body. Her back was tabby: from above or the back, she was a pretty tabby kitten, in grey and cream. But her front and stomach were a smoky-gold, Siamese cream, with half-bars of black at the neck. Her face was pencilled with black—fine dark rings around the eyes, fine dark streaks on her cheeks, a tiny cream-coloured nose with a pink tip, outlined in black. From the front, sitting with her slender paws straight, she was an exotically beautiful beast. She sat, a tiny thing, in the middle of a yellow carpet, surrounded by five worshippers, not at all afraid of us. Then she stalked around that floor of the house, inspecting every inch of it, climbed up on to my bed, crept under the fold of a sheet, and was at home.

S. went off with H. saying: Not a moment too soon, otherwise I wouldn't have a husband at all.

And he went off groaning, saying that nothing could be as exquisite as being woken by the delicate touch of a pink tongue on his face.

The kitten went, or rather hopped, down the stairs, each of which was twice her height: first front paws, then flop, with the back; front paws, then flop with the back. She inspected the ground floor, refused the tinned food offered to her, and demanded a dirt box by mewing for it. She rejected wood shavings, but torn newspaper was acceptable, so her fastidious pose said, if there was nothing else. There wasn't: the earth outside was frozen solid.

She would not eat tinned cat food. She would not. And I was not going to feed her lobster soup and chicken. We compromised on some minced beef.

She has always been as fussy over her food as a bachelor gourmet. She gets worse as she gets older. Even as a kitten she could express annoyance, or pleasure, or a determination to sulk, by what she ate, half-ate, or chose to refuse. Her food habits are an eloquent language.

But I think it is just possible she was taken away from her mother too young. If I might respectfully suggest it to the cat experts, it is possible they are wrong when they say a kitten may leave its mother the day it turns six weeks old. This cat was six weeks, not a day more, when it was taken from its mother. The basis of her dandyism over food is the neurotic hostility and suspicion towards it of a child with food problems. She had to eat, she supposed; she did eat; but she has never eaten with enjoyment, for the sake of eating. And she shares another characteristic with people who have not had enough mother-warmth. Even now she will instinctively creep under the fold of a newspaper, or into a box or a basket— anything that shelters, anything that covers. More; she is overready to see insult; overready to sulk. And she is a frightful coward.

Kittens who are left with their mother seven or eight weeks eat easily, and they have confidence. But of course, they are not as interesting.

As a kitten, this cat never slept on the outside of the bed. She waited until I was in it, then she walked all over me, considering possibilities. She would get right down into the bed, by my feet, or on to my shoulder, or crept under the pillow. If I moved too much, she huffily changed quarters, making her annoyance felt.

When I was making the bed, she was happy to be made into it; and stayed, visible as a tiny lump, quite happily, sometimes for hours, between the blankets. If you stroked the lump, it purred and mewed. But she would not come out until she had to.

The lump would move across the bed, hesitate at the edge. There might be a frantic mew as she slid to the floor. Dignity disturbed, she licked herself hastily, glaring yellow eyes at the viewers, who made a mistake if they laughed. Then, every hair conscious of itself, she walked to some centre stage.

Time for the fastidious pernickety eating. Time for the earth box, as exquisite a performance. Time for setting the creamy fur in order. And time for play, which never took place for its own sake, but only when she was being observed.

She was as arrogantly aware of herself as a pretty girl who has no attributes but her prettiness: body and face always posed according to some inner monitor—a pose which is as good as a mask: no, no, *this* is what I am, the aggressive breasts, the sullen hostile eyes always on the watch for admiration.

Cat, at the age when, if she were human, she would be wearing clothes and hair like weapons, but confident that any time she chose she might relapse into indulged childhood again, because the role had become too much of a burden—cat posed and princessed and preened about the house and then, tired, a little peevish, tucked herself into the fold of a newspaper or behind a cushion, and watched the world safely from there.

Her prettiest trick, used mostly for company, was to lie on her back under a sofa and pull herself along by her paws, in fast sharp rushes, stopping to turn her elegant little head sideways, yellow eyes narrowed, waiting for applause. 'Oh beautiful kitten! Delicious beast! Pretty cat!' Then on she went for another display.

Or, on the right surface, the yellow carpet, a blue cushion, she lay on her back and slowly rolled, paws tucked up, head back, so that her creamy chest and stomach were exposed, marked faintly, as if she were a delicate subspecies of leopard, with black blotches, like the roses of leopards. 'Oh beautiful kitten, oh you are so beautiful.' And she was prepared to go on until the compliments stopped.

Or she sat on the back verandah, not on the table, which was unadorned, but on a little stand that had narcissus and hyacinth in earthenware pots. She sat posed between spikes of blue and white flowers, until she was noticed and admired.

Not only by us, of course; also by the old rheumatic tom who prowled, grim reminder of a much harder life, around the garden where the earth was still frostbound. He saw a pretty half-grown cat, behind glass. She saw him. She lifted her head, this way, that way; bit off a fragment of hyacinth, dropped it; licked her fur, negligently; then with an insolent backwards glance, leaped down and came indoors and out of his sight. Or, on the way upstairs, on an arm or a shoulder, she would glance out of the window and see the poor old beast, so still that sometimes we thought he must have died and been frozen there. When the sun warmed a little at midday and he sat licking himself, we were relieved. Sometimes she sat watching him from the window, but her life was still to be tucked into the arms, beds, cushions, and corners of human beings.

Then the spring came, the back door was opened, the dirt box, thank goodness, made unnecessary, and the back garden became her territory. She was six months old, fully grown, from the point of view of nature.

She was so pretty then, so perfect; more beautiful even than that cat who, all those years ago, I swore could never have an equal. Well of course there hasn't been; for that cat's nature was all tact, delicacy, warmth and grace—so, as the fairy tales and the old wives say, she had to die young.

Our cat, the princess, was, still is, beautiful, but, there is no glossing it, she's a selfish beast.

The cats lined up on the garden walls. First, the sombre old winter cat, king of the back gardens. Then, a handsome black-and-white from next door, his son, from the look of it. A battle-scarred tabby. A grey-and-white cat who was so certain of defeat that he never came down from the wall. And a dashing tigerish young tom that she clearly admired. No use, the old king had not been defeated. When she strolled out, tail erect, apparently ignoring them all, but watching the handsome young tiger, he leaped down towards her, but the winter cat had only to stir where he lay on the wall, and the young cat jumped back to safety. This went on for weeks.

Meanwhile, H. and S. came to visit their lost pet. S. said how frightful and unfair it was that the princess could not have her choice; and H. said that was entirely as it should be: a princess must have a king, even if he was old and ugly. He has such dignity,

227

said H.; he has such presence; and he had earned the pretty young cat because of his noble endurance of the long winter.

By then the ugly cat was called Mephistopheles. (In his own home, we heard, he was called Billy. Our cat had been called various names, but none of them stuck. Melissa and Franny; Marilyn and Sappho; Circe and Ayesha and Suzette. But in conversation, in love-talk, she miaowed and purred and throated in response to the long-drawn-out syllables of adjectives—beeeooooti-ful, delicious puss.

On a very hot weekend, the only one, I seem to remember, in a nasty summer, she came in heat.

H. and S. came to lunch on the Sunday, and we sat on the back verandah and watched the choices of nature. Not ours. And not our cat's, either.

For two nights the fighting had gone on, awful fights, cats wailing and howling and screaming in the garden. Meanwhile grey puss had sat on the bottom of my bed, watching into the dark, ears lifting and moving, tail commenting, just slightly at the tip.

On that Sunday, there was only Mephistopheles in sight. Grey cat was rolling in ecstasy all over the garden. She came to us and rolled around our feet and bit them. She rushed up and down the tree at the bottom of the garden. She rolled and cried, and called, and invited.

'The most disgraceful exhibition of lust I've ever seen,' said S. watching H., who was in love with our cat.

'Oh poor cat,' said H. 'If I were Mephistopheles I'd never treat you so badly.'

'Oh, H.,' said S., 'you are disgusting, if I told people they'd never believe it. But I've always said, you're disgusting.'

'So that's what you've always said,' said H., caressing the ecstatic cat.

It was a very hot day, we had a lot of wine for lunch, and the love play went on all afternoon.

Finally, Mephistopheles leaped down off the wall to where grey cat was wriggling and rolling—but alas, he bungled it.

'Oh my God,' said H., genuinely suffering. 'It is really not forgivable, that sort of thing.'

S., anguished, watched the torments of our cat, and doubted, frequently, dramatically and loudly, whether sex was worth it. 'Look at it,' said she, 'that's us. That's what we're like.'

'That's not at all what we're like,' said H. 'It's Mephistopheles. He should be shot.'

Shoot him at once, we all said; or at least lock him up so that the young tiger from next door could have his chance.

But the handsome young cat was not visible.

We went on drinking wine; the sun went on shining; our princess danced, rolled, rushed up and down the tree, and, when at last things went well, was clipped again and again by the old king.

'All that's wrong,' said H., 'is that he's too old for her.'

'Oh my God,' said S., 'I'm going to take you home. Because if I don't, I swear you'll make love to that cat yourself.'

'Oh I wish I could,' said H. 'What an exquisite beast, what a lovely creature, what a princess, she's wasted on a cat, I can't stand it.'

Next day winter returned; the garden was cold and wet; and grey cat had returned to her fastidious disdainful ways. And the old king lay on the garden wall in the slow English rain, still victor of them all, waiting.

The White and Black Dynasties

THÉOPHILE GAUTIER

A CAT brought from Havana by Mademoiselle Aïta de la Penuela, a young Spanish artist whose studies of white angoras may still be seen gracing the printsellers' windows, produced the daintiest little kitten imaginable. It was just like a swan's-down powder-puff, and on account of its immaculate whiteness it received the name of Pierrot. When it grew big this was lengthened to Don Pierrot de Navarre as being more grandiose and majestic.

Don Pierrot, like all animals which are spoilt and made much of, developed a charming amiability of character. He shared the life of the household with all the pleasure which cats find in the intimacy of the domestic hearth. Seated in his usual place near the fire, he really appeared to understand what was being said, and to take an interest in it.

His eyes followed the speakers, and from time to time he would utter little sounds, as though he too wanted to make remarks and give his opinion on literature, which was our usual topic of conversation. He was very fond of books, and when he found one open on a table he would lie on it, look at the page attentively, and turn over the leaves with his paw; then he would end by going to sleep, for all the world as if he were reading a fashionable novel.

Directly I took up a pen he would jump on my writing-desk and with deep attention watch the steel nib tracing black spider-legs on the expanse of white paper, and his head would turn each time I began a new line. Sometimes he tried to take part in the work, and would attempt to pull the pen out of my hand, no doubt in order to write himself, for he was an aesthetic cat, like Hoffman's Murr, and I strongly suspect him of having scribbled his memoirs at night on some house-top by the light of his phosphorescent eyes. Unfortunately these lucubrations have been lost.

Don Pierrot never went to bed until I came in. He waited for me inside the door, and as I entered the hall he would rub himself against my legs and arch his back, purring joyfully all the time. Then he proceeded to walk in front of me like a page, and if I had asked him, he would certainly have carried the candle for me. In this fashion he escorted me to my room and waited while I undressed; then he would jump on the bed, put his paws round my neck, rub noses with me, and lick me with his rasping little pink tongue, while giving vent to soft inarticulate cries, which clearly expressed how pleased he was to see me again. Then when his transports of affection had subsided, and the hour for repose had come, he would balance himself on the rail of the bedstead and sleep there like a bird perched on a bough. When I woke in the morning he would come and lie near me until it was time to get up. Twelve o'clock was the hour at which I was supposed to come in. On this subject Pierrot had all the notions of a concierge.

At that time we had instituted little evening gatherings among a few friends, and had formed a small society, which we called the Four Candles Club, the room in which we met being, as it happened, lit by four candles in silver candlesticks, which were placed at the corners of the table.

Sometimes the conversation became so lively that I forgot the time, at the risk of finding, like Cinderella, my carriage turned into a pumpkin and my coachman into a rat.

Pierrot waited for me several times until two o'clock in the morning, but in the end my conduct displeased him, and he went to bed without me. This mute protest against my innocent dissipation touched me so much that ever after I came home regularly at midnight. But it was a long time before Pierrot forgave me. He wanted to be sure that it was not a sham repentance; but when he was convinced of the sincerity of my conversion, he deigned to take me into favour again, and he resumed his nightly post in the entrance-hall.

To gain the friendship of a cat is not an easy thing. It is a philosophic, well-regulated, tranquil animal, a creature of habit

and a lover of order and cleanliness. It does not give its affections indiscriminately. It will consent to be your friend if you are worthy of the honour, but it will not be your slave. With all its affection, it preserves its freedom of judgement, and it will not do anything for you which it considers unreasonable; but once it has given its love, what absolute confidence, what fidelity of affection! It will make itself the companion of your hours of work, of loneliness, or of sadness. It will lie the whole evening on your knee, purring and happy in your society, and leaving the company of creatures of its own kind to be with you. In vain the sound of caterwauling reverberates from the house-tops, inviting it to one of those cats' evening parties where essence of red-herring takes the place of tea. It will not be tempted, but continues to keep its vigil with you. If you put it down it climbs up again quickly, with a sort of crooning noise, which is like a gentle reproach. Sometimes, when seated in front of you, it gazes at you with such soft, melting eyes, such a human and caressing look, that you are almost awed, for it seems impossible that reason can be absent from it.

Don Pierrot had a companion of the same race as himself, and no less white. All the imaginable snowy comparisons it were possible to pile up would not suffice to give an idea of that immaculate fur, which would have made ermine look yellow.

I called her Seraphita, in memory of Balzac's Swedenborgian romance. The heroine of that wonderful story, when she climbed the snow peaks of the Falberg with Minna, never shone with a more pure white radiance. Seraphita had a dreamy and pensive character. She would lie motionless on a cushion for hours, not asleep, but with eyes fixed in rapt attention on scenes invisible to ordinary mortals.

Caresses were agreeable to her, but she responded to them with great reserve, and only to those of people whom she favoured with her esteem, which it was not easy to gain. She liked luxury, and it was always in the newest armchair or on the piece of furniture best calculated to show off her swan-like beauty, that she was to be found. Her toilette took an immense time. She would carefully smooth her entire coat every morning, and wash her face with her paw, and every hair on her body shone like new silver when brushed by her pink

tongue. If anyone touched her she would immediately efface all traces of the contact, for she could not endure being ruffled. Her elegance and distinction gave one an idea of aristocratic birth, and among her own kind she must have been at least a duchess. She had a passion for scents. She would plunge her nose into bouquets, and nibble a perfumed handkerchief with little paroxysms of delight. She would walk about on the dressing-table sniffling the stoppers of the scent-bottles, and she would have loved to use the violet powder if she had been allowed.

Such was Seraphita, and never was a cat more worthy of a poetic name.

Don Pierrot de Navarre, being a native of Havana, needed a hot-house temperature. This he found indoors, but the house was surrounded by large gardens, divided up by palings through which a cat could easily slip, and planted with big trees in which hosts of birds twittered and sang; and some-times Pierrot, taking advantage of an open door, would go out hunting of an evening and run over the dewy grass and flowers. He would then have to wait till morning to be let in again, for although he might come mewing under the windows, his appeal did not always wake the sleepers inside.

He had a delicate chest, and one colder night than usual he took a chill which soon developed into consumption. Poor Pierrot, after a year of coughing, became wasted and thin, and his coat, which formerly boasted such a snowy gloss, now put one in mind of the lustreless white of a shroud. His great limpid eyes looked enormous in his attenuated face. His pink nose had grown pale, and he would walk sadly along the sunny wall with slow steps, and watch the yellow autumn leaves whirling up in spirals. He looked as though he were reciting Millevoye's elegy.

There is nothing more touching than a sick animal; it submits to suffering with such gentle, pathetic resignation.

Everything possible was done to try and save Pierrot. He had a very clever doctor who sounded him and felt his pulse. He ordered him asses' milk, which the poor creature drank will-ingly enough out of his little china saucer. He lay for hours on my knee like the ghost of a sphinx, and I could feel the bones of

his spine like the beads of a rosary under my fingers. He tried to respond to my caresses with a feeble purr which was like a death rattle.

When he was dying he lay panting on his side, but with a supreme effort he raised himself and came to me with dilated eyes in which there was a look of intense supplication. This look seemed to say: 'Cannot you save me, you who are a man?' Then he staggered a short way with eyes already glazing, and fell down with such a lamentable cry, so full of despair and anguish, that I was pierced with silent horror.

He was buried at the bottom of the garden under a white rosebush which still marks his grave.

Seraphita died two or three years later of diphtheria, against which no science could prevail.

She rests not far from Pierrot. With her the white dynasty became extinct, but not the family. To this snow-white pair were born three kittens as black as ink.

Let him explain this mystery who can.

Just at that time Victor Hugo's *Misérables* was in great vogue, and the names of the characters in the novel were on everyone's lips. I called the two male kittens Enjolras and Gavroche, while the little female received the name of Eponine.

They were perfectly charming in their youth. I trained them like dogs to fetch and carry a bit of paper crumpled into a ball, which I threw for them. In time they learnt to fetch it from the tops of cupboards, from behind chests or from the bottom of tall vases, out of which they would pull it very cleverly with their paws. When they grew up they disdained such frivolous games, and acquired that calm philosophic temperament which is the true nature of cats.

To people landing in America in a slave colony all negroes are negroes, and indistinguishable from one another. In the same way, to careless eyes, three black cats are three black cats; but attentive observers make no such mistake. Animal physiognomy varies as much as that of men, and I could distinguish perfectly between those faces, all three as black as Harlequin's mask, and illuminated by emerald disks shot with gold.

Enjolras was by far the handsomest of the three. He was remarkable for his great leonine head and big ruff, his powerful shoulders, long back and splendid feathery tail. There was something theatrical about him, and he seemed to be always posing like a popular actor who knows he is being admired. His movements were slow, undulating and majestic. He put each foot down with as much circumspection as if he were walking on a table covered with Chinese bric-à-brac or Venetian glass. As to his character, he was by no means a stoic, and he showed a love of eating which that virtuous and sober young man, his namesake, would certainly have disapproved. Enjolras would undoubtedly have said to him, like the angel to Swedenborg: 'You eat too much.'

I humoured this gluttony, which was as amusing as a gastronomic monkey's, and Enjolras attained a size and weight seldom reached by the domestic cat. It occurred to me to have him shaved poodle-fashion, so as to give the finishing touch to his resemblance to a lion.

We left him his mane and a big tuft at the end of his tail, and I would not swear that we did not give him mutton-chop whiskers on his haunches like those Munito wore. Thus tricked out, it must be confessed he was much more like a Japanese monster than an African lion. Never was a more fantastic whim carved out of a living animal. His shaven skin took odd blue tints, which contrasted strangely with his black mane.

Gavroche, as though desirous of calling to mind his namesake in the novel, was a cat with an arch and crafty expression of countenance. He was smaller than Enjolras, and his movements were comically quick and brusque. In him absurd capers and ludicrous postures took the place of the banter and slang of the Parisian gamin. It must be confessed that Gavroche had vulgar tastes. He seized every possible occasion to leave the drawing-room in order to go and make up parties in the backyard, or even in the street, with stray cats,

'De naissance quelconque et de sang peu prouvé,'

in which doubtful company he completely forgot his dignity as cat of Havana, son of Don Pierrot de Navarre, grandee of Spain of the first order, and of the aristocratic and haughty Doña Seraphita.

Sometimes in his truant wanderings he picked up emaciated comrades, lean with hunger, and brought them to his plate of

food to give them a treat in his good-natured, lordly way. The poor creatures, with ears laid back and watchful side-glances, in fear of being interrupted in their free meal by the broom of the housemaid, swallowed double, triple, and quadruple mouthfuls, and, like the famous dog Siete-Aguas (seven waters) of Spanish *posadas* (inns), they licked the plate as clean as if it had been washed and polished by one of Gerard Dow's or Mieris's Dutch housewives.

Seeing Gavroche's friends reminded me of a phrase which illustrates one of Gavarni's drawings, 'Ils sont jolis les amis dont vous êtes susceptible d'aller avec!' ('Pretty kind of friends you like to associate with!')

But that only proved what a good heart Gavroche had, for he could easily have eaten all the food himself.

The cat named after the interesting Eponine was more delicate and slender than her brothers. Her nose was rather long, and her eyes slightly oblique, and green as those of Pallas Athene, to whom Homer always applied the epithet of γλαυκῶπις. Her nose was of velvety black, with the grain of a fine Périgord truffle; her whiskers were in a perpetual state of agitation, all of which gave her a peculiarly expressive countenance. Her superb black coat was always in motion, and was watered and shot with shadowy markings. Never was there a more sensitive, nervous, electric animal. If one stroked her two or three times in the dark, blue sparks would fly crackling out of her fur.

Eponine attached herself particularly to me, like the Eponine of the novel to Marius, but I, being less taken up with Cosette than that handsome young man, could accept the affection of this gentle and devoted cat, who still shares the pleasures of my suburban retreat and is the inseparable companion of my hours of work.

She comes running up when she hears the front-door bell, receives the visitors, conducts them to the drawing-room, talks to them—yes, talks to them—with little chirruping sounds, that do not in the least resemble the language cats use in talking to their own kind, but which simulate the articulate speech of man. What does she say? She says in the clearest way, 'Will you be good enough to wait till monsieur comes down? Please look at the pictures, or chat with me in the meantime, if that will amuse you.' Then when I come in she discreetly retires to an armchair or a corner of the piano, like a well-bred animal who knows what is correct in good society. Pretty little Eponine gave so many proofs of intelligence, good disposition and sociability, that by common consent she was raised to the dignity of a *person*, for it was quite evident that she was possessed of higher reasoning power than mere instinct. This dignity conferred on her the privilege of eating at table like a person instead of out of a saucer in a corner of the room like an animal.

So Eponine had a chair next to me at breakfast and dinner, but on account of her small size she was allowed to rest her two front paws on the edge of the table. Her place was laid, without spoon or fork, but she had her glass. She went right through dinner dish by dish, from soup to dessert, waiting for her turn to be helped, and behaving with such propriety and nice manners as one would like to see in many children. She made her appearance at the first sound of the bell, and on going into the dining-room one found her already in her place, sitting up in her chair with her paws resting on the edge of the tablecloth, and seeming to offer you her little face to kiss, like a well-brought-up little girl who is affectionately polite towards her parents and elders.

As one finds flaws in diamonds, spots on the sun, and shadows on perfection itself, so Eponine, it must be confessed, had a passion for fish. She shared this in common with all other cats. Contrary to the Latin proverb,

'Catus amat pisces, sed non vult tingere plantas,'

she would willingly have dipped her paw into the water if by so doing she could have pulled out a trout or a young carp. She became nearly frantic over fish, and, like a child who is filled with the expectation of dessert, she sometimes rebelled at her soup when she knew (from previous investigations in the kitchen) that fish was coming. When this happened she was not helped, and I would say to her coldly: 'Mademoiselle, a person who is not hungry for soup cannot be hungry for fish,' and the dish would be pitilessly carried away from under her nose. Convinced that matters were serious, greedy Eponine would swallow her soup in all haste, down to the last drop,

polishing off the last crumb of bread or bit of macaroni, and would then turn round and look at me with pride, like someone who has conscientiously done his duty. She was then given her portion, which she consumed with great satisfaction, and after tasting of every dish in turn, she would finish up by drinking a third of a glass of water.

When I am expecting friends to dinner Eponine knows there is going to be a party before she sees the guests. She looks at her place, and if she sees a knife and fork by her plate she decamps at once and seats herself on a music-stool, which is her refuge on these occasions.

Let those who deny reasoning powers to animals explain if they can this little fact, apparently so simple, but which contains a whole series of inductions. From the presence near her plate of those implements which man alone can use, this observant and reflective cat concludes that she will have to give up her place for that day to a guest, and promptly proceeds to do so. She never makes a mistake; but when she knows the visitor well she climbs on his knee and tries to coax a tit-bit out of him by her pretty caressing ways.

Midshipman, The Cat

JOHN COLEMAN ADAMS

THIS is a true story about a real cat who, for aught I know, is still alive and following the sea for a living. I hope to be excused if I use the pronouns 'who' and 'he' instead of 'which' and 'it,' in speaking of this particular cat; because although I know very well that the grammars all tell us that 'he' and 'who' apply to persons, while 'it' and 'which' apply to things, yet this cat of mine always seemed to us who knew him to be so much like a human being that I find it unsatisfactory to speak of him in any other way. There are some animals of whom you prefer to say 'he,' just as there are persons whom you sometimes feel like calling 'it.'

The way we met this cat was after this fashion: It was back somewhere in the seventies, and a party of us were cruising east from Boston in the little schooner-yacht *Eyvor*. We had dropped into Marblehead for a day and a night, and some of the boys had gone ashore in the tender. As they landed on the wharf, they found a group of small boys running sticks into a woodpile, evidently on a hunt for something inside.

'What have you in there?' asked one of the yachtsmen.

'Nothin' but a cat,' said the boys.

'Well, what are you doing to him?'

'Oh, pokin' him up! When he comes out we'll rock him,' was the answer, in good Marblehead dialect.

'Well, don't do it anymore. What'a the use of tormenting a poor cat? Why don't you take somebody of your size?'

The boys slowly moved off, a little ashamed and a little afraid of the big yachtsman who spoke; and when they were well out of sight the yachtsmen went on, too, and thought no more

about the cat they had befriended. But when they had wandered about the tangled streets of the town for a little while, and
paid the visits which all good yachtsmen pay, to the grocery
and the post office and the apothecary's soda fountain, they
returned to the wharf and found their boat. And behold, there
in the stern sheets sat the little gray-and-white cat of the
woodpile! He had crawled out of his retreat and made straight
for the boat of his champions. He seemed in no wise disturbed
or disposed to move when they jumped on board, nor did he
show anything but pleasure when they stroked and patted
him. But when one of the boys started to put him ashore, the
plucky little fellow showed his claws; and no sooner was he set
on his feet at the edge of the wharf than he turned about and
jumped straight back into the boat.

'He wants to go yachting,' said one of the party, whom we
called 'the Bos'n.'

'Ye might as wal take the cat,' said a grizzly old fisherman
standing on the wharf. 'He doesn't belong to anybody, and ef
he stays here the boys'll worry him t'death.'

'Let's take him aboard,' said the yachtsmen. 'It's good luck to
have a cat on board ship.'

Whether it was good luck to the ship or not, it was very clear
that pussy saw it meant good luck to him, and curled himself
down in the bottom of the boat, with a look that meant
business. Evidently he had thought the matter all over and
made up his mind that this was the sort of people he wanted to
live with; and, being a Marblehead cat, it made no difference to
him whether they lived afloat or ashore; he was going where
they went, whether they wanted him or not. He had heard the
conversation from his place in the woodpile, and had decided
to show his gratitude by going to sea with these protectors of
his. By casting in his lot with theirs he was paying them the
highest compliment of which a cat is capable. It would have
been the height of impoliteness not to recognize his distinguished appreciation. So he was allowed to remain in the boat,
and was taken off to the yacht.

Upon his arrival there, a council was held, and it was
unanimously decided that the cat should be received as a
member of the crew; and as we were a company of amateur
sailors, sailing our own boat, each man having his particular

duties, it was decided that the cat should be appointed midshipman, and should be named after his position. So he was at once and ever after known as 'Middy.' Everybody took a great interest in him, and he took an impartial interest in everybody —though there were two people on board to whom he made himself particularly agreeable. One was the quiet, kindly professor, the captain of the *Eyvor*; the other was Charlie, our cook and only hired hand. Middy, you see, had a seaman's true instinct as to the official persons with whom it was his interest to stand well.

It was surprising to see how quickly Middy made himself at home. He acted as if he had always been at sea. He was never seasick, no matter how rough it was or how uncomfortable any of the rest of us were. He roamed wherever he wanted to, all over the boat. At mealtimes he came to the table with the rest, sat up on a valise, and lapped his milk and took what bits of food were given him, as if he had eaten that way all his life. When the sails were hoisted it was his especial joke to jump upon the main gaff and be hoisted with it; and once he stayed on his perch till the sail was at the masthead. One of us had to go aloft and bring him down. When we had come to anchor and everything was snug for the night, he would come on deck and scamper out on the main boom, and race from there to the bowsprit end as fast as he could gallop, then climb, monkey-fashion, halfway up the masts, and drop back to the deck or dive down into the cabin and run riot among the berths.

One day, as we were jogging along, under a pleasant southwest wind, and everybody was lounging and dozing after dinner, we heard the Bos'n call out, 'Stop that, you fellows!' and a moment after, 'I tell you, quit! Or I'll come up and make you!'

We opened our lazy eyes to see what was the matter, and there sat the Bos'n, down in the cabin, close to the companion-way, the tassel of his knitted cap coming nearly up to the combings of the hatch; and on the deck outside sat Middy, digging his claws into the tempting yarn, and occasionally going deep enough to scratch the Bos'n's scalp.

When night came and we were all settled down in bed, it was Middy's almost invariable custom to go the rounds of all the berths, to see if we were properly tucked in, and to end his

inspection by jumping into the captain's bed, treading himself a comfortable nest there among the blankets, and curling himself down to sleep. It was his own idea to select the captain's berth as the only proper place in which to turn in.

But the most interesting trait in Middy's character did not appear until he had been a week or so on board. Then he gave us a surprise. It was when we were lying in Camden Harbor. Everybody was going ashore to take a tramp among the hills, and Charlie, the cook, was coming too, to row the boat back to the yacht.

Middy discovered that he was somehow 'getting left.' Being a prompt and very decided cat, it did not take him long to make up his mind what to do. He ran to the low rail of the yacht, put his forepaws on it, and gave us a long, anxious look. Then as the boat was shoved off he raised his voice in a plaintive mew. We waved him a good-bye, chaffed him pleasantly, and told him to mind the anchor, and have dinner ready when we got back.

That was too much for his temper. As quick as a flash he had dived overboard, and was swimming like a water spaniel, after the dinghy!

That was the strangest thing we had ever seen in all our lives! We were quite used to elephants that could play at seesaw, and horses that could fire cannon, to learned pigs and to educated dogs; but a cat that of his own accord would take to the water like a full-blooded Newfoundland was a little beyond anything we had ever heard of. Of course the boat was stopped, and Middy was taken aboard drenched and shivering, but perfectly happy to be once more with the crew. He had been ignored and slighted; but he had insisted on his rights, and as soon as they were recognized he was quite contented.

Of course, after that we were quite prepared for anything that Middy might do. And yet he always managed to surprise us by his bold and independent behavior. Perhaps his most brilliant performance was a visit he paid a few days after his swim in Camden Harbor.

We were lying becalmed in a lull of the wind off the entrance to Southwest Harbor. Near us, perhaps a cable's-length away, lay another small yacht, a schooner hailing from Lynn. As we drifted along on the tide, we noticed that Middy was growing very restless; and presently we found him running along the rail and looking eagerly toward the other yacht. What did he see—or smell—over there which interested him? It could not be the dinner, for they were not then cooking. Did he recognize any of his old chums from Marblehead? Perhaps there wee some cat friends of his on the other craft. Ah, that was it! There they were on the deck, playing and frisking together—two kittens! Middy had spied them, and was longing to take a nearer look. He ran up and down the deck, mewing and snuffing the air. He stood up in his favorite position when on lookout, with his forepaws on the rail. Then, before we realized what he was doing, he had plunged overboard again, and was making for the other boat as fast as he could swim! He had attracted the attention of her company, and no sooner did he come up alongside than they prepared to welcome him. A fender was lowered, and when Middy saw it he swam toward it, caught it with his forepaws, clambered along it to the gunwale, and in a twinkling was over the side and on the deck scraping acquaintance with the strange kittens.

How they received him I hardly know, for by that time our boat was alongside to claim the runaway. And we were quite of the mind of the skipper of the *Winnie L.*, who said, as he handed our bold midshipman over the side, 'Well, that beats all *my* going a-fishing!'

Only a day or two later Middy was very disobedient when we were washing decks one morning. He trotted about in the wet till his feet were drenched, and then retired to dry them on the white spreads of the berths below. That was quite too much for the captain's patience. Middy was summoned aft, and, after a sound rating, was hustled into the dinghy which was moored astern, and shoved off to the full length of her painter. The punishment was a severe one for Middy, who could bear anything better than exile from his beloved shipmates. So of course he began to exercise his ingenious little brain to see how he could escape. Well under the overhang of the yacht he spied, just about four inches out of water, a little shoulder of the rudder. That was enough for him. He did not stop to think whether he would be any better off there. It was a part of the yacht, and that was home. So overboard he went, swam for the rudder, scrambled on to it, and began howling piteously to be

243

taken on deck again; and, being a spoiled and much-indulged cat, he was soon rescued from his uncomfortable roosting place and restored to favor.

I suppose I shall tax your powers of belief if I tell you many more of Middy's doings. But truly he was a strange cat, and you may as well be patient, for you will not soon hear of his equal. The captain was much given to rifle practice, and used to love to go ashore and shoot at a mark. On one of his trips he allowed Middy to accompany him, for the simple reason, I suppose, that Middy decided to go, and got on board the dinghy when the captain did. Once ashore, the marksman selected a fine large rock as a rest for his rifle, and opened fire upon his target. At the first shot or two Middy seemed a little surprised, but showed no disposition to run away. After the first few rounds, however, he seemed to have made up his mind that since the captain was making all the racket it must be entirely right and proper, and nothing about which a cat need bother his head in the least. So, as if to show how entirely he confided in the captain's judgment and good intentions, that imperturbable cat calmly lay down, curled up, and went to sleep in the shade of the rock over which the captain's rifle was blazing and cracking about once in two minutes. If anybody was ever acquainted with a cooler or more self-possessed cat I should be pleased to hear the particulars.

I wish that this chronicle could be confined to nothing but our shipmate's feats of daring and nerve. But, unfortunately, he was not always blameless in his conduct. When he got hungry he was apt to forget his position as midshipman, and to behave just like any cat with an empty stomach. Or perhaps he may have done just what any hungry midshipman does under the circumstances; I do not quite know what a midshipman does under all circumstances and so I cannot say. But here is one of this cat midshipman's exploits. One afternoon, on our way home, we were working along with a head wind and sea toward Wood Island, a haven for many of the small yachts between Portland and the Shoals. The wind was light and we wee a little late in making port. But as we were all agreed that it would be pleasanter to postpone our dinner till we were at anchor, the cook was told to keep things warm and wait till we were inside the port before he set the table. Now, his main dish

244

that day was to be a fine piece of baked fish; and, unfortunately, it was nearly done when we gave orders to hold back the dinner. So he had closed the drafts of his little stove, left the door of the oven open, and turned into his bunk for a quiet doze—a thing which every good sailor does on all possible occasions; for a seafaring life is very uncertain in the matter of sleep, and one never quite knows when he will lose some, nor how much he will lose. So it is well to lay in a good stock of it whenever you can.

It seems that Middy was on watch, and when he saw Charlie fast asleep he undertook to secure a little early dinner for himself. He evidently reasoned with himself that it was very uncertain when we should have dinner and he'd better get his while he could. He quietly slipped down to the stove, walked coolly up to the oven, and began to help himself to baked haddock.

He must have missed his aim or made some mistake in his management of the business, and, by some lucky chance for the rest of us, waked the cook. For, the first we knew, Middy came flying up the cabin companionway, followed by a volley of shoes and spoons and pieces of coal, while we could hear Charlie, who was rather given to unseemly language when he was excited, using the strongest words in his dictionary about 'that thief of a cat!'

'What's the matter?' we all shouted at once.

'Matter enough, sir!' growled Charlie. 'That little cat's eaten up half the fish! It's a chance if you get any dinner tonight, sir.'

You may be very sure that Middy got a sound wigging for that trick, but I am afraid the captain forgot to deprive him of his rations as he threatened. He was much too kindhearted.

The very next evening Middy startled us again by a most remarkable display of coolness and courage. After a weary thrash to windward all day, under a provokingly light breeze, we found ourselves under the lee of the little promontory at Cape Neddick, where we cast anchor for the night. Our supply of water had run very low, and so, just after sunset, two of the party rowed ashore in the tender to replenish our water keg, and by special permission Middy went with them.

It took some time to find a well, and by the time the jugs were filled it had grown quite dark. In launching the boat for the return to the yacht, by some ill luck a breaker caught her and threw her back upon the beach. There she capsized and spilled out the boys, together with their precious cargo. In the confusion of the moment, and the hurry of setting matters to rights, Middy was entirely forgotten, and when the boat again was launched, nobody thought to look for the cat. This time everything went well, and in a few minutes the yacht was sighted through the dusk. Then somebody happened to think of Middy! He was nowhere to be seen. Neither man remembered anything about him after the capsize. There was consternations in the hearts of those unlucky wights. To lose Middy was almost like losing one of the crew.

But it was too late and too dark to go back and risk another landing on the beach. There was nothing to be done but to leave poor Middy to his fate, or at least to wait until morning before searching for him.

But just as the prow of the boat bumped against the fender on the yacht's quarter, out from under the stern sheets came a wet, bedraggled, shivering cat, who leaped on board the yacht and hurried below into the warm cabin. In that moist adventure in the surf, Middy had taken care of himself, rescued himself from a watery grave, got on board the boat as soon as she was ready, and sheltered himself in the warmest corner. All this he had done without the least outcry, and without asking any help whatever. His self-reliance and courage were extraordinary.

Well, the pleasant month of cruising drew to a close, and it became a question what should be done with Middy. We could not think of turning him adrift in the cold world, although we had no fears but that so bright and plucky a cat would make a living anywhere. But we wanted to watch over his fortunes, and perhaps take him on the next cruise with us when he should have become a more settled and dignified Thomas. Finally, it was decided that he should be boarded for the winter with an artist, Miss Susan H——, a friend of one of our party. She wanted a studio cat, and would be particularly pleased to receive so accomplished and traveled a character as Middy. So when the yacht was moored to the little wharf at Annisquam, where she always ended her cruises, and we were packed and ready for our journey to Boston, Middy was tucked into a

246

basket and taken to the train. He bore the confinement with the same good sense which had marked all his life with us, though I think his feelings were hurt at the lack of confidence we showed in him. And, in truth, we were a little ashamed of it ourselves, and when once we were on the cars somebody suggested that he be released from his prison just to see how he would behave. We might have known he would do himself credit. For when he had looked over his surroundings, peeped above the back of the seat at the passengers, taken a good look at the conductor, and counted the rest of the party to see that none of us was missing, Middy snuggled down upon the seat, laid his head upon the captain's knee, and slept all the way to Boston.

That was the last time I ever saw Middy. He was taken to his new boarding place in Boylston Street, where he lived very pleasantly for a few months, and made many friends by his pleasing manners and unruffled temper. But I suppose he found it a little dull in Boston. He was not quite at home in his aesthetic surroundings. I have always believed he sighed for the freedom of a sailor's life. He loved to sit by the open window when the wind was east, and seemed to be dreaming of faraway scenes. One day he disappeared. No trace of him was ever found. A great many things may have happened to him. But I never could get rid of the feeling that he went down to the wharves and the ships and the sailors, trying to find his old friends, looking everywhere for the stanch little *Eyvor*; and, not finding her, I am convinced that he shipped on some East Indianman and is now a sailor cat on the high seas.

The Best Bed

SYLVIA TOWNSEND WARNER

T HE cat had known many winters, but none like this. Through two slow darkening months it had rained, and now, on the eve of Christmas, the wind had gone round to the east, and instead of rain, sleet and hail fell.

The hard pellets hit his drenched sides and bruised them. He ran faster. When boys threw stones at him he could escape by running; but from this heavenly lapidation there was no escape. He was hungry, for he had had no food since he had happened upon a dead sparrow, dead of cold, three days ago. It had not been the cat's habit to eat dead meat, but having fallen upon evil days he had been thankful even for that unhealthy-tasting flesh. Thirst tormented him, worse than hunger. Every now and then he would stop, and scrape the frozen gutters with his tongue. He had given up all hope now, he had forgotten all his wiles. He despaired, and ran on.

The lights, the footsteps on the pavements, the crashing buses, the swift cars like monster cats whose eyes could outstare his own, daunted him. Though a Londoner, he was not used to these things, for he was born by Thames' side, and had spent his days among the docks, a modest useful life of rat-catching and secure slumbers upon flour sacks. But one night the wharf where he lived had caught fire; and terrified by flames, and smoke, and uproar, he had begun to run, till by the morning he was far from the river, and homeless, and too unversed in the ways of the world to find himself another home.

A street door opened, and he flinched aside, and turned a corner. But in that street, doors were opening too, every door

letting out horror. For it was closing-time. Once, earlier in his wanderings, he had crouched in by such a door, thinking that any shelter would be better than the rainy street. Before he had time to escape a hand snatched him up and a voice shouted above his head. 'Gorblime if the cat hasn't come in for a drink,' the voice said. And the cat felt his nose thrust into a puddle of something fiery and stinking, that burned on in his nostrils and eyes for hours afterwards.

He flattened himself against the wall, and lay motionless until the last door should have swung open for the last time. Only when someone walked by, bearing that smell with him, did the cat stir. Then his nose quivered with invincible disgust, his large ears pressed back upon his head, and the tip of his tail beat stiffly upon the pavement. A dog, with its faculty of conscious despair, would have abandoned itself, and lain down to await death; but when the streets were quiet once more the cat ran on.

There had been a time when he ran and leaped for the pleasure of the thing, rejoicing in his strength like an athlete. The resources of that lean, sinewy body, disciplined in the hunting days of his youth, had served him well in the first days of his wandering; then, speeding before some barking terrier, he had hugged amidst his terrors a compact and haughty joy in the knowledge that he could so surely outstrip the pursuer; but now his strength would only serve to prolong his torment. Though an accumulated fatigue smouldered in every nerve, the obdurate limbs carried him on, and would carry him on still, a captive to himself, meekly trotting to the place of his death.

He ran as the wind directed, turning this way and that to avoid the gusts, spiked with hail, that ravened through the streets. His eyes were closed, but suddenly at a familiar sound he stopped, and stiffened with fear. It was the sound of a door swinging on its hinges. He snuffed apprehensively. There was a smell, puffed out with every swinging-to of the door, but it was not the smell he abhorred; and though he waited in the shadow of a buttress, no sounds of jangling voices came to confirm his fears, and though the door continued to open and shut, no footsteps came from it. He stepped cautiously from his buttress into a porch. The smell was stronger here. It was

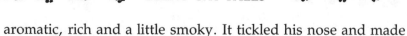

aromatic, rich and a little smoky. It tickled his nose and made him sneeze.

The door was swinging with the wind. The aperture was small, too small for anything to be seen through it, save only a darkness that was not quite dark. With a sudden determination the cat flitted through.

Of his first sensations, one overpowered all the others. Warmth! It poured over him, it penetrated his being, and confused his angular physical consciousness of cold and hunger and fatigue into something rounded and indistinct. Half-swooning, he sank down on the stone flags.

Another sneezing fit roused him. He jumped up, and began to explore.

The building he was in reminded him of home. Often, hunting the river-side, he had strayed into places like this— lofty and dusky, stone-floored and securely uninhabited. But they had smelt of corn, of linseed, of tallow, of sugar: none of them had smelt as this did, smokily sweet. They had been cold. Here it was warm. They had been dark; and here the dusk was mellowed with one red star, burning in mid-air, and with the glimmer of a few tapers, that added to the smoky sweetness their smell of warm wax.

His curiosity growing with his confidence, the cat ran eagerly about the church. He rubbed his back against the font, he examined into the varying smell of the hassocks, he trotted up the pulpit stairs, sprang on to the ledge, and sharpened his claws in the cushion. Outside the wind boomed, and the hail clattered against the windows, but within the air was warm and still, and the red star burned mildly on. Over against the pulpit the cat came on something that reminded him even more of home—a wisp of hay, lying on the flags. He had often seen hay; sometimes borne towering above the greasy tide on barges, sometimes fallen from the nosebags of the great draught horses who waited so peacefully in the wharfingers' yard.

The hay seemed to have fallen from a box on trestles, cut out of unstained wood. The cat stood on his hind legs, and tried to look in, but it was too high for him. He turned about, but his curiosity brought him back again; and poising himself on his clustered paws he rocked slightly, gauging his spring, and

then jumped, alighting softly in a bed of hay. He landed so delicately that though the two kneeling figures at either end of the crib swayed forward for a moment, they did not topple over. The cat sniffed them, a trifle suspiciously, but they did not hold his attention long. It was the hay that interested him. A drowsy scent rose out of the deep, warm bed as he kneaded and shuffled it with his fore-paws. This, this, promised him what he had so long yearned for: sound sleep, an enfolding in warmth and softness, a nourishing forgetfulness. He paced round in a small circle, burrowing himself a close nest, purring with a harsh note of joy. As he turned he brushed against a third figure in the crib; but he scarcely noticed it. Already a rapture of sleepiness was overcoming him; the two kneeling figures had done him no harm, nor would this reposing one. Soon the bed was made to his measure. Bowing his head upon his paws, he abandoned himself.

Another onslaught of hail dashed against the windows, the door creaked, and at a gust of wind entering the church the candle flames wavered, as though they were nodding their heads in assent; but though the cat's ears flicked once or twice against the feet of the plaster Jesus, he was too securely asleep to know or heed.

Acknowledgements

The Publisher has made every effort to contact the Copyright holders, but wishes to apologise to those he has been unable to trace. Grateful acknowledgement is made for permission to reprint the following:

Lillian by Damon Runyon. Copyright renewed 1957 by Damon Runyon, Jr. and Mary Runyon McCann as children of the author. Published by special arrangement with American Play Company, Inc., Sheldon Abend, President, 19 West 44 Street, Suite 1206, New York, New York 10036.

The Fat Cat by Q. Patrick. Reprinted by permission of Curtis Brown Ltd. Copyright © 1944 by Q. Patrick.

Ming's Biggest Prey by Patricia Highsmith. Reprinted by permission of William Heinemann Limited and Penzler Books.

'Mrs Bond's Cats' from *All Things Bright and Beautiful* by James Herriot. Reproduced by permission of David Higham Associates Limited and St Martin's Press, Inc., New York. Copyright © 1973, 1974 by James Herriot.

A Cat Affair by Derek Tangye. Reproduced by permission of Michael Joseph Limited and Peters Fraser & Dunlop Group Ltd.

Kym by Joyce Stranger. Reproduced by permission of Michael Joseph Limited and Aitken & Stone Ltd. Illustrations on pages 80, 125 and 153 by permission of Michael Joseph Limited.

A Fine Place for a Cat by Margaret Bonham. Reproduced by permission of Curtis Brown Limited.

The Blue Flag by Kay Hill. Reprinted by permission of Curtis Brown Ltd. Copyright © 1942 by Kay Hill.

'*The Story of Webster*' from *Mulliner Nights* by P.G. Wodehouse. Reproduced by permission of A.P. Watt Ltd on behalf of the Trustees of the Wodehouse Trust No 3 and Century Hutchinson Limited.

Cats in the Belfry by Doreen Tovey. Reproduced by permission of the author and Michael Joseph Limited.

'*Heathcliff*' from *Quorum of Cats* by Lloyd Alexander. Reproduced by permission of A.M. Heath & Company Limited and Brandt & Brandt Literary Agents, Inc. *My Five Tigers* by Lloyd Alexander. Copyright, 1956 by Lloyd Alexander. Copyright renewed © 1984 by Lloyd Alexander.

A Ship of Solace by Elinor Mordaunt. Reprinted by permission of William Heinemann Limited.

Particularly Cats by Doris Lessing. Reproduced by permission of Michael Joseph Limited and Simon & Schuster, Inc. Copyright © 1967 by Doris Lessing Productions Limited

The Best Bed by Sylvia Townsend Warner. Reproduced by permission of the Estate of Sylvia Townsend Warner and Chatto & Windus Limited.

Illustration on page 171 courtesy Julia Macrae.

FINE WORKS OF FICTION AVAILABLE IN QUALITY PAPERBACK EDITIONS FROM CARROLL & GRAF

☐ Asch, Sholem/THE NAZARENE $10.95
☐ Asch, Sholem/THREE CITIES $10.50
☐ Ashley, Mike (ed.)/THE MAMMOTH BOOK OF
    SHORT HORROR NOVELS $8.95
☐ Balzac, Honoré de/CESAR BIROTTEAU $8.95
☐ Balzac, Honoré de/THE LILY OF THE VALLEY $9.95
☐ Bellaman, Henry/KINGS ROW $8.95
☐ Bernanos, George/DIARY OF A COUNTRY PRIEST $7.95
☐ Brand, Christianna/GREEN FOR DANGER $8.95
☐ Céline, Louis-Ferdinand/CASTLE TO CASTLE $8.95
☐ Chekov, Anton/LATE BLOOMING FLOWERS $8.95
☐ Conrad, Joseph/SEA STORIES $8.95
☐ Conrad, Joseph & Ford Madox Ford/ROMANCE $8.95
☐ Coward, Noel/A WITHERED NOSEGAY $8.95
☐ Cozzens James Gould/THE LAST ADAM $8.95
☐ Dos Passos, John/THREE SOLDIERS $9.95
☐ Feuchtwanger, Lion/JEW SUSS $8.95
☐ Feuchtwanger, Lion/THE OPPERMANNS $8.95
☐ Fitzgerald, Penelope/OFFSHORE $7.95
☐ Flaubert, Gustave/NOVEMBER $7.95
☐ Fonseca, Rubem/HIGH ART $7.95
☐ Fuchs, Daniel/SUMMER IN WILLIAMSBURG $8.95
☐ Gold, Michael/JEWS WITHOUT MONEY $7.95
☐ Greenberg & Waugh (eds.)/THE NEW
    ADVENTURES OF SHERLOCK HOLMES $8.95
☐ Greenfeld, Josh/THE RETURN OF MR.
    HOLLYWOOD $8.95
☐ Greene, Graham & Hugh/THE SPY'S BEDSIDE BOOK $7.95
☐ Hamsun, Knut/MYSTERIES $8.95
☐ Hardinge, George (ed.)/THE MAMMOTH BOOK
    OF MODERN CRIME STORIES $8.95
☐ Hugo, Victor/NINETY-THREE $8.95
☐ Huxley, Aldous/EYELESS IN GAZA $9.95
☐ Jackson, Charles/THE LOST WEEKEND $7.95
☐ James, Henry/GREAT SHORT NOVELS $11.95
☐ Lewis, Norman/DAY OF THE FOX $8.95
☐ Lowry, Malcolm/ULTRAMARINE $7.95
☐ Macaulay, Rose/CREWE TRAIN $8.95
☐ Macaulay, Rose/DANGEROUS AGES $8.95

- [ ] Macaulay, Rose/THE TOWERS OF TREBIZOND $8.95
- [ ] Mailer, Norman/BARBARY SHORE $9.95
- [ ] Mauriac, François/VIPER'S TANGLE $8.95
- [ ] Mauriac, François/THE DESERT OF LOVE $6.95
- [ ] McElroy, Joseph/LOOKOUT CARTRIDGE $9.95
- [ ] McElroy, Joseph/A SMUGGLER'S BIBLE $9.50
- [ ] Moorcock, Michael/THE BROTHEL IN ROSENTRASSE $6.95
- [ ] Munro, H.H./THE NOVELS AND PLAYS OF SAKI $8.95
- [ ] Neider, Charles (ed.)/GREAT SHORT STORIES $11.95
- [ ] Neider, Charles (ed.)/SHORT NOVELS OF THE MASTERS $12.95
- [ ] O'Faolain, Julia/THE OBEDIENT WIFE $7.95
- [ ] O'Faolain, Julia/NO COUNTRY FOR YOUNG MEN $8.95
- [ ] O'Faolain, Julia/WOMEN IN THE WALL $8.95
- [ ] Olinto, Antonio/THE WATER HOUSE $8.95
- [ ] Plievier, Theodore/STALINGRAD $8.95
- [ ] Pronzini & Greenberg (eds.)/THE MAMMOTH BOOK OF PRIVATE EYE NOVELS $8.95
- [ ] Rechy, John/BODIES AND SOULS $8.95
- [ ] Sand, George/MARIANNE $7.95
- [ ] Scott, Evelyn/THE WAVE $9.95
- [ ] Singer, I.J./THE BROTHERS ASHKENAZI $9.95
- [ ] Taylor, Peter/IN THE MIRO DISTRICT $7.95
- [ ] Tolstoy, Leo/TALES OF COURAGE AND CONFLICT $11.95
- [ ] Wassermann, Jacob/CASPAR HAUSER $9.95
- [ ] Werfel, Franz/THE FORTY DAYS OF MUSA DAGH $9.95
- [ ] Winwood, John/THE MAMMOTH BOOK OF SPY THRILLERS $8.95

Available from fine bookstores everywhere or use this coupon for ordering.

Carroll & Graf Publishers, Inc., 260 Fifth Avenue, N.Y., N.Y. 10001

Please send me the books I have checked above. I am enclosing $_____ (please add $1.00 per title to cover postage and handling.) Send check or money order—no cash or C.O.D.'s please. N.Y. residents please add 8¼% sales tax.

Mr/Mrs/Ms _____

Address _____

City _____ State/Zip _____
Please allow four to six weeks for delivery.